Ь

By John Peel

Dragonhome Books
New York

This book is a work of fiction. Any resemblance to actual events, places or person is entirely coincidental.

Dragonhome Books, New York
ISBN# 9780615726007

Book of Time

For Carla Jadrich

John Peel

Prologue

The Great Wizard Jagomath studied his books with deep concentration. Here in his mystic lair, he was surrounded by his weighty tomes, and here he hatched his plans and schemes that were to make him the sole ruler of the Diadem.

The Diadem... He had not even suspected its existence until some six months ago. Then he had come across his mystic stone, and this had expanded his senses, revealing much to him of matters he'd been completely unaware. Working with the stone, his powers had grown, and then he had met *her*. The one imprisoned in the rock, condemned to live out a pitiful life, and yet –

She knew so much! And, because of his powers, she had been called back into being. She could never stay long in his world, but each time she came, she brought him fresh knowledge. She it was who had revealed the existence of the Diadem to him, and given him fresh territories to manipulate and conquer.

The Diadem – a universe of worlds, linked together by magical portals. The Outer Circle consisted of worlds where magic was weakest, but those with power could cross into the next circle, where magic was stronger and more was possible. Next came the Inner Circuit, where the power was so strong it burnt out all but the most skilled users. And finally, at the center of it all, the world known as Jewel. This held the mightiest of power, and whoever held Jewel controlled all of the Diadem.

The captive had revealed that the Diadem was currently in the control of four magicians of varying skills and abilities. There was their odd leader, Score, a young man from Earth. He was the son of a criminal and followed in his father's footsteps. He had been instrumental in building up his own empire, one much larger and viler than that of his father. Then there was Helaine Votrin, daughter of Lord Votrin, despot from the medieval world of Ordin. A cold, heartless wench with delusions that her noble birth meant that she should rule *everyone*. There was her servant, Jenna, a small-time witch who had seized her chance at power by infatuating the final member of the group – Pixel, a scientist without morals who dealt with computers and machinery. Together, the four of them had overthrown the lawful governments of a dozen worlds and taken them into their own power. And they had slaughtered or imprisoned any who refused to accept their evil sway.

Such as his imprisoned mentor. She had tried to fight the evil quartet and failed. They had sought to slay her, but she had managed to escape death, only to be imprisoned instead, her soul fettered within a bleak ball of rock. The same rock that had fallen from the skies and into his possession.

He glanced at his chronometer again. She could only appear to him once a day and it was almost time. He had no idea what he might learn from her this day, but he knew that his aim was to free the captive – and for that he needed more power. He had to overcome and destroy the villainous four, and only then could he set her free.

He could feel the magic building, the power flowing through him. It excited him, as it always did, and he could feel that fate was reaching out, using him to destroy the evil ones, and enabling him to take his rightful place as the ruler of the Diadem. Each day he was stronger, better, smarter. Each day meant that the hour of judgment on Score, Pixel, Jenna and Helaine was drawing closer.

For the longest time, they had no clue that he even existed, and he was able to work carefully and cleverly without their interference. But then they had somehow stumbled across his plans on that ocean world… What was it called again? No matter, it was in his notes somewhere, and he could find it if he needed it. The merchants of that world had been supplying him with gemstones, jewels that were able to amplify his powers, and he had aided them in their fight against the quartet. The four villains had somehow discovered what he was doing and had interfered. He wasn't entirely certain what they had done, but he was completely unable to contact any of his former allies. They were most likely dead, and his supply of magical enhancing gems had been cut off.

But not soon enough to be a real problem. He had a stockpile of them in hiding, more than the quartet possessed, and enough for him to be able to defeat them if they interfered with him again.

It was almost time.

Jagomath moved to where he had hidden his magical stone. He had made certain that no one else would be able to find and use it, and was careful only to bring it out when he was alone, and it was time for his magical muse to appear. He lifted the stone from its hiding place, smiling happily to himself. It didn't look like much - a dark stone, almost a foot across, shaped like a potato, with heat-searing on it. If he'd passed it in the fields, he wouldn't have given it a second glance. But this was a special rock, as he'd known when he'd seen it descending from the skies in a fireball. He'd watched the impact, and then waited for it to cool sufficiently for him to be able to wrap it in his coat and carry it back. He'd known it was special, but until the captive had managed to materialize herself, he had had no idea just *how* special.

It was time.

He began the incantation under his breath, the one to aid her in her materialization. He didn't know where she went when she left him, or if she was even really alive when she was gone. She said she had to conserve her strength, that being almost slaughtered had taken too much of her life energy from her, and she needed to replenish it. He supposed that resting aided her in that in some way. But he could feel the power building up again, as it always did when he was with her, and he knew that she was coming.

And then, as always, she was there. Tall, slender, dark-haired, vaguely exotic, and quite young. Her face lit into a smile, and he knew she was stronger.

"Jagomath," she purred. Whenever she said his mystic name, it always gave him a thrill. She was beautiful, and kind, and in desperate need of his help. He knew he was falling in love with her, and that this might be a mistake. But he simply couldn't help himself - even captive as she was, and chained magically to the rock, she was the most thrilling and delightful person he had ever known. One day she would be free, and then... Well, who knew? Romance wasn't out of the question.

"My lady," he replied, bowing slightly. "It is good to see you again. It seems to me that you are stronger this evening."

"Yes," she agreed. "Yes, I am - and it is all thanks to you. I have been able to send my mind out, out from captivity and back into the Diadem. And I can sense that our great time of opportunity is fast approaching. Our enemies are preparing to cast a new and powerful spell, one that will aid them in their vile conquests. But we are ready, you and I!" She laughed in delight, and reached out as if to take his hands. But, as always, there was that disappointment as her intangible fingers passed clear through his flesh. Her face fell for a moment, but then she shook her head and smiled again. "Soon, soon, we will break their power, and then I shall become corporeal again. Then we can touch... And, I promise you, you will not regret it."

He could hardly wait - it sounded as if she was as hungry for his touch as he was for hers... But, first of all, there had to be the defeat of the foursome. "They are preparing a new spell?" he asked. "One that we will be able to affect?"

"Yes," she replied. "It will happen very soon, so you must be ready. I believe I can manifest myself a second time this evening, when the spell is to be cast. Together, Jagomath, you and I will be able to warp their magic, and twist it to suit our purposes and not theirs. They plan conquest, but we shall be able to weave the spell and turn it into captivity for them - and, ultimately, freedom for me and for all of the other souls they have in their evil thrall."

"That's excellent!" He grinned happily. "I shall be ready, I swear."

"I know you will." The dark-haired girl smiled again, and then laughed. "Oh, you are so *good*, Jagomath! Without your help, they would have conquered - and now they will pay for all of their evil plans!"

"Yes," he agreed, content. "Yes, Destiny - together we shall make certain their doom."

And Destiny - beautiful, honest, Destiny - laughed with delight.

Chapter One

Score was sitting alone in the courtyard, feeling perfectly miserable, and enjoying it. Actually, he was reveling in it. It seemed as if his life had gone completely down the toilet, and taken him with it. How much worse could things get?

"Score?" Helaine peered down at him, concern written all over her face. "What is wrong with you? Why are you hiding like this?"

"Leave me alone," Score mumbled. "I'm feeling sorry for myself, and you're not helping."

Helaine sighed, and crouched down to look at him. "I wish to help. I'll admit that I am a little... unused to the concept of being anyone's girlfriend, but you *did* call me that, didn't you?"

"That's right, rub in *all* of my mistakes," Score complained.

"*Mistakes*?" Helaine looked furious. "You think having me as a girlfriend is a *mistake*?"

"Yes," he answered. "I'll only drag you down. You deserve somebody better than me."

"Oh, you conceited jackass!" Helaine snapped. "I'll make my own mind up about who is right for me - and I won't let you argue me out of it." Then she reached out a hand and gently touched his cheek. Score enjoyed the touch, and then tried to bury the feeling. "I *am* your girlfriend, whether you like it or not - and you had *better* like it! And, as your girlfriend, I think I have certain responsibilities. One of them, I believe, is that I should attempt to help you solve problems when you have them. And I think you clearly have a problem, otherwise you wouldn't be out here, skulking in a dark little spot."

"I am not skulking," Score replied. "I'm sulking. There's a difference."

"Well, whatever you are doing, you are clearly unhappy. And I do not wish you to be unhappy with me."

"Oh, you idiot," Score said. "I'm not unhappy with *you*. I could never be unhappy with you. Mad, yes. Annoyed, yes. Even screaming in frustration. But never unhappy."

"Then perhaps you will tell me what this is about," Helaine said.

"Isn't it obvious?"

Helaine growled. "If it was obvious, would I be asking? Is it permissible for a girlfriend to punch the daylights out of her idiot boyfriend?"

"Hey, I'm new to this whole routine myself," Score replied. "I don't know much about the rules of it. But I do think that beating up on the other is out." He held up his hands as she started to growl again. "Okay, if you really don't know what's wrong with me - it's Shanara."

Helaine blinked, surprised. "Shanara? But you have just discovered that she is your mother. Surely that must please you? You had long believed your mother to be dead."

Score stared at Helaine in amazement. "Where has your head been the past few hours?" he asked her. "*Pleased*? Why would I be *pleased* that Shanara's finally admitted she's my mom? She's only kept it from me for - oh, I don't know - ever since we met her! Oh, yes, and she just tried to kill me, remember? Trapping me on that planet with all of the mutant killer plants. Do you think all of that would *please* me?"

"Oh. I think I understand the problem."

"Oh, good. I am *so* glad you finally get it." Score settled down to feeling miserable again.

"Yes," Helaine said, cheerfully. "You need to talk to Shanara and let her explain her actions."

"Lady," Score growled, "you are out of your mind if you think I want to hear anything more from that... traitor. Don't you get it? She lied to me, she betrayed me and she tried to kill me. I don't ever even want to see her face again - whichever face it is she's wearing right now."

"Her own," Helaine replied. "Ever since Jenna cured her of those dreadful scars that covered her body, she seems to be happy looking just the way she actually is, instead of hiding behind one of her illusions."

"Oh, wow, I am *so* glad that psycho-mom is happy. That's one of us. Now go away and let me feel sorry for myself in peace."

Helaine shook her head. "I do not think I can do that. As you know, I take all of my responsibilities very seriously. As you are now officially my boyfriend, I have no option but to help you, whether you wish me to or not."

"Great. So now I'm your project of the day." Score glared at her. "If I'd known you'd be this intent about it, I'd never have said you were my girl."

Helaine stiffened. "Do you wish to retract your statement?" she asked. "I should warn you that I don not take rejection very calmly."

Score laughed. "Yeah, I'd kind of guessed that bit. And I know that if it came down to a fight, you could take me without breaking a sweat."

"Indeed," Helaine agreed. "But I do not wish to force you to accept a relationship that is unpleasant for you. If you truly do not wish me for your girlfriend, I will agree to release you from your promise."

"Promise?" Score was getting confused. "What promise? All I did was to say you were my girlfriend." A sudden thought came to him. "Wait a minute - is this another of your crazy medieval ideas? Look, where I come from, being boyfriend and girlfriend means we hang out together, go on dates, smooch some and maybe get a little frisky. And you might get a little daring and allow me to see your naked ankle. It doesn't mean anything more than that."

"Oh." Helaine actually looked disappointed. "Then perhaps I *do* have an incorrect understanding of what you had said. I had believed that it meant you wished to wed me."

"Wed you?" Score was shocked out of his sulking. "Look, Helaine, I'm fond of you and all, but... *marry* you?"

She glared at him, furiously. "Am I not marriageable?" she demanded.

"Well, yes, probably," he stammered. "But *I'm* not. I'm an idiot. I'm a loner - mostly. And I'm *definitely* not ready to settle down and be a husband and maybe father. I'm just a teenager! And so are you."

"We marry young on my world," Helaine answered. "I am already past marrying age. My father is most disappointed with me."

"Yeah, well, in New York we wait until we're a lot more mature," Score answered. "When we're twenty or thirty, maybe. Before then, we just explore, play the field, find out who's right for us and who isn't."

Helaine gave him a cold stare. "I understand. So, let me be certain I have this right. You wish to *smooch* me, play the field with me and sample me to decide whether you wish to remain with me or not? Is that correct?"

Score realized he was getting into very deep waters here. Helaine had such completely different ideas than he, thanks to her very straight-laced upbringing. Plus, she was certainly a girl who knew her own mind. She had evidently decided that she and Score were to marry... He was starting to feel suddenly very confined in his hideaway. "Ah, that's not quite what I meant," he said, trying to think of a safe way out of this situation. "It's just that on my world, we do things differently to the way they're arranged on Ordin."

"Yes, I had noticed that," Helaine said, coldly. "Such as girls running about virtually naked, with no apparent modesty."

"Bikinis and halter tops aren't *virtually naked*," Score protested. "Honest, they're considered to be perfectly acceptable. It's just that things are different there than you're used to..."

"Yes, I had gathered as much," Helaine agreed. She took a long, deep breath. "I understand that you are not used to the customs of my world, and you must understand that I am unused to your ways, also. So, therefore, I think we should talk to one another about the entire matter, and be certain that we both mean the exact same thing when we refer to our relationship."

Score had a horrible suspicion that he was about to enter a minefield, and that, whatever he said or did, things were going to explode in his face. "Such as?"

"Such as my manner of dress," Helaine replied. "I feel that it is demeaning and immoral to appear unclothed in public, and yet you seem to be imagining that I will walk about naked with you. This is not going to happen."

"Not *naked*!" Score protested. "Just... well... you could go for less than the whole armor-plated look." He gestured at her chain-mail tunic and thick leggings. "All I can see of you is your face and hands. Would it be so dreadful to wear a skirt sometimes, and show off those legs of yours?"

"I am a warrior," Helaine said firmly. "I dress this way because it is the way that a warrior dresses."

"Well, that's fine for fighting trolls, or sea-monsters," Score agreed. "But not for going on dates, or just hanging out. I'd need a can opener to get to first base with you."

"First base?" she asked. "Where is that? And why would we go there?"

Score flushed. "Uh, we'd better discuss that some other time," he said. "But you see the problem? We have different expectations. Maybe this whole idea was crazy to begin with. Maybe you should be dating one of the nobles from your own world, and not some jerk from New York City."

"You *are* a noble from my world," Helaine pointed out. "In fact, you are *supposed* to be the king."

Score had almost forgotten that he had managed to get himself declared hereditary heir of Ordin. Naturally, Helaine had not. "Well, I don't act like one. And I don't feel like one. All I want us to do is to hang about and have fun. Go on dates." He slapped his forehead. "Hey, we live in a castle on a magical world. No cinemas, no clubs, not even a fast food franchise - where the heck would we go on a date anyway?"

"We could try a picnic," Helaine suggested.

"Which would probably end with us getting attacked by a sea serpent or something," Score complained. "Hey - wait a minute - Jenna's getting real good at making portals. Maybe I could take you back to New York for a *real* date! But you'd have to agree to wear something less..."

"Enclosing?" Helaine suggested, icily.

"Armored," Score replied. "I'm sure we can whip up something we'd both like to see you in. Compromise, remember? You give a little, I give a little, and we try and live with it."

Helaine sighed. "I believe I could agree to that. But I will not be baring skin beyond my neckline or wrists, so don't get your hopes up."

"Jeez, it's like trying to date a nun," Score muttered. "Okay, whatever you say. I guess we can get Shanara to scry up a view of some clothing for you..." His voice trailed off as he realized what he had just said. "Oh, right, I'm still furious with her, aren't I? That's why I'm out here sulking. You *almost* made me forget it by getting me worked up about a date."

"You only need to speak with her," Helaine suggested. "And try and see things from her point of view. Compromise - that seems to be your favorite word today, anyway."

"With *you* I'll compromise," Score said, coldly. "Not with that traitor."

"Score, she's your mother - you have to give her a chance to explain."

"Right, like she gave me." He snapped his fingers. "No, wait, she tried to kill me instead of talking to me. Maybe I should return the favor."

"Do you really wish to kill her?" Helaine asked.

"No. I don't wish *anything* of her!" Score turned away, angry again. "I don't want to have anything to do with her, period."

There was a low cough, and then Jenna's voice asked: "Have I arrived at a bad time?"

Score looked around, and saw the other young girl from Ordin. Unlike Helaine, though, Jenna was low-born, daughter and heir of a hedge-witch. The two girls had loathed each other at the start, but had now become - well, perhaps not exactly *friends*, but they at least liked and tolerated one another.

"What's this?" he demanded. "Gang up on Score day?"

Jenna glanced at Helaine. "He's in his usual ill-temper, I take it?" she asked.

"Yes," Helaine agreed. "He's sulking over Shanara and the fact that I won't walk around naked for him."

"For a girl who won't take off her suit of armor, you sure do like that word *naked*," Score grumbled.

Jenna laughed. "If she is to be your girl-friend, I think she had probably better remain in the armor. It might be safer for her. I am fortunate that Pixel understands my beliefs, and caters to them."

"Pixel is a wimp," Score snapped. "He's completely under your thumb."

Jenna raised an eyebrow. "I have not heard him complaining."

"He *never* complains about anything," Score said. "He's just too agreeable."

"Unlike you," Helaine pointed out. "You do enough complaining to make up for six normal people."

"It's a gift," Score replied. He stared at Jenna rudely. "So, why are you here, anyway? To gang up with Helaine against me?"

"No," Jenna said, ignoring his rudeness. "I merely came to tell you that Shanara has fixed a meal. I thought the two of you might be hungry."

"I don't want anything from that woman," Score growled, ignoring the way his stomach reacted to the word *food*. He hadn't eaten in hours.

"Oh." Jenna sighed. "You're still acting irrationally, then?"

"I *like* being irrational!" Score yelled.

"So I see." Jenna glanced at Helaine. "Can't you control your boyfriend?"

"Don't take that tone with me," Helaine snapped. "He's not as compliant as Pixel. It's easy for you. Besides, he has a mind of his own, and I would not change that."

"Gee, thanks," Score said. "I can't believe I'm listening to you two discussing *controlling* us guys."

"I do not seek to control you," Helaine yelled back. "I merely wish you'd behave more rationally sometimes. Like over Shanara."

"Okay, fine," Score said. "If it'll make you feel better, I'll go and listen to what weaselly excuse she has for her behavior, and then I'll go back to hating and ignoring her. Will that make you happy?"

"Fine!" Helaine yelled. "And *then* we can go on a date!"

"Fine!" Score agreed, and stomped off toward the living quarters. His hearing was acute enough to catch what the girls said to one another as he left.

"How was *that* for controlling him?" Helaine asked, smugly.

"Loud and aggressive," Jenna replied. "But it seems to be how the two of you relate to one another in pretty much every case."

They were *still* at it... Score almost felt like going back and yelling out the girls - but what was the point? He was already mad enough at Shanara - he didn't really want to alienate Helaine and Jenna also. Pixel was bound to take their side, and he'd be out on his own if he started another fight.

Besides, he *wanted* that date with Helaine. She was insufferably proud, arrogant and repressed about showing an inch of skin - but she was also the person he trusted the most in any world, and she was beautiful and he liked being with her - even when they were fighting. But he had absolutely no intention of letting her know that...

And, anyway, he knew that, deep down, he *did* want to talk to his mother, to hear what she had to say. He had believed her dead for so long, it was... well, maybe not *wonderful* to discover she was alive, but it was amazing. He didn't want to hate her. He could only hope that whatever excuse she came up with, it was a good one.

He really wanted to be able to love her again, as he had when he was a child...

Chapter Two

Helaine followed Score back to the dining room of the castle they shared, trying to ignore Jenna beside her. It wasn't that she *disliked* Jenna, exactly. It was just that... well, they were so different. It wasn't simply that Jenna was low-born while she was a noble - it was their personalities, too. Jenna was low-key and gentle, sympathetic and pacifistic - none of which qualities Helaine could claim to share. They just had so little in common - besides the ability to perform magic, the knack of getting into danger, and that Jenna was in love with Helaine's second-best friend, Pixel.

So, rather than think about Jenna, Helaine thought about Score. In many ways she could sympathize with his feelings of betrayal. She knew he was going through a very rough patch, and that she should be more supportive of him. She grinned secretly to herself. Though she made a big fuss about it, she wasn't *really* that averse to trying some of those Earth clothing styles. Some of them actually looked rather intriguing - okay, maybe a bit more feminine than she was used to, but there was probably nothing wrong with that. She'd go on this date with Score, and let him "talk her" into wearing one of the outfits he'd help her pick out. Of course, she'd make a great deal of noise about how terribly immodest it was - she didn't want Score to get *too* used to her being agreeable! - but it might actually be fun to try something a little daring... Surely allowing her arms to show couldn't be *that* wicked?

It would make Score happy, and it wouldn't be too much of a strain on her... Right now, he definitely needed to be cheered up. Helaine wasn't absolutely certain what this whole boyfriend/girlfriend thing entailed, but trying to make Score feel better surely had to be a part of it. She hated seeing him so depressed like this, because he was normally the happiest and most silly of them all.

Besides, seeing him hurt made her hurt too, somehow.

Score, having made up his mind to talk to his mother, was striding along purposefully. Helaine had long legs, but it was hard for her to keep up with him. Jenna - smaller and lighter - wasn't even trying to keep up with Helaine. They marched through the corridors of the castle to the room where they normally took breakfast. Shanara was there, of course, and so was Pixel. Both had finished eating and were sitting, lost in their own thoughts. On the table,

Shanara's magical helper, Blink, the red panda, had curled up on an empty plate and was sleeping soundly. No surprise there - all he ever did was eat and sleep, unless Shanara needed him to assist in her spells.

Shanara was looking good. She was still in her "real" face - being the mistress of illusions, she had in the past tended to look different every time they saw her. They had only recently discovered that the reason for this was that she had been horribly scarred by Traxis, and she had used her powers to appear beautiful again. Since Jenna had healed her, though, Shanara was happy to simply be herself again. She had a curly mass of dark hair, and a very pretty smile. This smile was noticeably missing when she looked up and caught Score's eye.

"Are you still angry with me?" she asked.

"Hey, get used to it," Score snapped. "But I'm here to listen to your side of the story. She -" he pointed over his shoulder toward Helaine with a jerk of his thumb "- convinced me to give you a chance. So, start talking."

Pixel unfolded himself from his chair. "Score, you're not being fair," he objected. "You're not giving her a chance. It's quite clear that you're not going to accept *anything* she says as the truth because your feelings are still hurt."

"Butt out of this, bat-ears," Score said rudely. "This is between my *mom* and me."

"That's hardly called for, Score," Shanara said. "Pixel is -"

"Right," Score finished. "Pixel is *always* right. But I don't want to hear that now, and not from him. Or you. I just want you to tell me why you lied to me all this time. The trying to kill me thing - well, that hurts, but I can almost understand it. What I *can't* understand is why you didn't tell me you were my mother much earlier than this."

Helaine wasn't too good at understanding other people's emotions, but even she could hear the hurt in his voice and feel the pain he was going through. Shanara looked to be on the verge of tears, too.

"At first, I didn't know," she said, softly. "When we first met, all I knew was that the three of you were young, brash magicians, but had the possible power to take on the Three Who Rule. How could I even imagine that you *were* the Three? When they escaped their fate and became children again, born a second time as you,

Helaine and Pixel - well, I wasn't the only one who didn't know. It was only later, when I discovered that you were Traxis reborn that I understood that you were my son."

"You knew I was from New York!" Score yelled. "You knew you'd left your son there!"

"Score," Shanara said, gently, "New York is a big place. It never occurred to me that you might be Matthew Caruso, my son - until later. I knew you only as Score, remember? It was only much later that I discovered your real name. Don't forget, knowing someone's real name gives you power over them – so you didn't tell me it for a long while."

"And you didn't *tell* me once you knew who I was," Score said, bitterly.

"No. I was afraid. Score - Matt! - you have to understand! Traxis did some very terribly things to me. He scarred my body, but he also scarred my soul. When I discovered you were my son, and had all this magical power... I panicked. I couldn't handle it. So I stayed quiet. I agree - it was the wrong thing to do. But I was so scared!"

Helaine's heart went out to Shanara. There was a ring of sincerity in everything the woman was saying. "Score," she said, gently. "You should listen to her."

"I *am* listening to her!" Score yelled. "But how do I know she's telling the truth? She's the Magician of Illusions - and all of her words could simply be more illusions she's spinning around us!"

"That's not fair," Helaine said.

"Actually, it is," Shanara contradicted her, surprisingly. "I understand what he means, and he's right - why should he believe anything I say? He's right - if I wanted to lie to him, I've had a long time to invent a story. But how can I convince him that I'm not lying? Certainly not just by words." Shanara gazed at Score, and Helaine could feel the pain in her voice. "I need to *prove* that I'm telling the truth."

"And how do you plan on doing that?" Jenna asked. "Is there somebody else who can verify what you say?"

"Well, there's Oracle, of course." Shanara saw the look on Score's face. "And I know you don't really trust him to tell you the truth, either," she added hastily. "No, I don't think there's anybody who can vouch for me whose word Score would accept. He *has* been lied to a lot, and disappointed even more."

"Stop trying to sound like you even care," Score said bitterly.

"I *do* care," Shanara said. "But I have to prove that to you, and there's only one way that I can think of that would work. By magic."

"Whoa, lady!" Score said, quickly, throwing up his hands. "What part of *mistress of illusions* makes you think I'd trust anything your magic conjured up either?"

"Not *my* magic - well, not entirely - but your own, and that of your three friends," Shanara said. "What I propose is very simple - we join together, the five of us, and cast a spell. Since you will all be drawing on your own power to create it, you'll be able to be *certain* that it's doing exactly what I claim it's doing. If I tried to lie, you'd be able to detect it in the spell, wouldn't you?"

"Yes," said Helaine, firmly, before Score could think of any objections - or simply shoot off his mouth, as he liked to do. "We can detect anything that goes wrong with our spells. If we're part of what you cast, then we'll know it."

"But what can you possibly cast that can prove your story?" Jenna asked.

Shanara smiled. "Something I think Pixel will understand, and perhaps appreciate - a very special illusion. One that will draw on my own memories and experiences and form all about us. It will be like... what do you call those things you do on those computer machines of yours, Pixel?"

"Ah!" The blue-skinned boy grinned. "Holograms! You'll be using a spell to cast a form of virtual reality about us."

"That's it exactly," Shanara agreed. "We will be able to witness what actually happened. It will look real to us, but it won't *be* real. We won't be able to touch anything, or interact with it. It will simply be a very realistic illusion of how events actually unfolded." She looked at Score. "For the first time, Matthew, you will see *exactly* what happened, and learn the truth about your own past. How we ended up on Earth, who your father is - everything."

"Who my father is?" Score scowled darkly. "I *know* who my father is - Bad Tony Caruso."

"He's your step-father," Shanara said. "Not your father."

Score stared at her, open-mouthed. Helaine could understand why - Score was bitterly ashamed of his... step-father, it now seemed. Bad Tony was a law-breaker and - what was that Earth term? - oh, yes, gangster. Score had always been afraid he might have inherited his father's evil. But if what Shanara was saying was true...

"It's a lot to take in," Shanara said gently. "But don't worry, Score - it will all become clear to you." She glanced around the room until her eyes rested on Blink. "Blink, you lazy creature - up!"

The red panda didn't move, except to open one bleary eye. "I'm sleeping," he protested. "I need my rest."

"You've had more than enough sleep!" Shanara exclaimed. "Up, and get busy - we have work to do."

"How I hate that word," Blink complained. "*Work*! They should ban the whole concept." He stretched out, and yawned wide, showing his sharp little teeth. "Can I at least have breakfast first?"

"You've had breakfast," Shanara replied. "Twice."

"Then it must be lunch time!" Blink said, brightly.

"No, between breakfast and lunch it's work time." Shanara scooped him up. "Once we're done, I promise you'll be able to eat to your heart's content."

"Ha!" Blink scoffed. "I could *never* eat until my heart was content. There's not enough food in the world for that."

Helaine smiled, and reached over to stroke Blink's fur. The panda and Shanara were constantly arguing, but they clearly loved each other. "I've always wondered how you and Blink got together," she said. "Will that be a part of your story?"

"It could be," Shanara agreed. "As long as none of you ever tell the Bronx Zoo that one of their red pandas is actually a very long-lasting illusion..."

"What's a Bronx Zoo?" Jenna asked.

"We'll go there some time," Score said, gruffly. "It's actually kind of neat, and I'm sure you'd all get a kick out of it. They have animals from all over Earth there."

Jenna's eyes opened wide. "Amazing! A collection of magical creatures."

"They're not magical," Score explained. "Well," he added, eyeing Blink, "at least, I don't think any more of them are. They're just really cool and interesting."

"Oh." Jenna looked slightly disappointed. "Well, later, then."

"Quite," Shanara agreed. "Right now, we need to cast the spell. Are you all ready to join with me in this?"

"Yes," Helaine said, and heard Score, Pixel and Jenna echo her. Blink, of course, said "No."

"Good." Shanara ignored the panda, who was squirming in her arms. "Now, we'll all need to concentrate and focus. All of you, draw on the magical fields about you, and bring them into focus. Blink, you link them all together, and keep them in hand. I'll open my memories, and feed them into the matrix that we're creating." Helaine could feel the power starting to flow through the room, and tapped into her own strengths, bringing her abilities up to full strength. The magical fields of force swirled about them all, and she could feel the focus starting to sharpen. "Don't forget!" Shanara called out. "None of what will materialize about us is real - but it will *appear* to be. We can only watch what happens, and not join in." She glanced at Score. "But, as you can tell, I'm casting only the illusion of reality over the room - my memories are *not* being clouded or shaded in any way. What will appear is what happened, untouched by lies or illusions."

Helaine could tell quite clearly that Shanara was telling the absolute truth - there would be no lies in any of this. It was going to work - Score would see what actually happened. Hopefully, that would be enough to make him believe Shanara, and understand why she had done what she had.

All around them, the magical power intensified. She could feel her power reach out to link with Score, first of all. Though he was standing beside her, it was as if she could see within him - and she saw his strengths and weaknesses. His overwhelming emotion at the moment was a need to believe. He *wanted* this all to be true, he wanted to be able to believe and trust his mother. But he was also afraid - afraid that it wouldn't happen and that he'd be disappointed in her once again.

She could feel Pixel, also - tall, strong, confident and bright - as well as naive and unworldly. Then there was Jenna - calm, gentle, healing Jenna, but with a tinge of her anger and resentment at how she'd been treated in the past. Helaine wondered what the others were feeling about her - could they sense all of her own fears and insecurities? There was Shanara - tormented, but strong, and ferocious in her desires to protect. Helaine could even feel Blink's hunger-pangs.

And then there was something else - something from outside of their spell. She could feel another personality, a strong one, filled with a desire to *hurt* and twist. It was impossible to tell where it was coming from, or why, but she could feel the power that this person was pouring into their spell. It was making the casting shift and change, to become something else.

Their spell was being rewoven, somehow, into something else. Helaine tried to cry out a warning, but she could tell that the others all felt the wrongness also. Power sizzled about and through them, more power than even she could handle safely.

Something had changed - but what?

Her senses were simply overloaded. A bright, crisp white light flared up, burning through her entire body. She felt as if she were somehow naked from the inside out, as if every nerve and cell of her body was somehow twisted outside, as if she was about to explode. She imagined that this must be what happened to a magician who went closer to the ultimate source of magical power than they could control. It was as if she was being fried from her soul outward. She tried to scream, but she couldn't tell if she succeeded or not.

Everything was pain. She could no longer see or feel the room, or the others about her. Whatever was happening to them had cut her off from her companions. She felt time and space twisting, and then she felt herself being spat out.

With a crash that rocked her body, she hit the ground, stunned. Every muscle of her body ached, every nerve crawled with pain. Her eyes were open, and gradually she could start to make out things about her.

She was on her stomach on a stone floor. She lifted her head, and saw the walls of a castle about her. But it didn't look like the room she had been standing in moments earlier. The illusion must have worked, then!

Except... it didn't seem right.

Then she realized why. She was there, and Score was next to her, groaning, and trying to get to his feet.

They were completely alone. There was no sign at all of Pixel, or Jenna or Shanara...

Chapter Three

Pixel felt as if a mule had kicked him in the head - from the inside. He groaned and rolled over. When he could force his eyes to see again, he could make out that he was in some sort of castle, and that only Jenna and Shanara were with him. Both of them were lying on the floor, unmoving. Pixel couldn't find the strength to stand, but he managed to drag himself across to where Jenna lay. To his relief, her eyes were open, though she looked very dazed.

"How are you feeling?" he asked her.

"As if somebody rammed a large branch in one ear and out the other," she replied. "What happened?"

"I don't know. I feel much the same way. Shanara -" he glanced across at her, and saw she was stirring also "-appears to be with us now. Maybe she knows what happened." He cradled Jenna's head in his lap. Jenna smiled at him and then winced in pain. She was quite pale, and showed no inclination to move.

"Actually," Shanara said, forcing herself up on her elbows, "I was just about to ask you if you knew what went wrong. I felt some kind of force just as we cast the spell, and then..." She shook her head. "Oh. Bad idea." She rubbed her temples. "I feel like I'm in some sort of mental fog. It's hard to concentrate."

"Me too," Pixel agreed. "Whatever happened to us, it really affected us. But it seems to have affected Score and Helaine much worse."

Shanara glanced around. "Where are they? We should be able to still see them here."

"No idea," Pixel said. "If they're here, they're cloaked under your spell somehow, and are invisible and inaudible. Is that possible?"

"Theoretically? No." Shanara shrugged. "Theoretically, we shouldn't have been hurt, either - but we were." She glanced around further. "This isn't the illusion I was planning - but it *somehow* looks vaguely familiar. I just can't place it."

"Probably because you can't think straight," Pixel said. "It *must* be somewhere you know, because this whole thing is conjured up from your mind." He looked around the place. They seemed to be in some sort of a cellar, by the feel of the dank air. There were racks all around holding various bottles, so it might be a wine cellar. "But why would we appear to be here instead of where you planned?"

"The magic that attacked us could have changed the setting," Shanara suggested. "I got the impression that it was quite a powerful wizard who cast that spell - though who it was, or why he or she did it, I don't know."

"Maybe if we look around we'll find a clue," Pixel said. He looked down at Jenna. "Can you sit up?"

"Yes," she said. "I just don't want to. I rather like it where I am."

He grinned at her. "I like having you here, too. But I think we had better put our personal enjoyment aside, and see what's happened to us."

"Spoilsport." But she sat up, rubbing her temples. "But we can continue that later."

"Absolutely," Pixel agreed. He stood up slowly. His head was spinning a little, but he was starting to return to normal. "Shanara, this is some illusion. If I didn't know better, I'd swear it was absolutely real." He walked across to the closest of the racks, and reached out a wondering hand.

And touched a bottle.

He jerked back immediately. "Uh... didn't you say we could *see* your illusions but not interact with them?"

"Yes," Shanara agreed.

"I thought you did." He reached out and gripped a bottle, pulling it free and holding it up. "Then how come I can do this? It feels perfectly solid to me. This is *some* illusion."

Shanara looked worried. She staggered to her feet, and put out a hand to support herself on the closest wall. She didn't fall through it. "That's because it *is* real," she said, slowly. "Nothing here is my illusion - I would be able to tell if it was. This is all *real*."

"How can that be?" Jenna asked.

"I don't know," Snahara replied, worried.

"The magic that hit us," Pixel said. "It must have been some sort of a transportation spell. It brought us - well, wherever *here* is. And, I guess, it took Score and Helaine somewhere else, which is why they're not visible – it's because they aren't here."

"That makes a sort of sense," Shanara agreed. "Except I don't know why anyone would do that."

"Nor do I," Pixel agreed. "But it's what *must* have happened." He reached into his pocket. "I still have my gemstones - how about you, Jenna?"

Jenna felt the pouch tied to her waist. "Yes, mine are here."

"So we aren't powerless - I hope." Pixel took the ruby from his pocket and held it tight. "Score," he muttered. The ruby enhanced his natural ability to be able to find things - and people. This should tell him where Score was.

Only it didn't. There wasn't the slightest tingle. He tried it again for Helaine, and came up just as empty.

"Where's Blink?" Shanara asked. "Without him, I still have my powers, but they're not as strong."

Pixel tried to find Blink also, with the same result. "We're on our own," he told the others. "I can't find any of them. Whatever happened to them, they were transported somewhere out of the range of my abilities to discover them."

"Do you think they're all right?" Jenna asked, concerned.

"Probably as much as we are," Pixel decided. "Just not here." He frowned. "Okay - we're facing some unknown enemy. He or she wants us separated for whatever reasons. And he or she has made sure we came *here* - wherever here is. I assume not for any good motives. We'd better be on our guards. Something tells me that we're in for a whole bunch of trouble."

Shanara nodded. "I agree. But there doesn't seem to be too much trouble here in this wine cellar. Maybe if we explore a little, we might get some idea of where we are and why we're here - and what our unseen enemy has planned for us."

"Makes sense to me," Pixel agreed. He glanced around and saw a flight of stairs in one corner. "And that sure looks like an exit to me." He took hold of Jenna's hand, which was always nice. "Come on." He led the way to the stairs, and then up. Shanara trailed behind them.

At the top of the stairs was a door, thankfully unlocked. Beyond it, they found themselves in a corridor. "Just like a computer game," he muttered to himself. "Exploring a strange place, ready for trouble..." The corridor led in both directions. There were torches lit in sconces on the walls, showing simple stone with no decorations. There were a bunch of other doors, all closed. To their left was a flight of stairs leading upward; to their right another flight leading down.

"This doesn't tell us much," Jenna said. "So - which way should we go?"

"Up," Pixel and Shanara said at the same moment. Pixel

grinned. "Great minds think alike," he murmured. "No windows, so we're probably still below ground level." He led off again. Then he stopped and sniffed. "I smell cooking," he announced.

"Yes," Jenna agreed. "I recognize several of the spices. There must be someone in the kitchen we can talk to."

"Absolutely." Pixel followed his nose, and then could hear the sound of low conversations and the rattle of pots and pans. They came to a large door, open, and passed through.

The kitchen was huge - a good eighty feet deep, and twenty wide. There was a huge, blazing fire on the left, and a number of armatures holding metal pots in or close to the flames. Several large tables were set up in the center of the room, most of them filled with foodstuffs, vegetables, pans, and cooking implements. Down the right-hand wall were a series of cupboards and barrels. At the far end of the room were several more doors.

And there were people here, too - quite a number of them. There were women chopping, dicing, mixing and blending. There were maids scurrying to fetch and carry. There were several men by the fire, each checking on the cooking. And there was one man overseeing everything - tall, and slender, with a worried look about him.

"Quick, quick, quick!" he cried. "Everything must be just right!" He glanced around and saw Pixel and his companions. "You three - what are you doing?" He frowned. "I don't recognize you."

"We're new here," Pixel said, truthfully.

"Oh dear. I *do* wish the Mistress would inform me when she's going to bring in new servants. It is *so* difficult..." He caught himself abruptly. "Not that I'm criticizing *her*, of course, you understand."

"Of course not," Shanara agreed, darkly. "You wouldn't dare, would you?" Before he could say anything, she continued: "Now, where can we be the most help?"

The nervous man thought for a moment. "Waiting on the tables. I do hope you know your manners. It's too much to hope that you'll be trained for that."

"I am," Shanara said. "And my companions are good are taking instructions. I'll keep them out of trouble."

"Thank the Three!" the man said. "Very well, you'll find fresh clothing two doors down. Go and change immediately."

Pixel and Jenna followed Shanara out of the bustling kitchen. "Do you have any idea what's going on?" he asked the sorceress.

"Some sort of dinner party, by the look of things," Shanara replied. "I've attended enough of them in my time to know how they should be served. We can bluff our way through this without too much trouble. And it should give us some idea of where we are and what's going on."

"Do you have any idea who this Mistress is?" Jenna asked.

"None at all," Shanara replied. She grinned. "But I could tell that man was scared of her, so a little bluffing was a safe bet." They had reached the door he'd told them about, and it opened at Shanara's touch. Inside were racks of servants' clothing. She breezed through them, and then pulled out a couple of long dresses, handing one to Jenna. "These should do for us," she decided. "Pixel, that rack over there has the men's outfits. Pick out one that will fit you. It's important to look the part - that way whoever is in charge here isn't likely to pay any attention to you. No high and mighty Mistress ever concerns herself with the help."

Jenna looked dubiously at the bright blue and yellow dress. "I'm very fond of Pixel," she said. "But I am not removing my clothing while he watches." Pixel felt himself blushing at the thought.

"Behind the racks," Shanara said firmly. "I'm not as fond of him as you are, and I'm certainly not stripping in front of him." She stared at Pixel. "You do the same behind your own rack - and keep your eyes averted."

"Absolutely!" Pixel promised. He had no desire to embarrass either of the females - or himself!

His own outfit was a tunic of blue and yellow leggings. The shoes had ornate buckles on them, and there was a cravat for around his neck. He felt gaudy and foolish, but imagined he would blend in. Jenna and Shanara were waiting for him when he was finished. Their dresses matched his own color scheme - the skirts of yellow, the tops of blue - and they also had shoes with ornate buckles.

"I *know* I've seen these outfits before," Shanara said. "But I can't quite recall where or when." She shook her head. "Like I said, nobody pays much attention to the servants. Well, we'll discover what is going on soon enough, I suppose."

They returned to the kitchen, where the worried man looked them up and down critically. "Well, you clean up decently enough," he sniffed.

"Argone," one of the cooks called, "the soup is ready."

"Very well," the nervous man replied. "Well, let's see if the three of you are really as good as you claim. You may take the soup in and serve it."

"Of course," Shanara agreed. She led Pixel and Jenna to the preparation table. The cook and her assistant were pouring the soup from a large pot into a fat tureen. It appeared to be some sort of seafood broth, and it smelled wonderful. Pixel wasn't hungry yet, but if this was any indication, they might be eating quite well here.

Argone took a small spoon and tasted a sample. "That's acceptable," he decided. "Well?" he added, pointedly in Shanara's direction.

Shanara found a large tray and handed it to Pixel. "You carry," she said, and placed the tureen on the tray. She added a ladle from the table. "Jenna and I will serve when we get into the dining room. Speaking of which - where might that be?" she asked Argone.

He gestured to the large door at the end of the kitchen. "Through there, then first door on your right. There is a footman, of course."

"Of course." Shanara nodded to Pixel, and he led the females the way he'd been told. Once they were out of Argone's hearing, Shanara said: "Whatever happens, don't show any reaction. There will be a table and, judging by the size of this pot, several people there. Just follow my lead, and I'll try and keep us out of trouble."

"Fingers crossed," Pixel said, though he obviously couldn't make the gesture carrying the heavy tureen.

Once outside the kitchen, they were in a short corridor. As Argone had said, there was a liveried servant at the door on the right. As they approached, he opened the door and stood absolutely still, holding it open. Shanara gestured Pixel forward, and they stepped into the dining room.

It was large - a good forty feet long, and almost as wide and high. There were large windows at the far end of the room, filled with stained glass that cast a rosy glow about the room. There were candelabras on the one large table and others placed several feet behind each of the seats. All held glowing candles, giving a soft cast to the light in the room.

The table was long, and only about half of the chairs had people in them - well, *people* wasn't perhaps the best description for some of the guests. There were four of them, and Pixel recognized them instantly - they were Beastials. Two were bird-based, with feathered heads and backs, and sharp, curved beaks instead of noses. One was male, one female. Facing this couple were a whale-man and a leopard-woman. The man was mostly black, but with white on his front and up to his chin. The woman had soft brown fur, with faint dark patches.

Next to them sat two people that looked quite human - which didn't mean that they were, of course. And, at the head of the table, sat a tall, imposing woman in a flared robe.

Pixel's heart almost stopped beating. He had known the Beastials by sight because they had been the first creatures he had ever met in the Diadem. But this woman - he knew her *very* well, and he had hoped that he would never see her again.

"Eremin," he breathed. One of the Three Who Rule. The despot that Helaine might one day become...

Chapter Four

Jenna could feel the tension that flooded through Pixel's body as he stood beside her, and she realized that it was because he had recognized the woman at the head of the table. Jenna didn't have a clue who she was, so it had to be somebody that he'd met before they had been together. Judging from his reaction, he wasn't anything like happy to see this woman.

"Steady," hissed Shanara. Jenna blinked as she looked at the sorceress - she had altered her own appearance again. Not a lot - her dark hair was now a lot lighter, with golden highlights, and her face was a little rounder, her eyes now a pale blue. Clearly, then, this woman was somebody who knew Shanara - and who might have recognized her in her undisguised form...

Who *was* this person?

The Beastials were not so much a surprise to her, as she'd met some of their kind on a short trip she'd taken with her three friends, but she knew they weren't exactly a common sight off their own planet, Treen. So, did that mean that she and her companions had been transported to Treen? Or that these Beastials were simply out visiting another world?

"We have to serve the soup," Shanara muttered. "Don't look at *her*, whatever you do - she wouldn't like it. Come on." She led the way to the table, and stood behind the woman's chair. Pixel was almost trembling, so Jenna stepped in to serve the soup. The woman ignored her completely, and they moved on to the person on her left.

This was a tall man, darkly handsome, but with unpleasant eyes. Pixel served him, thankfully. The unpleasant eyes flickered over Jenna for a moment, and then away, which was a relief. They served the Beastials last, and then Shanara led Jenna and Pixel back to the entrance door. There was a table set there, and she placed the soup tureen down on it.

"Stay here," she whispered. "Listen to whatever is being said. I *knew* I should have recognized this place."

The woman at the table glanced across at them, and the three of them stood firmly at attention. The woman's gaze turned back to her dining companions. She barely touched the soup, but there was an unpleasant smile lurking at the corners of her mouth.

"Well, Cha'kka," she said, coldly. "Have your people come to any decision yet? Will they submit, or will they fight?"

The hawk-like Beastial stared at her. "You know that we cannot fight," he replied. "The Three are too powerful for us to challenge your rule."

"It's about time you understood that," the man growled.

"Be quiet, Restar," the woman said, not even bothering to look at him. "I'm sure they've thought this over very carefully. Haven't you?"

"We have no choice but to submit," Cha'kka said. "But we do not like it. You may have the power to do as you wish, but you cannot order our hearts. We will obey - but we will never do so willingly."

"I don't care whether you like it or not," the woman growled. "I don't care if it makes you molt - as long as you shed somewhere else. All the Three want is your complete, unquestioning obedience. And if we don't get it, you will die. *All* of you. Is that understood?"

"Of course it is understood," the leopard woman snarled. "Why else would we ever bow our knees to such as you?"

"My, aren't we the feisty one?" The woman laughed. "You'd like to use those sharp claws and fangs on me, wouldn't you?"

"Nothing would give me greater pleasure." The leopard woman raised a paw and there was a *snick* as the claws extended. They looked extremely lethal. But then the catwoman sheathed them again. "But I know I would never be able to reach you."

"No, you wouldn't. You'd be dead the second your furry butt left that chair. And, a few seconds after that, so would your kittens in my dungeons downstairs."

The leopard woman's eyes went hard. "There is no longer any need for you to keep them captive. We have agreed to submit to you. One of the terms was that the hostages were to be released." She inclined her head slightly.

"So it was," the woman agreed. "And never let it be said that I am not a woman of my word." She glanced sharply at the man beside her. "Restar, go and order the guards to free the hostages."

"I haven't finished my soup yet," he muttered. "Can't they wait?"

The woman's face turned furious. "How *dare* you question any of my orders? Go *now* - or I'll give her permission to use her claws on *you*."

The man paled, and jumped to his feet. He hurried across the room, and through the door Jenna and the others stood beside. He looked quite terrified.

"I don't know," the woman said to the table in general. "Take a man to your bed, and they start getting uppity. He's about to lose interest for me - and you all know how dangerous that can be." She finished her soup, and then waved her hand. "You, over there - take these dishes away and bring the next course."

Shanara inclined her head, and ushered Jenna and Pixel forward. They collected the soup bowls - only the woman's was empty, and two looked completely untouched - and then hurried out. Once they were in the corridor outside the room, Shanara breathed a sigh of relief. "Thank the good god I wasn't recognized!"

"Or me," Pixel added.

"She's not met you yet," Shanara replied. "But she knows me very well - Traxis always brings me along when he visits *her*."

"Who is she?" Jenna asked.

"Eremin," Pixel said. "One of the Three Who Rule. The woman Helaine might once have grown up to become."

Jenna shuddered. "I'm not Helaine's best friend," she said, softly, "but even I can't see any likeness between the two of them. Helaine's only stuck-up and proud - this woman is *evil*."

"It's what can happen when you can wield unstoppable power, and don't have friends to help keep you grounded," Shanara said. "The seeds of Eremin are there in Helaine's nature - but, thankfully, Helaine keeps a *very* tight rein on them."

"The same way that Nantor is me," Pixel added.

"You're nothing like him!" Jenna insisted.

"Not now," Pixel agreed. "I have friends - and I have *you*. Now I won't ever grow into that cold, heartless creature - because you keep my heart so warm."

Jenna reached to take his hand - she couldn't help loving him. He was so gentle and considerate -

Shanara brushed her hand aside. "Now is not the time for romance," she said, sternly. "I know now where we are - this is Eremin's castle on Treen. It's one of several on various worlds she controls. This is the time when the Three forced the Beastials to serve them, obviously. And things are going to get very bad very quickly."

"What do you mean?" Pixel asked.

"This is the start of their decline," Shanara explained. "Sarman makes his move on them in the very near future, and destroys them - or, at least, so he thinks. For some reason, we've been sent here at a very critical moment in time. And that scares me."

"Why?" Jenna was confused. "I mean, Eremin is unpleasant, but she's doomed, isn't she? All we have to do is to stay out of her way until we can work out how to get back home again."

"It's not that simple," Shanara said. "For one thing, the Diadem is completely under the sway of the Three. *Anyone* here might betray us at any moment if they think there's any advantage in it for themselves. It's a very dangerous time to be here. And then there's the worse aspect of it..."

"Which is?" Pixel prompted.

"I can't imagine it's simply a coincidence that we're here at this exact moment in time. Whoever interfered with our spell sent us here and now for some specific reason. And I don't think it's a very nice reason."

"Oh." Pixel paled. "You think whoever did this sent us back here so that we'll change things somehow?"

"Yes. And because we don't know what or how, there's a chance that we might just change all of history without meaning to do so. We might be here to keep the Three in power - and that would mean that you, Helaine and Score might never be born..."

"I'd kill her rather than allow that to happen!" Jenna exclaimed. The thought of losing Pixel was unbearable.

"Which is *exactly* what we can't do," Shanara snapped. "We can't change *anything* - not the slightest detail. The past *has* to play out as it once did, No matter what happens, we *must* remain calm, and do nothing to change anything."

Jenna paled. "But I don't know what happened!" she said. "Only whatever Pixel and the others told me. I could do something wrong at any moment."

"I know," Shanara said. "I was - am - here, somewhere. But even I don't know every detail. Any of us could make a mistake..."

It was a terrible thought, and one that made them all shudder.

"We have to get out of this place," Jenna said.

"Agreed," Pixel replied. "But *how*? We can't just create a portal - one would just transport us through space, not time. We have to get back to our own time - and I don't have the slightest idea how we'd go about that!"

"Nor do I, I'm afraid," Shanara admitted. "Despite my skill at creating portals, I've never even thought about making one to join two different times together. But obviously *somebody* knows how to do it, because we're here."

"There's only two possibilities for that," Pixel agreed. "First, somebody wants us here, at this specific time and place, for some reason. Second, we're here by accident, simply because somebody *didn't* want us where and when we were."

Jenna sighed. "How can we tell which it is?" she asked.

"We wait," Pixel replied. "If we're here for a purpose, then it should become obvious to us shortly. Perhaps whoever sent us here wants us to change the past; perhaps it's for a completely different reason. Either way, I'm sure it will become obvious. And if there's no sign of us being here to do something specific, then we'll know we've just been sent here to get rid of us from the future, and then we'll have to try and find out why. And while we're here... we'd better take every opportunity to look around. We already know that there's some way to create a time portal - and I imagine if anyone knows how to do that, it must be the Three. So perhaps we can find a way back in Eremin's files somewhere."

Jenna shivered. "That woman scares me," she confessed. "I always thought that Helaine was... well, the enemy. A noble, stuck-up and all. But seeing what she might turn into..." She shivered. "I realize what she must be fighting inside herself."

"Yes," Pixel said, gently. "Helaine is terrified of one day becoming Eremin, as I am terrified of becoming Nantor. The Three are so... soulless. None of us ever want to become those people. We'd all sooner die."

Jenna kissed him. "You could *never* become a monster like that. You're *far* too loving."

"This is not the time for that," Shanara said. "We'd better get the food - Eremin isn't the most patient person in the world, and we *really* don't want to get her mad at us. Come on." She led the way back to the kitchen, where Argone was impatiently waiting.

"Where have you been?" he asked. Then he blinked and looked at Shanara curiously. "Didn't you used to be a brunette?"

"I hate being the same all the time," Shanara replied, brightly. "We'd better get along - Eremin is waiting."

Argone clapped his hands together. "Come along, people," he cried. "Let's get it all together now!" He appeared to have dismissed Shanara's odd change of appearance. Well, he'd probably seen stranger - and more dangerous - things in this place.

Taking the next set of dishes, Shanara led Jenna and Pixel back to the dining hall. Things had changed slightly while they were gone - Restor was back, and had brought a dozen Beastial children with him. There were four of each species, two male and two female each of leopards, whales and hawks. They all cowered close to the table. Jenna could feel the tension in the air - they all wished to rush to the adult Beastials, but none of them dared move without word from Eremin.

Who was seated in her chair as if it was a throne, smiling maliciously to herself, watching the terror and frustration with evident pleasure. Jenna felt an utter disgust for the woman. She didn't care a whole lot for Helaine, but she couldn't imagine what might possibly have happened to turn someone like Helaine into a monster like this. If *this* was somewhere in Helaine's psyche, then Jenna had to marvel at how well Helaine was keeping it in check. Perhaps she should in future be nicer and more supportive to the other girl.

Eremin glanced around and saw the trio. She waved them to a halt. "Business before pleasure," she murmured. "Then again, when the two are one..." She glared at the Beastials. "As I promised, your children are returned to you. However, I wouldn't wish you to get the wrong message from this gesture - that I can be sweet and kind and merciful. I can't. But I *do* keep my word. Nothing will happen to your brats. But I didn't say anything about *you*." With a sudden gesture, she reached forward, curving her left hand into a claw and hissing a few words under her breath.

The male leopard-man gave a cry, and fell to his knees, pawing at his chest. His eyes bulged and he gave a keening scream. Blood began to trickle from his mouth, his nose, his eyes and his ears. Then his eyes rolled, and he fell, unmoving, to the floor.

"Clean that up," Eremin ordered Restor, gesturing to the body. Then she turned to the stunned and grief-stricken female leopard. "I trust the point has been made perfectly clear? You will do the will of the Three without question and without hesitation. Otherwise you will suffer. Including your cubs next time. Now, get out of here, all of you. I'm sick of looking at your moronic faces."

The leopard woman was clearly restraining her fury and grief for the sake of the kits. She huddled them close to her, as did the other Beastials, and then they rushed as fast as they could from the hall. They left the male's body, and Restor gestured for two soldiers to remove it.

Jenna had been too startled to react up until now, but she felt the anger and disgust within her growing. She didn't realize how obvious it had to be on her face until she felt Pixel's hand on her arm.

"Jenna," he whispered. "Control yourself. We can't affect what has already happened. And all of this happened a long time before either of us was even born."

She couldn't understand why he wasn't as sickened as she was, and she honestly didn't care right now. All of her life, she had been raised to venerate life, to care for the sick and injured, to help the helpless. It went completely against her nature to watch such an act of violence without acting. She didn't care what Pixel was saying, or how foolish she was being - she just couldn't help herself.

And it was obvious that Eremin could read all of this on her face. The magician laughed. "What's this?" she asked, mockingly. "One of my servants disapproves of my actions?"

"There was no need for that," Jenna hissed, savagely, furiously. Shanara touched her arm, but Jenna shook it off.

"There was *every* need for it," Eremin replied. "And there's need for more, it would appear. You're new here, obviously, or else you'd have known by now that *nobody* questions my actions." She leaned forward again, and made the same gesture she had toward the Beastial, and began her incantation.

Jenna knew she was seconds away from death. Her hand, almost without thinking, slipped to clutch her aquamarine, and then she felt Eremin throw her spell. It crashed against the hastily-erected barrier Jenna had thrown up - aquamarine enhanced survival - but didn't entirely dissipate. The fury of the blast knocked Jenna from her feet and dazed her - but didn't kill. Jenna was on her knees, gasping for air, and shaking - mostly from pain and shock, but also from a savage fury she had never felt before. She used her carnelian to repair the damage that Eremin's spell had caused and slowly staggered to her feet.

Eremin was stunned. "You *survived* that? Obviously, girl, you aren't the witless slave you are playing." Eremin gestured again, and Jenna found her feet leaving the floor as some powerful, invisible force grasped her and thrust her into the air. "I think it's time for another lesson..." *Something* shook Jenna as if she were a rag doll, stunning her. She couldn't think, couldn't react. All she could do was hold on and pray she survived. She heard a cry from Pixel as if from a far-off distance, but couldn't manage to focus on it. Her whole attention was taken up by Eremin, who rose from her seat and strode across the hall toward her. "This is going to be fun," the sorceress purred. "I haven't tortured anyone to death for simply ages..."

Chapter Five

Score managed to sit up finally and look about him. "Well, the illusion seems to be working," he commented. "I can't see what *was* here a minute or so back. Including Pixel, Jenna and Shanara..."

"I cannot see or hear them," Helaine stated. She was on her feet, looking a little groggy, but managing to stand upright without falling. She was moving about the walls of the room they were in, running her hands across the stone. "Because they are not here. Nor is this an illusion."

"What are you talking about?" Score managed to get unsteadily to his feet. "It's got to be an illusion - that's what we were casting."

"I'm tempted to bang your head against this stone wall to prove that it's real," Helaine growled. "But I don't want to damage the stones."

"Ha ha." Score scowled. "Then - something's gone wrong?"

"Your brain appears to be functioning at its normal low-powered level," Helaine said. "Yes, something has indeed gone wrong. We're alone here on Ordin."

"Ordin?" Score looked around the room. "We're in an empty room made of stone and you somehow *know* this is Ordin?"

"Of course. Would you not know it if we were in New York? You would not mistake any other city for it, would you?"

"No," Score agreed. "Especially not Toronto or one of those other Canadian cities they try and convince you is New York in low-budget movies. Those mountains in the background are a dead giveaway." Seeing the blank look on her face, he added: "No, I wouldn't. You're right. So I accept that you can tell we're on Ordin, even in this boring room. So, do you know the date? The time? When dinner is being served?"

"I assume you're being sarcastic again," Helaine said. "We need to find a room with clothing in it before we do anything else."

"Relax, babe," Score told her. "You're not showing any skin, so you won't get arrested, or put in the stocks, or whatever they do on this planet to immodest teenage girls."

"That's not what I meant," Helaine said, rolling her eyes. "I'm a girl, remember?"

"Well, even though it's hard to tell when you're inside your armor, yes, I *am* aware of your basic femininity."

"You idiot," she snapped. "That's the whole point. On Ordin, as a girl I am supposed to wear a dress. In this outfit, I must return to playing Renald until we discover where exactly we are, and what is happening."

"Oh, right." He had almost forgotten that on this medieval world women were supposed to do only domestic chores and have babies. "Okay, I guess we'd better get out of here, then, and start hunting hats." With her long hair tucked into a hat, Helaine could play a boy again with reasonable conviction. It wouldn't fool Score, but it was good enough for anyone who didn't know her.

Helaine opened the door carefully and peered out. "There's nobody about. Come on." She led the way into the corridor, glanced about and then headed off down to the left. Score sighed and followed. There was no point in asking her if she was sure she was going the right way - Helaine was *always* sure of herself. Generally with very good reason.

A few minutes later, she opened another door and peered inside. "Barracks," she said, cheerfully. "Come on." He followed her into a room with a dozen beds in two rows. At the foot of each bed was a wooden chest. "There should be a cap in one of these chests," she said. "Help me look." She opened the first on the left, so he took the first on the right.

There were items of clothing in them. He held up a tunic. It had some sort of a coat of arms on it. "Maybe I should change into one of these?" he suggested. "I'm a bit conspicuous in jeans and a T-shirt."

"Score, even dressed properly, you would *never* be able to pose credibly as a swordsman," Helaine replied. "Leave that to me, and stay the way you are."

"You don't think I could play a dumb fighting man?" Score asked. "I'm hurt."

"You would be. I doubt you even know how to use a sword."

"It's easy - you hold the blunt end and try to stick the pointy part into your enemy. Or is that the other way around?"

"That's my point - a swordsman would *never* joke about his weapon."

Score rolled his eyes. "Give me a break. You fighting people are *way* too serious. Anyway, here's a hat. Is it your color?" He held up a cap in dark green. It looked large enough to hold her mass of hair.

"It will suffice," Helaine agreed, taking it from him. She bent forward, swept up her cascade of locks and managed to slide them all into the cap. When she stood up again, she raised an eyebrow. "How do I look?"

"Nowhere near as cute as with your hair down, but definitely more like a boy." Score grinned. "There's just something so sexy about a girl in uniform..."

To his surprise, Helaine grinned. Then she leaned forward and kissed him. "I am glad you still find me attractive," she murmured.

"And how," he said, his heart racing. Despite their constant bickering, she was definitely the most attractive female he'd ever met. He kissed her back, enjoying the moment.

Then the door opened, and someone poked his head inside. "You two boys - stop kissing and get back to work!" The intruder vanished again.

Score jerked away from Helaine, startled. "Oh, great!" he exclaimed. "We're going to be in for trouble now." His face was burning.

Helaine frowned. "Why?"

"He must think we're gay!" Score yelped. "It *looked* like there were two guys making out! He doesn't know you're a girl!"

"So? Why would it make us happy if we were two boys?"

Language differences again. "I don't mean gay as in happy - I mean gay as in two boys attracted to one another. It's just an Earth expression." He shook his head. "So, what's going to happen to us now?"

"Nothing, as long as we start looking like we're busy," Helaine said. She scowled. "What is *wrong* with you?"

"Helaine -"

"Renald!" she snapped. "While we're here, I am *always* Renald!"

"Renald," Score said. "Two guys. Kissing."

"So?"

He stared at her. "This is medieval world, remember? What do they do to homosexuals on this planet? Whip them? Boil them in oil? Cut off their..." He shuddered.

"Why should anybody do anything because of that?" Helaine seemed genuinely puzzled. "If two boys like one another, why shouldn't they kiss? Isn't it allowed in New York?"

"Trust me, it's quite common," he replied. "But... well, it didn't use to be. At one time, you could get seriously damaged if you were gay. If not killed. And it still happens. Besides, I don't want anyone to think I like *boys*."

"There's not much danger of *that*," Helaine commented. "A couple of minutes talking with you and anyone would know it's only half-naked girls that hold any interest for you." She stared at him, fascinated. "You're *afraid* of being taken for... gay, aren't you?"

"Yes!" Score admitted. "It can get you into serious trouble where I'm from. You have to be macho." He couldn't believe he was having a discussion like this with Helaine. Or that he was, somehow, losing.

"Then perhaps your world is not as civilized as you would wish me to believe," she said. "Here, you are what you are, and there is no shame in it. So if you wish to continue to kiss me in public, you will not be whipped or anything, even if everyone assumes I'm a boy."

"Believe me, I am *not* kissing you in public while you're Renald," he assured her.

"You and your bizarre moral codes." Helaine shook her head. "Come on." She led the way out of the room.

Score grabbed her arm. "So... does that apply to girls, as well?"

"Does what apply to girls as well?"

"You know - the same sex thing."

Helaine sighed. "Of course - why wouldn't it? If two girls like one another, they can follow their love's urging, just as two boys can."

"Whoo..." Score said. "Then you and another girl could..."

Helaine glared at him. "We *could* - but I *wouldn't*," she replied. "I happen to be attracted to you, and not another girl. Though sometimes I have to wonder why."

"Rats. So there's no chance that you and Jenna might...." His voice trickled off as he caught a look at the expression on her face. "I guess not."

"Even if I *were* attracted to another girl," Helaine growled, "it would not be *her*. Whatever crazy ideas you have rattling around in that head of yours - get rid of them. Now. I do not wish to *ever* hear them again."

"Spoilsport," he muttered.

"I mean it," she told him. "Honestly, you Earth boys are crazy. Now we'd better look busy, or we could be in serious trouble. Come on." She led the way that the man who had surprised them had gone.

Score followed, seriously confused. A world where showing a naked ankle was considered scandalous - and yet had no problems with people being gay? It just seemed so... odd. He knew he was judging their world by the standards of his own again, but he couldn't help it. And, he had to admit, she *did* have a point. He didn't consider himself to be prejudiced against gays, but the thought of kissing another boy made him feel disgusted. Kissing Helaine, on the other hand, set his heart racing.

Maybe he *wasn't* civilized... But that didn't mean that Ordin was!

They exited the corridor into a courtyard, where there were a bunch of armed men, and a number of young warriors their age. The man who had ordered them about halted in front of the soldiers, and glanced around as Score and Helaine hurried over. His eyebrows rose as he studied Score.

"What kind of a soldier are you?" he asked, incredulously.

"He's not a soldier," Helaine said, quickly, making her voice slightly gruff to add to the impression she was male. "He's my cousin, just visiting."

"Then he'd better stand aside," the man decided. "This is no place for a civilian." He gestured Helaine to take a place with the other youths. "Honor guard - at the ready."

The older soldiers formed lines and came smartly to attention. The younger ones fell in beside them in their own ranks. Score noted that Helaine was as quick and smart as any of them. He watched, curiously.

Their leader glared at him. "I assume you're his *retarded* cousin," he growled. "Get out of here!"

"Touchy," Score muttered. But he moved to lean against the nearest wall, watching as the leader put his men - and one girl! - through their paces. Score was quite impressed that Helaine had absolutely no problem keeping up with the others. Of course, it all seemed rather pointless to him, but they seemed to place great store by it all.

"Right," the squad leader finally decided, "I don't think you'll let House Votrin down too badly." Score could see Helaine start a little in surprise - this was her own home! Score had only visited it once, so it didn't look familiar to him. It was odd, though, that Helaine hadn't recognized it immediately. There had to be a reason for that... "Now, remember, you're an honor guard for the king - so keep your movements fluid and sharp. Honor to Votrin!"

"Honor to Votrin!" the troops echoed.

"Right - take five," the leader said. The armed men immediately relaxed and started talking amongst themselves. Helaine hurried over to Score again, her face creased by a frown.

"Castle Votrin," Score said, before she could speak. "How come you didn't spot this as home immediately?"

"Because this is *not* Castle Votrin," Helaine answered. "At least, not *my* castle. Now I look around, I can see that it has the potential to *become* my home. But the East Tower is missing, as well as the stables."

Score understood immediately, and he felt sick. "Hela-Renald, that means we're in the past, somehow. Before the tower and stables were built. And there's a visiting king, which there wouldn't be in our time. Shanara meant to *show* us the past, but somehow we've been actually transported into it."

"It's the only logical answer," she agreed. "I don't know how - or why. But this is Ordin's past. A few hundred years before our time, I'd guess."

"Now what do we do?" Score asked.

"Play along, for the moment," she suggested. "Until we discover how we got here, and why we're here - and how to get back again."

"I agree." He bit his lower lip in thought. "Look, you're obviously going to be tied up here with this honor guard thing, but I'm not wanted. Maybe I should take a look around, and see what I can discover."

"Great idea - except you don't really have much of a clue as to what to look for, do you? You don't know Ordin very well, so you're likely to get yourself into trouble." He was about to protest, but she shook her head. "Come on, Score - you *know* that's what you do best."

"Second best," he objected. "What I do best is get you *out* of trouble. Trust me - I'll be fine. I'll just play dim-witted if anyone asks me something I don't know."

"That would work - it's a believable pose for you."

"Gee, thanks." He started to move off, awkwardly. "See you later. And don't you *dare* kiss me goodbye!"

Helaine grinned, wickedly. "The thought had crossed my mind..."

"And you complain about *my* naughty thoughts," he muttered. He hurried off before she could do anything. He dived through the first door he came to, and then sighed with relief. She was taking a positively fiendish pleasure in this whole situation. Just wait till it was his turn for revenge... On that next trip to New York, he was *definitely* going to try and get her into a bikini...

"Watch where you're going, boy."

Score came to a halt and realized he'd be so lost on his thoughts he'd almost walked into a tall, scowling man. "Sorry," he apologized. "I was lost in thought."

"You're lost in other ways, too, it would seem," the man growled. "Who are you? What are you doing wandering about dressed in such outlandish fashion?"

Oh, great... "My name is..." He realized he couldn't use "Score" here, because it wasn't a local-sounding name. "Matthew," he finished. "I'm..."

"Obviously with the King's brother," the man said. "Nobody else would wear such... bizarre clothing."

"Right, King's brother," Score agreed, hastily. It was nice to have a good excuse for his odd behavior. "I'm a bit lost," he added, hoping that would cover everything he might do that could make him conspicuous.

Abruptly, the man grinned. "Castle Votrin can do that to the unwary," he said. "It's something of a maze. Come with me." He started off again, and Score had no option but to follow him.

The castle was quite busy - there were more guards, all looking alert, and servants of various sorts hurrying everywhere. Some carried cloth, others foodstuffs of varied sorts. There were no children to be seen, and the only females were clearly servants.

The man leading him came to a double set of doors eventually, which were flanked with pikesmen. The men saluted, and opened the door for Score's companion. Score followed him into the room, hoping he wasn't going to regret this.

His hopes were dashed almost immediately. It was clearly some sort of a meeting room. There was a dais at the end of the room, on which were four large chairs. The two in the center were the tallest, made of dark wood with thick cushions on them. In front of this were two long tables, set lengthwise. At the table on the left were seated about a dozen females, all talking amongst themselves. On the right, the table was mostly empty. The women stopped talking as they entered the room. At the head of the table, the eldest woman nodded. "Husband," she said, politely.

"Wife," the man greeted her, with a slight bow.

Standing, with his back to them, a tall man had been talking to the woman. Now he turned, and gave a deep bow of his own. "Lord Votrin," the man said. "It is such a pleasure to see you again."

Score felt sick and faint. He couldn't say the same about the man he was facing...

"Prince Sarman," Lord Votrin said, aimiably. "I believe I've found one of your lost servants." He gestured toward Score, who was still too much in shock to say a word.

"Yes," Sarman said, stroking his dark beard thoughtfully. "I've been wondering where he'd gotten to. We have a lot to talk about." He came closer, and placed a strong arm about Score's shoulders. "A great deal." He squeezed, hard.

Score winced. This was *definitely* not a good situation to be in...

Chapter Six

Helaine had been worried when Score had gone off without her. It wasn't that she doubted his abilities, exactly - he was more than capable of looking after himself - it was simply that he was so arrogantly sure he was better than anyone from a medieval world that he tended to do stupid things. Trouble followed him around like a lost puppy. She was certain that he was going to get himself into a bad situation somehow. But there was nothing that she could do about it at the moment. She'd been pulled into an honor guard for the King, and there was simply no way of getting out of it now.

And, truth be told, she didn't really want to get out of it. It had been so long since she'd been able to play Renald that she'd almost forgotten how much fun it was. It was good being taken for an equal again, rather than being judged as a female. In some ways, Score *was* right about Ordin being backward. They were extremely sexist - probably more so now she was a couple of hundred years at least before her own time. Girls here were being taught the gentle, womanly arts of needlepoint and looking after babies. That was fine for those suited for it, but she craved action. She'd rather hold a sword than a baby any day. So, now that she was drilling with the "other" boys and men, it felt as if she were home again, really, for the first time since she'd been exposed as a girl playing a boy - both long ago, and long in the future.

Then there came a blast of a trumpet from the main gate, and the squad leader yelled: "Right! Enough play-acting - it's time for the real thing! Honor guard to formation!"

Everyone moved into position. Though Helaine had no idea where she was supposed to be, she'd drilled enough in her own time to know how this was supposed to work. The men would be at the head of the line closest to the gate, the boys after that, and the officers at the end to greet the royal personages. She slipped into the line beside a tall, skinny boy. He gave her a puzzled frown.

"You're new," he muttered.

"Just arrived," she agreed. "Renald."

"I'm Damon. You seem to know what you're about, at least. Don't show up House Votrin."

"I would *never* shame the House of Votrin," Helaine said, sharply, and a little louder than she should have.

"Quiet in the ranks," the leader growled. "At the ready - the coach is almost here, lads."

Helaine stared straight ahead, hand on her sword hilt like the others. She waited, impatiently. Why was the King coming here? It could hardly be a coincidence that he was arriving at the same time she and Score had appeared here. *Something* important had to be happening...

There was another trumpet blast, and the main gates were swung open. At the other end of the courtyard, a tall, handsome man who looked vaguely like her father appeared from inside the castle. That must be the current Lord Votrin, she realized - her great-great-however-many-times-grandfather. It felt really strange looking at her own ancestor.

Then there was the sound of hooves, and a clatter, and the carriage drove in through the gate. It was drawn by six white horses, all beautifully matched and groomed. The coach itself was ornate and beautifully painted, with the shield of the Royal House painted on the doors on both side. Behind the coach came a second, and then a small party of soldiers, obviously the armed escort for the King. They all passed along the line of welcome. Helaine kept her face impassive, as she watched them all pass by.

The coach drew to a halt beside where Lord Votrin was waiting. Two servants, impeccably groomed, leapt out as the coach stopped. One grasped the lead horse, ensuring the animals wouldn't move further, while the second opened the coach door, and placed a small set of steps into position.

There was a moment's hesitation, and then the King appeared. He was smiling genially, and waved casually to Lord Votrin. Helaine gave a start, because she recognized the King - his portrait was hanging - would hang? - in the Castle Votrin she was from.

King Caligan...

Then *now* she knew when she was, for he had died some five hundred years before she'd been born. They were further back in time than she had imagined! He had been the last legitimate King of Ordin, but had been killed by his evil brother who had promptly stolen the throne...

Suddenly, she was *certain* she knew that the murder was due to take place at any time now. She couldn't understand exactly how she knew, but this had to be how Pixel felt when he figured something out. It was the only thing that made sense. She and Score were here, now to....

To *what*? To *save* the King from being murdered? But if that were so, then they would change history. To make certain he *would* be murdered? That would preserve history, but she knew it wasn't within her to simply stand by and allow anyone to die. But it was absolutely clear to her that this was their purpose in being here - if they could only work out which reason it was!

Maybe Score could do it, because he was actually pretty smart at such things. She was much better at handling action and battle plans than in working out what was going on. She'd have to find him again and tell him what she knew - before he stumbled and did something dumb.

"Lord Votrin," Caligan said, smoothly, extending his hand. The Lord knelt swiftly and kissed the King's ring.

"Majesty," he said. "Welcome to Castle Votrin! All I have is at your service."

"Thank you, old friend," the King replied. "It's good to be here again - though I wish we were back at Castle Bracklin. My wife is not feeling too well, I'm afraid."

"I'm sorry to hear that, sire," Votrin said. "I shall summon my physicians, and see if they can help."

"I doubt there's much they can do," Caligan answered. "It's her condition, I'm afraid. Traveling makes her sick."

"Then I'll have my wife and her ladies attend," the Lord said. "I'm sure they know what to do."

"Women's matters," the King murmured. "It's a shame they can't be more like men, isn't it?"

"But they wouldn't be half as much fun if they were, would they, majesty?"

The King laughed. "True enough, my friend! I wouldn't have my wife any less feminine, that's for certain. Well, shall we go in? I'm ready for a bite to eat and a cup of your good, honest mead. Nobody makes mead the way your craftsmen do."

"Our bees are the best in the region," Votrin said, with pride. "And their honey unequalled."

"No arguments from me on that score!" The King laughed, and the two of them made their way indoors.

Helaine and the men were not dismissed, so they all stayed where they were, at attention. A moment later, several women came from within the castle. They scurried to the coach. After a few moments fussing and heaving, they reappeared, helping to support a weak and pale figure.

Again, Helaine paled. She knew *this* person better than most. Shanara...

But not the Shanara she knew. This woman was no magician, really. Helaine could sense that there was power in her, but it was raw and unfocused. This was a Shanara who had not yet learned to use her abilities very much, one who was only just experimenting with her abilities.

One who didn't yet know Helaine.

Helaine was glad she was in her male disguise – which Shanara had never seen – so she wouldn't be recognized. When she had first met – *would* meet! – Shanara five hundred years in the future, Shanara had not known who she was. Helaine was certain that it was highly important that this remain true. Otherwise she might end up changing what had – or would! – happen! And who knew what disaster that might cause? All of this time traveling business was starting to give her a headache, but she was certain of one thing – that she *had* to make certain that what had happened in the past still happened. Changing even one detail might cause untold chaos in her own time. She was sure that Pixel would have a very logical, scientific explanation for this, but she was simply going on her gut instincts – and they were hardly ever wrong.

This Shanara looked quite similar to hers, though her hair was shorter, and she was certainly a lot sicker. Helaine had no idea why this should be so. Certainly, Shanara had never spoken of being ill. Then again, who would? It was probably just travel sickness – that coach, though it looked very rich and ornate – probably didn't have springs, and so would hardly be a comfortable ride. It was enough to make anyone ill.

The ladies helped Shanara into the castle. One of the servants turned to the waiting soldiers. "Help with the baggage," he ordered. The squad leader hesitated, because technically this wasn't a job for the soldiers. On the other hand, most of the servants were probably busy getting the place ready for the king. While the leader considered whether to refuse the ill-advised order, Helaine stepped forward.

"Permission to volunteer to help, sir," she said. To her surprise, Daman stepped forward also, and repeated what she had said. The leader looked relieved – he hadn't been forced to give what would have been an unpopular order to his men – who were proud of being warriors, not porters – and nodded. Helaine helped the coachman down with the first trunk, and Daman took the other end. It was heavy, but between them they should be able to manage it. They struggled inside with it, where one of the ladies in waiting saw them and gestured for them to follow her.

"Pretty smart, Renald," Daman said, softly.

"Smart?" Helaine asked. She hadn't really thought this out.

"Yes. I can tell you're ambitious – not one who's content to spend his life here in Castle Votrin. Get yourself noticed by the Queen, eh, and maybe a job in the palace?" He grinned. "I like the way you think."

Helaine smiled mysteriously back. It wouldn't hurt if the boy thought she was as crafty as he himself appeared to be. "It's time for carrying, not thinking," she muttered back.

Now that she knew that they were in Castle Votrin, Helaine was starting to recognize parts of it. The castle would change a lot in five hundred years, but the basic structure couldn't alter that much. They were heading for the guest suites in her father's wing of the castle, which made sense. Even in her time they were called the Royal Rooms, and now she understood why. Caligan and his wife had lodged there whenever they visited. Judging from the greeting he'd given the current Lord Votrin, that would appear to have been pretty frequently.

Helaine and Daman staggered along behind the royal party until they all reached the Royal Rooms. Here the ladies helped Shanara to sit on the large bed. She appeared to be drained from the journey and very pale.

"I just need to rest," she gasped. "I am very fatigued." She gestured at the trunk that Helaine and Daman had placed carefully at the foot of the large bed. "I need to change out of these traveling clothes, also. Something lighter, in there."

Lady Votrin turned to the "boys". "You two," she ordered. "Outside for now. Guard the door. I'll call for you when you're needed." They saluted, and went outside, shutting the door behind them.

"Nicely done," Daman said in a low voice, his face a wide grin. "We've been noticed now – rapid promotion no doubt on the way." Then, to Helaine's surprise, he leaned forward and kissed her on the lips. "You're my kind of a boy," he told her.

Helaine pulled back, startled. If Score were here, no doubt he'd find this highly amusing. Daman had kissed her – because he believed she was a boy! She must have looked startled, because Daman appeared slightly confused.

"I thought you liked boys," he said. "I mean, your cousin…" His eyes narrowed. "Unless there's something odd going on…" He thought a moment. "That cousin of yours isn't a girl in disguise, is he? Or she? I mean, he doesn't look like any boy I've ever seen."

It was all Helaine could do not to laugh. Score – a *girl*? That thought would have really annoyed him! "No," she said, with a straight face. "He's more of a boy than I am, trust me. It's just that… well, we're a couple. And I don't cheat."

"Oh." Daman nodded. "I can understand that. Well, if you two ever break up, look me up. You're just my type."

Not really, Helaine thought to herself. But she managed to keep her face impassive. "If we do, I'll let you know," she promised. "You're kind of cute yourself."

The door opened, and one of the ladies in waiting looked out. "You two," she snapped, "back inside. She's decent again."

Helaine was amused by that – it wouldn't have bothered her to have seen Shanara in a state of undress, and it wouldn't have affected Daman much, either! But she still managed to keep the grin off her face as they marched back inside.

Shanara was in a flowing gown now, and being helped into the bed by several of the clucking ladies, all trying to make sure she was comfortable. The lady who'd ordered Helaine is gestured at the trunk. "Put that under the window," she ordered. "We don't want the queen tripping over it if she has to use the chamber pot." Daman and Helaine hurried to obey, and then hung back.

Suddenly, Shanara started to retch. Helaine glanced about and saw a bowl. Snatching it up, she hurried to the bed, just in time to catch the dark stream Shanara threw up. One of the ladies hurried wiped the Queen's mouth, and Shanara smiled gratefully up at Helaine.

"Thank you," she said. "You're very quick-witted. I'm glad you're here. What's your name?"

"Renald," Helaine said, keeping her head bowed so that Shanara couldn't get a good look at her.

"Thank you, Renald. I'm not quite as ill as it might appear – it's just morning sickness."

Helaine paled. *Morning sickness*? Shanara was *pregnant*! And that could only mean…

That was *Score* in there! An embryonic Score…

Things had become more complex, just when she had thought that wasn't possible. Now she had even more reasons to be extremely careful what she was doing. There were *two* Scores here, now. As if one wasn't bad enough!

Shanara managed a weak smile. "Don't look so aghast," she said. "It's perfectly natural."

Helaine wasn't in agreement there – whatever this situation was, *natural* was definitely the wrong word to try and describe it. "Sorry, Majesty," she managed to say. "I wasn't aware the Queen was pregnant, is all."

"Not many people know," Shanara admitted. "Try not to spread the news if you can avoid it."

"Nobody who shouldn't know will learn about it from me," Helaine promised.

Shanara reached out to touch her hand. "Thank you, Renald. I'm glad you're here. Somehow I feel comforted that you're around."

"Comforted?" Lady Votrin said, looking worried. "You'll need all of that you can get, Majesty – I've just received word that the King's brother has arrived. He's on his way to speak with you, apparently." She didn't look thrilled with the news.

If she was bothered, Helaine was in agony. She knew, from her history lessons, that King Caligan had been killed by his brother, who had then stolen the throne for himself. The brother hadn't lasted long as king, but it had wrecked the proper line of succession and caused centuries of unease and war on Ordin. Soon she would see the traitor for herself.

"Don't worry," Shanara told the Lady. "He's mostly talk and bluster."

Lady Votrin scowled. "I know he's the King's brother and all, but I don't like that man. Not one bit."

"Not many people do," Shanara agreed. "He doesn't try and make himself pleasant, I know. But I'm sure he's harmless."

That's all you know, Helaine thought. She wished she could warn Shanara of what was to come – but that would alter all of history, and not necessarily for the better.

"Sister!" The voice was oily and almost purring as the King's brother entered the room. "I heard that you were ill, so I naturally hurried to see how you are."

"How kind of you, Traxis," Shanara said, managing a fake smile.

It was more than Helaine could achieve. Helaine stared in shock at the King's brother – the King's soon-to-be-killer.

Traxis… One of the Three Who Rule.

Traxis… who would become Score…

There weren't *two* Scores here.

There were *three*…

Chapter Seven

Pixel shook his head in a desperate attempt to clear it. When Eremin had attacked Jenna, he had tried to come to Jenna's aid. Almost casually, Eremin had swatted him aside, sending him crashing into one of the stone walls. He felt Shanara's arms about him, helping him into a sitting position.

"Do nothing!" she growled, softly. "I know it's Jenna - but you cannot fight Eremin!"

"I don't care who it is," Pixel gasped. "I won't allow Jenna to be harmed."

"And you dare not take the chance of hurting Eremin!" Shanara gasped. "If you do, all of history may be changed. Eremin *must* survive!"

"I don't care about history," Pixel said, stubbornly. "All I care about is Jenna."

"Then if you attack Eremin, you may condemn Helaine to oblivion - not to mention yourself and Score." Shanara glared at him. "If the Three don't become reborn as you three, then you won't exist! And you can't help Jenna if you wipe yourself out. Pixel, you're the smartest person I know - *think*!"

Much as he didn't want to consider it, Pixel knew in his heart that she was right - he didn't dare try and change anything that had once happened. To alter the time line might wreck everything. If he and the others were not created by the Three, then Sarman might well rule the Diadem forever - and he was as evil as the Three.

But - it was *Jenna*! How could he allow the girl he loved to be harmed?

He saw that Jenna was still managing to hold out somehow against Eremin's vicious attack. She had to be utilizing her aquamarine to protect herself. But how long could she manage to withstand this awful onslaught? Eremin was laughing, clearly sensing that she was breaking through Jenna's defenses.

There was movement across the room, and Restar inched his way toward Eremin. "My lady," he called, gently but firmly. "My lady, you must stop this."

"*Must*?" Eremin whirled to glare at him. "Have a care, worm - the fact that I take you to my bed for amusement confers no special privileges on you, and it certainly doesn't make you invulnerable."

"No, lady, I know that," Restar agreed, bowing. "But you

have an appointment, if you recall, and you do not have the time to spare to torture this foolish servant at the moment. She can wait until later."

"Appointment?" Eremin scowled. "Oh, that damned Nantor again!" She paused, clearly undecided. "He can wait my pleasure - I want my fun first."

"You *always* want you fun first," came a fresh voice from the doorway - one that Pixel knew only too chillingly well. It was Nantor, the member of the Three that Pixel was supposed to become. He had only recently vanquished Nantor - forever, he had hoped! - and now he was back with him again... A cold chill like a knife cut through him. He felt Shanara's gentle hand squeeze his shoulder in comfort.

"And you always enjoy spoiling it, don't you?" Eremin replied. She ceased her attack on Jenna. "Very well, I know how you are. She can wait until later."

"Now you're being sensible," Nantor replied. "How unlike you. You'll develop compassion next."

"Never toward *you*," Eremin muttered. She glared at Restar. "You - take charge here. I want these three to be available for my... pleasure... when I return. Else you'll be transferred from my bed to my rack. Do I make myself clear?"

"Always, my lady," Restar answered, bowing low.

"Good." Eremin turned her back on them. "Come on, Nantor - I don't wish to discuss important matters with slaves around. We'll go to my study." She strode from the room. Without a backward look, Nantor followed her.

Jenna had collapsed to the floor, sobbing. Pixel somehow managed to hobble over to her and held her tight. Jenna cried into his shoulder, her whole body spasming with her emotions.

"It's over for now," Pixel whispered, stroking her hair. "She's gone."

"What is wrong with you?" Restar demanded, towering over them. "Are you insane? Do you *want* to die? Confronting Eremin like that! I've never seen anything so foolish in my life."

"Get used to it," Shanara muttered. "These teens tend to behave that way all of the time."

"Not twice with Eremin," the consort snapped. "If she remembers you three, you won't survive. How could you be so mad? Are you with the Resistance also? If so, how is it that you're not better trained?"

Pixel was only vaguely aware of anything but the sobbing girl he held, but Restar's words filtered through to him. "*Also*?" he asked. "Then - you are a Resistance member?"

The man flinched, and bit his lip, but then nodded. "Of course. How could anyone with a conscience *not* be against her cruel and capricious ways?"

"And yet you sleep with her," Pixel said.

"I do what I must, even though it disgusts me," Restar replied. "She and the others of the Three must be brought down, otherwise the Diadem will be enslaved forever." He looked at each of them in turn. "You, too, are here to fight her?"

"No," Shanara said, heavily. "We are not. Fighting her is the very last thing that we want. We are here to ensure that events will unfold as they must. We cannot and will not fight either Eremin or the others of the Three."

Restar was clearly confused. "But - this girl defied her! Why would she do that if you are not here to fight?"

"Because she has compassion," Pixel said. "She has the most generous heart of any human being I have ever known. But she should not have fought - she should have accepted. As we did."

Jenna turned tear-filled eyes toward him. "Oh, Pixel," she gasped, "how could I *not* fight? She killed that poor being in front of his children. It was *evil*."

"Yes," Pixel agreed, sadly. "But it is an evil that has already happened. And we cannot change that. I do not wish Eremin to kill you, also, which is what she will do if you continue to fight."

"She is horrible," Jenna sighed. "Heartless and cruel. How can you stand it?"

"Because I must," Pixel replied. "Much as we might agree with Restar that she deserves to die, we cannot help in that. We cannot defy her, we cannot fight her. We must accept."

"Which is more than I can," Restar growled. "Each day, it grows more and more difficult to tolerate her behavior."

"Then I'll spare you that problem," Eremin said, standing in the doorway, a triumphant sneer on her face. "I allowed you to *touch* me, and this is how you repay me? By seeking my death?" Nantor, a smirk on his face, stood beside her.

Restar looked shocked, and then began to understand what Pixel had grasped instantly. "There was no meeting," he said, slowly.

"This was to test me."

"Yes," Eremin agreed. "Exactly. And you failed, miserably. I knew there was someone working against me, but at first I didn't suspect you. I never thought you had the spine for it." She ignored him for a moment, and stared down at Pixel and Jenna. "Though I confess you two surprised me. I was certain you'd be in on the plot also."

"Which is why you left us alone with Restar," Pixel said, understanding. "You wanted to see if we'd incriminate ourselves."

"But you didn't," Eremin said, wonderingly. "I'm amazed - I was *certain* you were traitors."

"And yet you see that they are not," Nantor snapped. "I'm sorry if it means that you don't have a legitimate reason to torture and kill them - but the lack of one has never stopped you from doing it in the past."

"Perhaps I'm more mature," Eremin said, a cold smile drawing across her face. "But I think I'll allow them to live - at least for the moment." She turned to Restar. "However - *you* have really disappointed and annoyed me. Now I'll have to find a new toy for bedtime."

Restar was clearly terrified, but he somehow managed to gather together all of his courage. "If you're going to kill me," he said, "go ahead and do it."

"Oh, I'm certainly going to kill you," Eremin replied. "It would set such a bad precedent if I allowed you to live. And I do so hate people who disappoint me - and you *have* disappointed me. But I'm not going to kill you immediately - that would be too swift and merciful."

"And you're not known for being swift and merciful," Jenna said, bitterly.

"No, I'm not," Eremin agreed cheerfully. "I'm known to be vindictive." She glared at Restar. "I have a new spell I've been dying to try on someone - and I think you'll make the perfect test subject." She glanced at Pixel. "Any objections?"

"I object to everything you are and everything you stand for," Pixel replied, striving to keep his temper. "But I cannot allow myself to give into my feelings. I won't fight you."

"Too scared?" Eremin mocked.

"Yes," Pixel admitted, candidly. "But not of you. Of what might happen if I do what I wish and destroy the pair of you."

Nantor raised an eyebrow. "The three of you have the stench of magic about you," he said. "But not strong enough to harm us. You don't know what you're saying."

"*She* couldn't kill Jenna," Pixel pointed out. "And it wasn't through a lack of will. I think we're stronger than you imagine."

"Yes," Nantor said, thoughtfully. "I think you are." He made an abrupt decision. "Eremin, I think I'll take these three with me when I leave. They bear some further study."

"I said I'd allow them to live," Eremin replied. "I didn't say you could have them. They're *my* slaves, and I wish to... play with them a little."

"Your idea of play tends to be a trifle lethal, my dear," Nantor said. "I *really* must insist that they accompany me - at least until I discover what they are and why they are here."

"They're *mine*," Eremin growled. "You take them over my dead body."

"That sounds agreeable to me," Nantor answered. His hand whipped up and he cast a spell.

Eremin, however, was ready, and she threw up a shield. His magics splashed harmlessly against it, and she fired a bolt of pure light back at him. He countered, and then they began to battle in earnest.

Pixel paled. "What are we going to do?" he asked.

Jenna smiled brightly. "I'm hungry," she announced. "I think I'll have something to eat." She wandered over to the table and started to help herself.

"How can you eat at a time like this?" Pixel asked. "Nantor and Eremin might kill each other."

"They won't," Jenna replied, munching on some cooked meat. "Because they *didn't*, did they?"

"That's right." Pixel sighed. He glanced at the dueling wizards, who were oblivious to everything else as they strove to beat each other. Sparks and fires flew. It looked worse than it was, he realized - neither of them was seriously intent on destroying the other. "The Three always hated one another, but they needed one another. They dare not cause too much damage."

"But while they're occupied," Shanara said, "perhaps we had better take advantage of their distraction." She glanced at Restar. "Now might be a good time to run for your life," she said, gently.

"How far do you think I'll get?" he asked, still shaking. "It will only anger her if I flee."

"She plans on torturing you to death," Pixel growled. "How much worse can it get? Run, while you can."

Restar hesitated, then nodded and dashed for the door. He never made it.

Eremin whipped around, and cast a spell in his direction. He barely had the time for a scream before he froze into place. Eremin glowered at him, her battle with Nantor temporarily halted. "Oh, no," she purred. "You don't escape me that easily." She gestured, and a jar made from thick glass flew into her hand from where it had been sitting on the table. Nantor seemed to be enjoying the respite from the battle, because he didn't attempt to continue his assault. Eremin glared at Pixel and then Shanara. "I thought you weren't going to fight me?"

"We're not," Pixel replied. "But that doesn't mean we won't oppose you - or try and help your victims."

Eremin's lips curled back in an unpleasant grin. "Are you going to fight me for him?"

"No," Shanara answered. Pixel could tell she disliked the decision as much as he did, but there was nothing they could do without possibly affecting history. "Not at the moment."

Eremin laughed. "Then you *are* cowards, after all!" She turned her back on them and stalked over to where Restar was frozen, unable to even struggle. "Restar, my love," she murmured, "I'm afraid you've lost all of your privileges. It's time to face up to the music and to dance to my tune." She made a strange gesture with her free hand, a twisting motion.

Restar managed somehow to scream as his body started to simply fall apart. It began to crumble into dust where he stood, pieces flaking and falling away, to decay into nothingness. In seconds all that was left of the unfortunate man was a wisp of yellowish smoke. Pixel fought back bile and fury. There was nothing he could do, and nothing he could have done.

"Fascinating," Eremin said. She raised the jar she held in her other hand, and removed the lid. Another gesture caused the smoke to float into the jar, and she slammed down the lid. "Bottled people," she announced, cheerfully. "Not alive - but neither is he fully dead."

Nantor snorted. "Where's the sport in that?" he asked her. "In that state he can't really be suffering, can he?"

"Not yet," Eremin agreed. "But I'm not quite done with him

yet. That's just the first part of the spell. Watch, and learn." She strode to the table, and set down the jar. Jenna had stopped eating, and stood there, glaring in helpless fury at the woman. Eremin gave her a dazzling smile. "You may find this... educational."

"I'm more likely to find it appalling," Jenna growled.

"Yes," Eremin agreed. "That, too." She concentrated, and started to weave her hands in the air, all of the time muttering words that Pixel couldn't quite catch. But there was a feeling of familiarity about the spell, even though he knew he had never heard it before, and wasn't at all sure what it was for. Nantor was watching with interest, his arms crossed, his eyes amused.

The air began to pucker and swirl. Blackness, inky and intense, started to materialize. Then it slowly took shape - human shape. A being of pure darkness at first, it gradually started to grow more focused.

Beside him, Shanara gasped, and he knew why. His heart was racing, and his mind swirling.

He recognized the form.

The blackness separated into clothing, and hair. Paler material filled out the shape, making it fully human now. Eremin gestured at the jar on the table, and the lid flew off. The yellowish smoke rose and then drifted across to the newly-formed body. For a moment, it seemed to hesitate, and then it flowed *into* the shape.

The eyes sprang open, and despair stared back at them all.

Pixel stared at the man. "Oracle," he breathed.

Chapter Eight

Jenna was filled with horror and fury. She could hardly believe that Eremin was so callous and evil. Even though she knew that Restar was still alive in some way as Oracle, what had been done to him was dreadful. She was so unused to hating anyone the way that she hated Eremin. She didn't like how it made her feel.

Nantor applauded slowly. "Oh, very good," he said, sounding bored. "So now you've remade him in a new form. Eremin, you're getting duller as you age, you know."

"Mind your manners," Eremin growled. "It's not as simple as you seem to think it. Try hitting him."

"Why would I want to do that?" Nantor asked. "I'd sooner cast a spell."

"Then try that." Eremin was barely able to conceal a smirk. She was obviously full of her own brilliance.

Nantor sent a fireball hurtling toward Oracle, who was still in a state of shock. The bored magician's eyes widened as the ball went *through* its intended target and splattered harmlessly across the far wall. "Now that's not bad," he conceded.

"He's completely immaterial," Eremin said, pleased with herself. "He can touch nothing in this universe - and nothing can touch him."

"Oh, *that's* clever," Nantor drawled. "You've made him indestructible? What a punishment!"

"Well, he does have *one* weakness," Eremin said, with a nasty grin on her face. "He has to do whatever I order him - he is bound to obey me. He can go anywhere I chose to send him. He has now become my untouchable messenger."

"The poor man," Jenna said, softly.

"He defied me," Eremin growled. "Any *nobody* does that and remains unpunished. Don't imagine that I've forgotten about the three of you, either." She glared at Jenna. "I'm inclined to kill you simply on general principles."

Pixel shook his head. "That wouldn't be very smart. We know things that might be of use to you. Things other people don't."

Nantor raised a lazy eyebrow. "Oh, please. How can the three of you possibly know anything that we don't know? Perhaps Eremin is right this once, and she should indulge her bloodthirsty nature."

"I know that you're under attack," Pixel said softly.

Eremin's eyes narrowed. "What are you talking about?"

"You have some unknown foe who is chipping away at your control over the Diadem," Pixel explained. "He's started to attack you - maybe not too obviously yet, but it is happening. And, clearly, this isn't something you're letting very many people know, is it?"

"So how is it that *you* know?" Nantor asked. "Are you saying that the three of you are the ones responsible? That you're trying to replace the Three Who Rule with the Three Who Want To Rule?"

"Trust me, we're most definitely not the ones who are attacking you," Pixel told him. "But we do have our sources of information that aren't available to you." Jenna knew what he was referring to - that, because he was from the future of this world, he knew what was going to happen.

"And you're offering to share that information with us - for a price?" Nantor asked, sounding almost amused.

"Something like that," Pixel agreed.

"Bah!" Eremin glared at him. "Nantor, why don't we simply torture them to get whatever pitiful information they might have?"

"Because," Pixel pointed out, "torture is *so* unreliable. We might say almost anything to avoid the pain, and you'd have no way of knowing whether what we were telling you was the truth or not."

"We have no way of knowing whether what you'll tell us *without* torture is the truth, either," Nantor said. "And we could simply separate the three of you and question you individually - and only believe what all three of you say." Jenna could see that Nantor was clearly as smart as Pixel - well, they *were* the same person, in effect, so that was hardly surprising. She couldn't guess which one of them would win this argument, though.

"Unless we've agreed to a lie beforehand," Pixel replied. "Besides, I doubt even Eremin's efforts at torture would work too well on us. You've already seen that her most powerful death-spell didn't kill Jenna. What makes you think that anything else you might do to us would have any greater chance of succeeding?" Jenna knew that this was a bluff - she had *barely* survived the attack, and was still quite weak. And she had managed even that little because of her special abilities - which neither Pixel nor Shanara shared. Pixel smiled, innocently. "Why don't you simply check my magical abilities? You'll find they're quite as powerful as your own."

"I *have* been checking them," Nantor answered. "I like to know my enemies. You and the young girl are both wizard-level.

Your… friend -" he eyed Shanara " - isn't quite as good. She's the weak link in your group. If we were to call Traxis, the three of us could take the three of you."

"*If* he came at your summons," Pixel said, smiling. "he's a bit… unpredictable, isn't he? And he's not too fond of either of you. He *might* just decide that he's better off on his own and leave the two of you to take on the three of us alone." Jenna could see by Nantor's expression that this was clearly a possibility. "And the two of you couldn't take the three of us." Pixel spread his hands, innocently. "But why even think of all of that? We're willing to be friendly, and help you in a few small ways. And I promise you that we have no intentions at all of attacking you - or of betraying you."

Jenna wondered if this was getting through to either Nantor or Eremin. Nantor was, like Pixel, very logical - but Eremin was highly emotional, and her emotions ran deep and dark. She might simply prefer to attack them even if she had no guarantee of winning. Jenna could see why Pixel was exerting all his logic toward Nantor - because he was the only one present who might be able to keep Eremin in check.

But would he do it?

"You're playing a very dangerous game, boy," Nantor growled.

Pixel glared at him. "This is no game, and we're not *playing*. People are dying, and more will, unless you listen to us and allow us to help you."

Eremin spat on the floor. "The day we need the help of a second-rate magician and two children is the day we *should* lose control of the Diadem. I say we kill them now, and have done with it."

Nantor didn't even look at her. "Well, your efforts in that direction haven't been too successful, have they? And *kill them all* seems to be the only thought you have these days in that nasty little mind of yours."

Eremin glowered at him. "I've had almost everything I can take from you," she told him. "Just give me an excuse, and I'll rip your insides out and feed them to the griffins."

"And *this* is exactly why you're losing control over the Diadem," Pixel said. "Because you can't get along together, some hidden foe is able to take you on and defeat you. And it's why you need our help."

Eremin laughed. "As if I would trust you!"

"You don't trust *anyone*," Jenna snapped. "I've had my fill of you, you bloodthirsty bitch." She turned to Pixel. "Let's get out of here and leave them to their fates." But even as she was saying this, she had her citrine clasped in her tight fist. It was her jewel of persuasion, and she was willing at the two adults: *Trust us…*

"Don't listen to Eremin," Nantor said. "Perhaps we are being a little too hasty in rejecting your offer of aid. You do seem to be sincere, and if you *are* intending to betray us - well, I think you know that we'd kill you. Quite slowly and painfully"

"I'm quite sure of it," Jenna agreed. All the time, she was focusing her strength on willing *trust us….* It was clearly getting through to Nantor, but was it having any effect at all on Eremin? She was the most dangerous one, with her unpredictable savagery. She might snap at any moment and try to murder them all. *Trust us…*

"You're a fool," Eremin finally said. "But I'll play along for now. They can live - just as long as there's no sign of them betraying us in any way." She stared at Jenna. "Trust me, the next time I want you dead, I'll gut you with my fingernails if nothing else works."

"I'm sure you'd try," Jenna agreed.

"Fine," Pixel said, quickly, before the two of them could start up again. "We'll try and help you identify who your hidden foe is, and see if there's anything we can do about it. Meantime, we'd all appreciate it if you could stop killing people."

"Beastials aren't people," Eremin sneered. "And Restar is still alive… technically." She snapped her fingers. "Pay attention," she told Oracle. "You and I have to see what sort of limitations there are on your abilities. Come along with me." She started to leave the room, then turned back to glare at Jenna one last time. "Stay out of my way," she said. "Your life will be longer and less painful if you do." Then she swept out of the room. Oracle walked straight through the door with her.

Nantor looked from one of them to another. "I don't agree with Eremin a lot," he said, softly. "But in this case, I find myself on her side. Show one hint of betrayal, and I'll help her gut the lot of you." He gave a half-smile toward Shanara." No matter how pretty." Then he left the room also.

As soon as they were alone, Pixel collapsed into a chair, shaking. "I *really* didn't think that was going to work," he admitted.

"You've Jenna to thank that it did," Shanara informed him.

"Couldn't you feel the force of her persuasion?"

"Yes." Pixel grasped Jenna's hand, and pulled her close and hugged her. "I don't know what I'd do without you," he said.

She bent down and kissed his forehead. "Don't ever try and find out," she advised him. "I'm just glad I could help out."

"Our position here isn't very secure," Shanara said. "Both of them are going to be watching us closely. And what are we going to do? I mean, I'm not complaining that we're still alive - but what next?"

"Next we try and find a way to get back home again," Pixel said. "We got here because someone managed to create a portal that goes through time as well as space. If it's possible, then there must be some information written down. The Three probably have a large collection of books of spells. We find their library and start hunting for it."

"They're going to want to see us make some progress in identifying their enemy," Shanara pointed out.

"That's not so hard," Jenna said. "We all know it's Sarman. He's supposed to be working for them, but the whole time he's working for himself and planning to slaughter them. Why don't we just tell them?"

"For two reasons," Pixel answered. "First, if we tell them it's Sarman, then they have no further use for us. Knowing Eremin, she'll promptly try and kill us. Second, we don't know *when* he's going to strike and defeat them. If we tell them too soon, then we might help them stop him - and change history. If the Three don't escape Sarman by becoming Score, Helaine and myself... Well, not only might the Diadem still be in their tyranny in our time - but we may actually wipe the three of us out. If the Three don't make themselves children again - Score, Helaine and I will never be born..."

Chapter Nine

Score was sweating and worrying. And there was no way to get out of this, as far as he could see. He was trapped in this meeting with Lord and Lady Votrin - and Sarman, of all people! It was a good thing that Sarman didn't have a clue as to who Score really was, because he'd already tried to kill him - or, rather, *would* try to kill him - in Sarman's future and Score's past. All of that was disturbing enough, but what was really bugging Score out was that Sarman claimed to know him…

Which meant one of two things: Sarman was either lying or telling the truth. He *had* to be lying - but *why*? It didn't make any sense. Why would Sarman claim to know Score if he really didn't? That left only the option that he was telling the truth. But he *couldn't* be, because the only way he could know Score was if he somehow knew the future…

And then a worse thought came to him: was Sarman somehow the one who had screwed up their spell and brought them back here in time? Was it all so that he could kill Score, Helaine and Pixel before they could finish him off in the future? The idea made Score's skin crawl. He had no clues yet as to what was going on.

And - Sarman was a prince? He was obviously a native of Ordin, and his rank presumably meant he was King Caligan's brother. Score didn't know much about the history of Ordin - obviously, that was Helaine's specialty - but he did know that according to legend Caligan was killed by his brother, who took over rule of Ordin and founded an evil dynasty that eventually died out, leaving Ordin without a legitimate ruler. So, was Sarman then the man who slew Caligan?

And was that why he was here in the palace at this moment with the king?

Score knew that he shouldn't mess with history, but things were getting *way* too complicated for his liking. Not for the first time, he wished Pixel were here. Pix was way better at figuring things out than he was, and he really needed help about now.

The first time he had visited Ordin - several hundreds of years in the future! - Score had seen a painting of King Caligan and his Queen… who had been the image of his dead mother. Only now Shanara claimed *she* was his mother, and had only faked her own death… Which meant that Shanara must have been Caligan's queen, and if Caligan was here…

"I trust the Queen is feeling better."

Score snapped back to paying attention to what was happening at the tables in the dining room. He was standing quietly behind Sarman's chair, as suited the supposed-servant he was playing. At the head of the table sat Lord Votrin, with his wife beside him. Sarman was seated to their left, and to the right was the man Votrin was addressing. With a start, Score recognized him from the painting.

King Caligan!

"I hope so," the King answered. "It is nothing, really. Just a touch of travel sickness, I'm sure. It is kind of you to ask after her."

"Not at all, your majesty," Votrin said. "She is a gentle and kind lady, and dear to everyone's hearts."

"Yes, I've always found her so," Caligan agreed. "She keeps me steady." He smiled at Sarman. "You need to find yourself a similar wife, cousin. It would make you happier."

Cousin… So Sarman wasn't the king's brother. Which meant he wasn't the king's killer, either. Scratch that theory…

"I am perfectly content as I am, sire," Sarman replied. "With all of the work I have to do, I would only neglect a wife. And women do not appreciate neglect."

"Indeed they do not!" Caligan agreed, laughing. "Which is a pointed and well-deserved rebuke of my own behavior." He stood up, so everyone else at the table was forced to do likewise. "I shall go and see how Cathane is faring. If you will all excuse me?" Naturally, there were no objections, and he swept from the room.

Cathane? Score was confused. He had believed that *Shanara* was Caligan's wife… Was this an earlier wife? Or had Shanara been lying all along? Score didn't know what to believe. It was all getting far too complicated for him to work out. Where was Pixel when he was really needed?

Sarman stood up and bowed to Lord Votrin. "I, too, had better retire to my room," he said. "Though I am not as affected by the trip as the Queen, I do feel tired."

"Of course, my prince," Votrin answered. "We shall look forward to seeing you again for supper."

Sarman turned, and looked down at Score. "Come along, boy." He strode from the room, and Score had no option but to follow. He wished he knew what was about to happen. Sarman had almost succeeded in killing him once, in the future, and that was when he'd had help from Helaine and Pixel. He didn't like the idea of facing Sarman alone. He slipped his hand into his pocket, and touched the four gemstones he carried there. The glow of power he felt from them restored a small amount of his waning confidence. If there was to be a fight, he'd go down fighting.

The problem was - he *would* go down. Sarman was far more powerful than he was. He was probably too powerful even if Helaine were here to help Score - and Score didn't like the thought of putting Helaine into harm's way, so he was sort of glad she wasn't. Except he always felt better when she was around, and he did miss her when she wasn't.

Whoa! Not the time to get sickly and romantic! Focus!

Sarman obviously knew his way around Castle Votrin, because he set off at a ferocious pace. Score had to hurry to keep up. Thankfully, Sarman didn't seem to want conversation as he marched down corridors and finally up a flight of stairs to a turret room. Once inside, he gestured for Score to close the door. With a thump like the crack of doom, Score shut himself in with one of his greatest enemies.

It was quite a pleasant room as much as any room in a cold, stone castle could be. There was a bed, a table, several chairs, three large trunks and a lot of candleholders. There was a blazing fire in the hearth that took the edge of the chill. Of course, matched against all the comforts was the presence of Sarman.

"Well, boy?" the magician demanded, impatiently. "What news do you have?"

"News?" Score didn't have to play ignorant.

"Don't act the fool with me," Sarman growled. "You *are* my spy inside this place, are you not?"

Uh-oh... So *that* was why Sarman had claimed to know him... There was a certain measure of relief in that knowledge. It meant Sarman *didn't* know he was facing one of the people who would kill him. But there was, of course, a huge problem. Score couldn't deny being the spy - he knew too much simply knowing one existed, and he was certain Sarman would slay him if he thought Score wasn't the spy... But, of course, Score didn't have a clue as to what information Sarman was after...

"Yes, sir," he said, quickly. "But... well, I'm not certain exactly what it is you're after."

"Damnation." Sarman glared at him. "Didn't she tell you?"

She? Score didn't know who *she* might be, but he had to improvise - and do so convincingly. He shook his head. "She just told me to keep my eyes and ears open, and that you'd tell me what I was supposed to do when you arrived. She didn't want to give me too much information in case anyone discovered who I was working for. I couldn't tell what I didn't know."

Sarman seemed mollified by this reply. "That sounds like her devious way of thinking," he agreed. "She's so twisted, one of these days she'll bite herself on her own backside. Alright, we'll get straight to it, then. First, though, you are certain that nobody has a clue what you're doing here?"

"Nobody," Score replied. *Especially me*, he added, mentally.

"And you do understand the political situation?"

Oh boy! "Well, as much as I can," Score said, carefully. He racked his brains for all the details he could remember from what Helaine had told him. "King Caligan rules, and is a popular monarch. His wife is Cathane, also well liked. But they have no heirs, and the king's brother is… interested in getting the throne for himself. The Lords in general are loyal to Caligan - Votrin especially, which is why the King is here."

"Where he feels safe," Sarman growled. "Yes, you've got the essence of it. We could never strike at him while he's home, so it has to be while he's on the road like this. Votrin is the perfect place to ambush him because he lets his guard down a little here. What I require from you is the perfect time and place when he will be unguarded - or, at least, not have his wife around."

"Huh?"

Sarman sighed. "You don't know that Cathane is a magician? That she has the power to change appearances?"

Score was startled - then Cathane *was* Shanara - it was highly unlikely that Caligan could have married two women with the exact same ability. Yes, it made sense now - Shanara had to be the name she adopted later, when she was trying to stay hidden from the Three, who would have known her as Cathane…

"Well, I knew *somebody* around here had that power," Score said.

Sarman's eyes narrowed. "There's the stink of magic about you, too," he said, surprised. "Quite a strong one."

"One reason I was chosen as your spy," Score lied, quickly.

"There's always the possibility that the Queen might cast a spell that would fool a normal spy into seeing something that isn't there."

"That makes sense. *She* has done her work well, then. Very well, you're not as unsuitable as I had worried. But be careful and report back to me as soon as possible."

"Don't worry," Score assured him. "As soon as I know what's happening, I'll be back to inform you." He wondered if he could push his luck a bit further. "But I don't understand why you're trying to kill the King. Even with him out of the way, there's still his brother between you and the throne."

"The throne?" Sarman laughed. "As if I care about *that*. No, my reward is better than a throne - the Book of Harmony."

A book of magic, obviously. Maybe the place where Sarman learned the spells that would make him dangerous enough to take on the Three… and win. Sarman's ambitions were always far-reaching. Why rule one small planet when you could rule the entire Diadem? Matters were making more sense now - and shadowing more danger. On the other hand, maybe the spell he and Helaine needed to return home would be contained in the Book of Harmony? Which meant that he needed to get a look at it. And if Sarman was going to get it as his reward, then there was only one person who could possibly possess it right now - the King's brother. He was the one paying off Sarman to kill the King.

But it wouldn't do for Score to appear to be interested in the book at all. "Books," he growled. "Boring."

"You'll learn better one day," Sarman told him. "If you live long enough to learn anything. Off with you now, and report back as soon as possible."

Score was glad of the dismissal. He almost ran from the room, and down the stairs. Then he paused, because he didn't have a clue as to where he was. He *really* needed to get a map of this place… Okay, so now what? He wanted to talk things over with Helaine very badly. Maybe together they could work out a plan. At the moment, he didn't have much of a clue as to what they could do. Maybe she'd found out information that could help them.

Of course, he didn't have a clue where Helaine might be. The person who would know was the guard captain who'd taken her off, and he had been in the courtyard the last Score had seen him. It was as good a place to start hunting as anywhere… if only he knew how to get there!

Luckily, he almost ran into a serving girl. She stammered apologies, which made Score realize she was used to getting beaten for getting in people's ways. "Relax," he told her. "I'm just trying to get to the courtyard, but I seem to have lost my way. This castle is very confusing."

"Yes, sir," she agreed. "You go down this corridor, and then take the first side-corridor on the left. That will take you to the courtyard."

"Thanks," he replied, grinning. "Off you go, then." She gave a delightful curtsy, and hurried off - quickly. "She'll run into somebody else at that rate," Score muttered to himself. But he at least knew where to go now.

He was relieved to make it outside without further problems. Of course, his luck was holding true to form - the honor guard had dispersed. Thankfully, there were more servants, all of whom seemed happy to answer his questions and guide him. He finally managed to stumble across the captain of the guard.

"You again," the man grumbled. "Now what do you want?"

"The… boy I was with," Score said, having caught his slip in time. "Do you know where he is?"

"Obeying orders, I hope," the soldier replied. "And attending the Queen. What's it to you?"

"He's my cousin," Score said, sticking to Helaine's earlier invention. "And I have an urgent family message for him. Don't worry, it won't distract him from his duties. I just need to find him."

"He's with the Queen - just ask for her rooms," the captain said.

"Doesn't anyone here have a map of the place?" Score cried in frustration. He wished - not for the first time - that he had Pixel's skills with a ruby, and could find things when they were needed.

"Ask one of the servants," the soldier said. "What else are they for?"

Quite a lot, Score thought to himself, but there was no point in arguing with the man. He sighed as he left. Time for more confusing directions… Why couldn't they run these places in a logical fashion? All they needed were big signs like those in malls with "you are here" written in big letters. "Stupid medieval planet," he muttered. How could Helaine possibly prefer a place like this over New York?

More questions, more directions and a lot more walking

finally brought him to the Queen's quarters. Needless to say, there were armed guards outside the doors, and he was instantly challenged. Score was starting to get very annoyed with all of this nonsense, but he knew that arguing with the guards would only cause trouble.

"I'm not here to see the Queen," he growled. "I'm here to see Renald. Can one of you fetch him here?"

The two guards looked at one another. "We're here to guard the Queen," one finally replied. "Not to carry messages."

Score held his temper in check - with difficulty. "Then summon one of the servants inside," he said, slowly. "And get them to deliver the message."

The two guards looked at each other and scowled. "That's not part of our job," the talkative one finally decided.

"That's it," Score snarled. "I've had it up to here with this stupid planet. Ask anyone, and they'll tell you I'm a patient, understanding sort of a guy. But I can only take so much…"

The two guards looked startled, and then they raised their spears to try and block him as he moved forward. Without pausing, he shot fireballs at them both, setting their spears alight. The two men howled and shrieked, and started batting their burning spears against the wall in an attempt to put out the flames. All they succeeded in doing was to set a tapestry afire.

Score, meanwhile, slipped past them and through the door -
- to almost run into a sword point.

"I'm annoyed enough already," he growled, knowing who had to be holding the sword in question. "Do you want me to spank you?"

"I'd like to see you try it," Helaine answered. She sheathed her sword, and turned to look over her shoulder. "It's not really a problem, your majesty," she said. "It's my half-witted cousin come visiting. It wasn't hard to recognize his style of doing things. Subtlety isn't one of his strong points."

There was a delightful laugh from further in the room, and a chill went through Score. The laughter was very familiar to him… He had a sudden memory from deep within his childhood. He had heard that ringing tone before…

And then he saw her. She was seated beside the bed, ladies about her. It was Shanara, but not the Shanara he knew. It was a younger woman, lively, happy and almost glowing. It was a Shanara

without the illusion of magic to disguise her.
    It was his mother…

Chapter Ten

Helaine had been caught off-guard by Score's sudden appearance, but it was typical of him - full of confusion. She managed to get the two guards outside of the door calmed down, and assured them that this was not an assassination attempt on the Queen. Closing the door, she turned back to Score, who was standing stiffly, absolutely stunned. Oh, of course... "That's not *our* Shanara," she hissed in his ear.

Her voice seemed to bring him back to himself. "I know," he said softly. "*That's* my mother." He stepped forward and managed quite a creditable bow. "Queen Cathane, please pardon my abrupt arrival."

Cathane? Helaine was confused, but she trusted everything would become clearer once she had a chance to talk with Score privately.

Shanara/Cathane smiled and nodded. "You certainly have a way of making an unforgettable entrance, young man," she said. "And who might you be?"

"Uh, my name is Matthew, your majesty," Score replied. Right - he couldn't use the name *Score* because when they first met Shanara, she didn't know who they were. He was using his given name, which he rarely did. "I'm Renald's cousin."

"Well, I hope you're as resourceful as he is, then," Cathane said. "I assume you do have some reason for this theatrical entrance?"

"I'm afraid I do." Score sighed. "You're in grave danger."

"I'm the Queen," Cathane replied. "There are always those who wish me ill."

"Well, this is a lot more than wishing," Score said. "I'm just come from meeting with Sarman."

"Sarman?" Helaine couldn't help showing her shock. "He's here, too?"

"Why shouldn't he be?" Cathane asked, puzzled. "He's my husband's cousin."

Score glanced at Helaine. "What do you mean *too*?"

Score didn't know, then... "The King's brother just left," she informed him. "Traxis."

"Oh, crap..." Score sighed. He looked really worried now. "So *he's* the one...What's he doing here, though, and not out loose in the rest of the Diadem?"

"Everyone has to start somewhere," Helaine said. "Obviously, this is where he begins."

"You are two of the strangest boys I've ever met," Cathane said, puzzled. "Why all of this surprise about my husband's relatives?"

"Because Sarman thinks I'm his spy," Score said. "I'm supposed to report back to him on the best time for him to kill you."

"What?" Cathane went pale again. "There must be some mistake…"

"Oh, there is," Score told her. "And he made it. I'm nobody's spy. But Sarman is in league with Traxis to kill you and your husband during your stay here, while you think you're safe. Then Traxis will seize the throne."

"But… but that *can't* be," Cathane protested. "I'm not fond of Traxis, but he would never kill his own brother."

"Lady," Score growled, "you have absolutely no idea what he's capable of. Killing his brother is small stuff compared to what he has planned."

"I find it hard to believe," Cathane protested.

"Yeah, I find the same problem with 3D movies," Score replied, in one of his usual confusing comments. "But they exist, and so does Traxis's mad ambitions. We have to make certain of your safety, your majesty, and that of the King."

Damon stepped forward and bowed slightly. "He'll need warning," the boy said. "I'll take him a message from you, my lady, if you wish."

Cathane looked bewildered and then somehow summoned her wits about her. "Yes, of course. Thank you." She beckoned one of the ladies in waiting. "Parchment and ink," she ordered. "I'll write him a note, so he'll know to believe you."

As she wrote, Score took Helaine aside. "What's going on here?" he asked her. "Everybody looked pretty tense even before I dropped my bombshell."

"The Queen's pregnant," Helaine hissed back. "Score, that's *you* inside her."

Score looked as if he were going to be the next person to throw up. "Oh, this just keeps on getting better and better. No wonder Sarman wants to attack now."

"Score…" Helaine didn't quite know how to say this. "Score,

we can't interfere with what's got to happen. We *know* that Traxis will kill King Caligan - we can't possibly prevent it. It's already happened."

Score shook his head. "Helaine, you don't understand - if that's *me* in there -" He gestured at Shanara's stomach "- then that means that Caligan is my real father. My *father…* And I've never even seen him. I don't care what it does to all of time, but I've *got* to save his life!"

Helaine could see the agony in his face, and she could both understand and empathize with it. But… "Score! We *can't* change anything! It could destroy our whole future! It could kill *us!*"

Score stared at her in agony. "I can't chance hurting you," he told her. "But… my *father!*"

"I know." She touched his cheek, tenderly. "I do know. But we can't save him. However, we *can* save your mother, and that's what we have to focus on. We know from history that she vanished while she was pregnant, so this has to be the time."

"Here." Cathane handed the letter she'd scribbled to Damon, who accepted it with a bow. "Warn my husband."

"I shall," he promised. He came over to Helaine, and abruptly kissed her again. "I'll see you later." He glared at Score, who gave him a foul look back. As Damon left the room, Score stared at Helaine.

"And what was *that* about?" he asked her. "Are you cheating on me already?"

"No!" she protested. "I didn't know he was going to do that. Score, he thinks I'm a *boy*. Otherwise he wouldn't be interested in me." Abruptly, she giggled. "And he thought you might be a girl in disguise."

"Me?" Score flushed. "Wow, this guy is *really* out of touch with reality. You can tell me all about your little romance later."

"It's not *my* romance," Helaine protested. But it actually felt kind of nice that Score was jealous. It meant that he really did care for her. Not that she had any idea of encouraging Damon just to provoke Score. But…

But back to business. She turned to the Queen. "Majesty, we have to be able to protect you," she said. "With both Sarman and Traxis in on this plot against your lives, I don't know if Castle Votrin is the safest place for you to stay."

Cathane looked sad. "It used to be," she said. "When I was a young girl, I loved to visit. But I can't set up the magical wardings here that I have at home, and Traxis is a lot stronger magically than I am. Most of my power is in illusions, whilst his is in active magic."

"Yeah," Score said. "We know first-hand what he's capable of - or, at least, what he will be capable of." He rushed on before the Queen could ask him what he meant by that remark. "But if we just try and leave the castle, won't that give them a perfect chance to attack?"

"You're finally starting to think like a soldier," Helaine said, approvingly. "Yes, that's exactly what would happen - *if* they attacked the right party."

Cathane managed a smile. "Well, my illusions should be strong enough to create the illusion of our party leaving. I can keep it going for about an hour, I imagine, which should lure them off and give us time to get out while they're distracted."

"No," Helaine said. "The *real* party leaves first - the illusion afterward. Sarman and Traxis are suspicious, so they'll assume that the first party will be an illusion if they see us fleeing."

"Good thinking," Score said, grinning happily. "That's my g-" He broke off before he could say any more and betray her secret.

Cathane laughed. "You were going to say *girl*, weren't you?" At their stricken look, she shook her head. "Come, now - my power is illusion. You don't think I can be taken in by someone wearing such a flimsy disguise, do you?"

Helaine hung her head. "Is it that obvious?" she asked.

"Not to others, I'm sure," the Queen said. "But I have a specialist's eye for seeing through disguises. Don't worry, I won't tell anyone your secret. To be honest, I wish I'd thought of doing something similar when I was your age - it's so dreadfully dull being prim and proper and wearing skirts all the time."

Score grinned. "There's still time for you to have an interesting childhood," he suggested. "Once this is all over."

"Perhaps so," Cathane agreed. "But we must get moving, now. My husband must have been warned, and he'll be getting ready to travel. We had better do the same." She thought for a moment. "I think we can leave almost everything behind. The ride to Bracklin Forest isn't that long, and we can probably find game and food on the way. Now, we need to send one of you to the stables with a servant to prepare horses for us."

There was a rap on the door, and they all tensed. It was

Damon, returning, looking concerned. "I delivered your message, majesty," he informed the Queen. "You're to be ready to travel. The King wishes to see the two strangers, though."

"Why?" asked Score, suspiciously.

"Because he's taking your word for it that there really is an ambush planned," Damon answered. "And he wants to be certain that it's not *you* leading everyone into a trap."

"That makes sense," Helaine agreed. "I'd be rather suspicious of us in his position also." She glanced at the Queen. "Go to the stables with Damon," she said. "We'll meet your husband and then see you there."

"Good." Cathane abruptly hugged her tightly. "Thank you for all of your aid, young man. Yours, too," she added to Score.

Helaine felt a little embarrassed. Her parents were never very affectionate with her, and it felt rather nice being appreciated. "Come on," she said to Score. "We have to move fast." He nodded and, with a last glance at his mother, followed her from the room.

Helaine led the way to the king's chambers, which were close by. There were two guards at the door there also. The men started to challenge them, but a voice from inside the room called out: "I'm expecting that pair - allow them in." The two guards then stood aside.

Score led the way into the room, and then stopped dead just inside. Helaine didn't understand why until she followed him in - and discovered that she was unable to move at all. She was frozen to the spot.

A trap…

"Oh, you two are *so* predictable…" Sarman stepped into view, which was a good thing as Helaine couldn't even turn her head. "I knew it would be simplicity itself to lure you here."

"What have you done?" Score demanded. Obviously the spell being used on them didn't affect their mouths.

"Did you *really* think that you had duped me into believing that you were my spy?" Sarman asked, scornfully. "I knew from the start that you were lying."

"Wow, how smart of you," Score growled.

"It *is* smart of me, yes," Sarman said. "I allowed you to think that you had fooled me because I saw a use for your foolish charade. It enabled me to contact the *real* spy."

With a sinking feeling, Helaine understood it all. "Damon,"

she snarled.

"Damon, yes." Sarman stared at her. "You know, there's something not quite right about you…" He walked over, and his hand swept out, jerking the cap from her head. Only the spell holding her prevented her hair from cascading down. "A girl, disguised as a boy. How very Shakespearean of you."

"How do you know about Shakespeare?" Score asked. He sounded very worried, understandably so. They were helpless, caught in this freezing trap.

"How do *you*?" Sarman countered. "It means that you've been to Earth also, doesn't it? I know this sorry little planet isn't all there is to the Universe, and I have ambitions that reach beyond its boundaries - ambitions the two of you will help me to fulfill."

"Where is the King?" Helaine demanded.

"He's here, in his room," Sarman replied. "Cathane's letter allowed Damon to get in here and… Well, take a look." He gestured over toward the bed. Now she was focused there, Helaine saw with a shock that there was a man's foot visible - and that there was blood seeping around it.

"You killed him," Score growled. "You murderer! You killed him!" Helaine could hear his agony - the father he had never met was already dead.

"Technically, no, it was Damon." Sarman smirked. "But it was my plan, so, yes, I'm responsible. The King is dead - long live the King. That would be Traxis, of course. And he's already off to take a Queen. That would be Cathane, who thinks she's escaping."

"What are you going to do?" Helaine demanded.

"Well, that rather depends on her response," Sarman said. "If she wants to stay Queen - and alive - she'll agree to marry Traxis. Otherwise… well, two state funerals are almost as cheap as one."

Score strained every muscle in an attempt to move, but was unable to budge. "You sadistic, cheap rat!" he screamed. "Everyone will know that Traxis is behind this coup - he'll never be accepted as King."

"Traxis behind it? My, what a thought! Why would anyone think *he's* behind it when the two killers have already been caught right here, red-handed, by a magical trap left by Cathane?" Sarman smiled. "Oops, that reminds me, I'd better finish adding the final touches." He drew Helaine's sword from its sheath, and then walked across to the bed. He bent down and stabbed several times, and then returned with her sword dripping blood. He slipped it into her hand and fastened her fingers about the hilt. "There we are - the perfect picture. As soon as Lord Votrin hears the commotion from this room, he'll hurry in - and find the King's murderer's caught in the act." He smiled again. "I'm sure your trial will be brief, and your executions will be a nice finishing touch to the whole thing. Oh, and they'll probably torture you first, to try and get you to tell them where the Queen is. And nobody will believe a word of your story…"

Score started to scream insults at him, but Sarman waved cheerfully and left the room.

Leaving them behind, unable to move a muscle while the Queen was being kidnapped…

Chapter Eleven

Pixel was deeply worried, but he tried not to show it. Of them all, Jenna was perhaps the most secure, because even if they *did* somehow change time so that the Three never did become himself, Score and Helaine, at least she would still be alive. Well, except for the fact that she was about to be murdered when he had first met her, and if he and the others hadn't rescued her, she might well have died then. So perhaps even she wasn't all that safe.

This changing-time business was giving even him headaches. It was so hard to know exactly what they could do without changing the whole course of history. Wiping himself out of existence might even be the least bad thing that might happen… Okay, from his perspective it was the worst, but for the Diadem as a whole, things could get *really* bad. If the Three were never defeated, or if Sarman was never vanquished - then everyone in the whole Diadem might still be under the yoke of tyranny… Jenna might be dead, and who knew what could have happened to Shanara. She might even have been tortured to death by Traxis instead of surviving the ordeal merely badly scarred - physically and emotionally.

And where were Score and Helaine anyway? Not for the first time, he clutched his ruby and sent the mental command to find them. As always, there was no response at all.

Jenna, always understanding his moods, reached over and touched his shoulder. "Trying to find them again?" she asked.

"Yes - without any luck."

"It doesn't prove anything," she told him. "Just that they aren't in range of your ruby. How far can you reach with it, anyway?"

"I don't know," he confessed. "At least a hundred miles, I think. I've not really tried it further than that."

"So all we know is that they're not within a hundred miles of here," Jenna said firmly. "You don't know any more than that."

"It's not what I *know*," Pixel admitted, miserably. "It's what I *fear*. What if Score and Helaine are missing because we've already done something that has wiped them from existence?"

For a second Jenna paled as she considered the thought. Then she shook her head firmly. "Pixel, I'm surprised at you! You're letting your fears overcome your logic! You, of all people! Think about it for a second - *if* we had somehow stopped them from ever being born, then we wouldn't even remember them, would we? But since we *do* remember them, it means we haven't changed history."

Pixel felt a little more reassured, and hugged Jenna tightly. "Thank you! Of course you're right." Then he sobered. "But it doesn't mean that they're still alive."

"We have no way of knowing that," Shanara said. "All we can do is to act as if they are, and trust that they can look after themselves, wherever they are. Meanwhile, we have a job to do, and the sooner we discover a way to return home, the better."

"Right." Pixel pulled himself together. But it was so hard not to worry about his best friends. After Jenna, there were no other people he cared about as much. Their mysterious disappearance was affecting him badly, he knew - but he also knew that he had to fight it, otherwise he'd be useless. He gripped his ruby, and ordered it to find the library.

A reddish line appeared in the air, visible only to him. He led the way through the castle until he reached the designated room. He halted in front of the door, and reached out with his senses. "Locked," he said.

"Which makes sense," Shanara said. "The Three wouldn't want just anyone to have access to their books of magic." She reached out a hand, and then jerked it back. "Ow! A pretty powerful pain spell."

"So how do we get in?" Jenna asked. "I don't think any of my talents are going to be much good here - they act mostly on living beings, and this door hasn't been living wood for a very long time."

"Wood burns," Pixel mused. He had control over the element of fire. "But I don't think Eremin and Nantor would appreciate my destroying their property. And we're in a delicate balance with them as it is. Air won't be much use, either. Maybe Summoning will be the answer." He gripped his jacinth. "Bring me the key," he ordered, focusing his will. "The way in…" He could feel the swirl of magic about him, and then a book appeared in the air in front of him. Jenna snatched it before it could fall.

"The counter-spell must be in this," she guessed. She opened the book and started to flick through it. "Hmmm… some interesting spells here. I wonder if they'd miss this?"

"Probably," Pixel said. "I can feel a property spell on it. If it's removed from the castle it will magically scream for help from the Three. I imagine all of their important books will have the same spell."

"But we can read it here," Jenna said. "And copy out anything that's handy."

"If it has the time-portal spell in it, I'll be happy," Shanara said.

"No, it's not in there," Pixel informed her. "I'm sure *that* spell is well-hidden, if they know it. This just contains the key to opening the library door." Using his ruby again, he was able to turn to the correct page.

"Unlocking spell," Jenna said, cheerily. "Right, this one I have to remember." She read the words aloud, pronouncing them carefully, and as she finished, the door swung slowly open. "There we are." She closed the book, and led the way into the library.

Pixel paused as he stood in the threshold. It was an amazing room, piled high with books of all shapes, sizes and age. There was a musty smell over the room that signaled neglect. If there was any order to the stacks, he couldn't see it. It was as if whoever had been reading a book had just tossed it aside into the nearest pile. There was a table at the center and a couple of windows to allow light in. There were also candelabras for reading lights, and several chairs.

"We have our work cut out for us here," Shanara said. "There doesn't seem to be any logic about this place."

"I imagine the Three know where whatever they want is," Pixel said slowly. "The lack of order would prevent any enemy from finding anything quickly."

"Which means *we* won't be able to find anything easily, either," Shanara pointed out. "I don't fancy looking through every book in here - there must be thousands and it could take us weeks. Can you use your ruby to find the right book?"

Pixel tried, and then shook his head. "That means there are two possibilities - that the book with the right spell in it isn't here... Or else there's a hiding spell on it."

"Well, if it isn't here, we're wasting our time," Jenna said. "So let's assume for the moment that it's been spelled. How do we find it?"

Pixel grinned. "Well, if I were the one hiding the book, I'd make certain it could hide itself no matter what."

"That's not reassuring," Jenna complained.

"Maybe not," Pixel conceded. "But that makes it a sort of

logic puzzle - how can you find something that doesn't want to be found? And I *really* like puzzles. Why don't the two of you start searching, and I'll just stand here and think."

"Well, that's as good an excuse as any I've ever heard to get out of work," Shanara said. But she was smiling as she made the comment, so she clearly didn't mean it. She picked up the closest book and examined it. "The Meditations of Dagma Poxit," she said. "Well, I don't know who he was, or is, or what he was thinking about. But it's not likely to be of any use to us." She started to put it down when Jenna reached out to grip her wrist.

"But if you were a powerful book of magic under a hiding spell, isn't that the sort of book you'd disguise yourself as?" she asked. "Something really dull-sounding so nobody would give you a second glance?"

"But it was on the top of the pile," Shanara objected. "If I were hiding something, I'd bury it in the middle somewhere."

"But isn't that the *obvious* place to hide it?" Jenna asked. "Wouldn't, then, the best place to hide something to be in plain sight?" She glanced to Pixel for support, but he was still deep in thought, and barely paying attention to the two of them.

"But by that sort of logic," Shanara objected, "we have to examine every single book in here. I know we can extend our lives magically, but I doubt even that would give us enough time to check out every book thoroughly." She opened the *Meditations* and started to read, "It's as boring as it sounds," she complained, slamming it shut.

"Unless it's just disguised to look boring," Jenna objected.

"That sort of thinking gets us nowhere!" Shanara protested. "If the book isn't only disguised on the outside but also the inside, what's the point of looking at any of them? We could be looking right at the book and not even know it!"

"We are," Pixel announced, having analyzed the problem to his own satisfaction. He was certain of his deductions. "If you wanted to hide a book, a library is the perfect place to do so. But then you'd want to hide it so it would never be found. There's always a small chance that a thief might accidentally lay his hand on the book - unless you can make it zero chance."

Jenna sighed and cocked her head to the side. "Okay, Pixel, we'll grant that you're a lot smarter than we are. Stop looking so smug and tell us what you've figured out."

"Am I looking smug?" Pixel felt a rush of guilt. He *was* acting smarter than they were, wasn't he? "I don't mean it like that."

"We know you don't," Shanara said. "You can't help being so clever, but dragging it out and making us beg for the solution isn't an endearing trait. Just *tell* us."

"If I were hiding a book," Pixel said, "and giving it a spell to disguise itself, I'd make certain that it didn't even look like a book."

"Oh." Jenna blinked. "I hadn't even thought of that. But it makes sense - anyone looking for the book would waste all their time examining the books, and not see the one they really want." She glanced around the room. But there's nothing else in here except the furniture."

"And the candelabras," Pixel said. "And if you examine them, you'll see all but one of them have candles in them. Only one is empty, because it's not really a candle-holder…"

"It's the book," Shanara finished. "And it couldn't take a chance somebody might try and light it!"

"Exactly," Pixel said, trying hard not to sound smug this time. "It must be what we're looking for." He reached out and grabbed it. "There's a definitely scent of magic about it," he said. "But how do we get it to change back?"

Shanara smiled. "Well, I'm not the magician of illusion for nothing," she said. "Let me see if I can figure this out." She took the fake candelabra from Pixel and examined it. "Yes, there's a powerful illusion spell on this object," she agreed. "But… it's not a book. I can't tell quite what it is, but it's very definitely disguised."

"Not a book?" Pixel felt himself blush. "But I was sure -"

"Relax, you haven't messed up," Shanara told him. "This is definitely what we're after, even if it isn't a book. Just give me a few minutes, and I'll crack the spell."

Pixel was embarrassed. He'd approached everything logically - and was completely wrong. He'd found something, but purely by accident, it would appear. So much for his pride in his thinking ability!

Jenna, knowing him so well, moved across to hug him. "Don't worry," she said, grinning mischievously. "Even if you're not as smart as you thought you were, I still love you."

"Thank you," he said, sighing. "But I feel like something of an idiot."

"Well, it'll stop you ever getting to be as arrogant as Nantor, then, and that's a good thing." Jenna kissed the tip of his nose. "A little humility now and then is good for the soul."

"I hope so," Pixel replied. "It's certainly not good for my ego."

"Got it," Shanara announced. "I've unlocked the key to the spell, and should be able to break it now." They both watched as she stared hard at the candelabra and muttered a spell in low tones.

There was a flash of light, and the object morphed into a large gemstone. Shanara started at it, puzzled. "A diamond? Why would anyone want to hide a diamond?"

Pixel wasn't sure of the answer, either. "Well, Score tells me that on Earth jewels like that are worth a lot of money. Maybe somebody was afraid that a thief would steal it.?"

Jenna snorted. "Wow, you're *really* not thinking straight today," she told him. "This isn't Earth, and we use gemstones like this ourselves to focus our magic, don't we?"

Pixel could have kicked himself - Jenna was right! "Of course! The diamond must be intended to be some sort of magical conduit."

"To what?" Shanara asked. "Or... to where?"

Pixel laughed happily. "The hidden object isn't a *book* with a spell to create temporal portals," he said. "It's a *jewel* to create a temporal portal! This has got to be what we need to get back home again!" He grinned at Shanara. "You and Jenna are the best at creating portals, so why don't the two of you see if you can trigger it?"

There was the slow sound of hands clapping, and a fresh voice said: "Well done, lover-boy. I knew you'd manage to find the portal stone - with a little encouragement."

Pixel whirled around. The voice had sounded very familiar... and he stared in astonishment at the person who was standing just inside the doorway to the library.

She was in her early twenties, almost a decade older than she had been the last time he had seen her. But there was no mistaking the beautiful looks of the Japanese girl. She was dressed in a shimmering low-cut black gown that made her look as if she'd just come from an incredibly elegant party - one at which she'd been the center of attention.

"Destiny," he whispered, shocked.

"I'm glad to see you still remember me, lover," she purred.

Then she glanced at Jenna. "And *this* is what you replaced me with? An under-dressed, unattractive common little hedge-witch. Pixel, I'm surprised at you."

"So am I," Jenna hissed, angrily. "Pixel, who is this... person?" Her eyes were almost sparking with anger and jealousy.

"Her name is Destiny," Pixel said, a cold sweat breaking out on his body. "But you don't understand."

"That *she* used to be your girlfriend?" Jenna was furious. "How is it that you neglected to mention such a..."

"Hottie?" Destiny suggested, with a grin. "Love goddess? Divine apparition?"

"I was thinking more *tramp*, actually," Jenna said, angrily. "Well?" she demanded of Pixel.

"Stop with this stupid jealousy for a moment!" Pixel cried. "Don't you understand? Don't either of you understand?" He looked at Shanara and then back to Jenna, and could see that they didn't. "We're back in time, and *this* is Destiny from back then. *Before* she became the girl I knew on Earth. Don't you see? There should be no way that she knows me yet! She won't meet me for at least another seventeen years!" He could see the understanding dawning on the faces.

"Bravo, lover," Destiny murmured. "You always were almost as smart as I am. You're quite right - this body is the Destiny of two hundred years ago - by my mind is the Destiny of just a couple of months after you killed me..."

Chapter Twelve

Jenna was shaken by what was happening. There was one part of her mind that registered what Pixel had said - that this woman standing before them was responsible for everything that was happening to them - but there was a larger part that was simply scared. This woman - Destiny - claimed she was Pixel's old girlfriend, and Jenna was feeling horribly inferior.

This was a real beauty! She looked utterly amazing, with cleavage, long legs, long, shining dark hair and a face that was absolutely perfect. She was like nothing and no one Jenna had ever seen. And she made Jenna feel shabby and insignificant. Now that Pixel had seen *this* woman, how could he ever bear to look at Jenna again? And if he did, how could he not make comparisons?

She was bound to lose him, if this woman wanted him back. And she didn't think life without Pixel would be bearable.

Then she saw the glint of knowledge and amusement in Destiny's eyes, and knew that this other person knew exactly what was going through her mind.

Shanara seemed to be oblivious to the undertones of this confrontation. "Where are Score and Helaine?" she demanded. "You sent us here, so you must have sent them to wherever they are."

Destiny wrenched her gaze from Jenna, and looked at Shanara. "I've no idea where they are," she replied. "I can find them when I want them, but I simply made sure that your spell separated you all. I should have no problem in dealing with the three of you but five might have been a bit too much."

"How did you manage it?" Shanara asked.

Destiny shook her head. "No, I'm not going to act like some stupid James Bond villain and spill the whole plot. I'll tell you only exactly as much as I want you to know before I humiliate and destroy you." She grinned at Pixel. "Though if cute cheeks here is really nice to me, I might let him live a little longer than you two losers."

Jenna was appalled again - this beauty *did* want Pixel back! And surely he'd want her, too?

"Be nice to you?" Pixel shook his head. "You're a… what is it that Score called you? Oh, yes - psycho bitch. Well, that was one of the more polite comments he made."

Jenna was astonished. "You don't want her back?" she asked.

Pixel tore his gaze from Destiny and looked at her. His anger softened. "Don't listen to what she's saying," he begged. "She's a liar and a manipulator. She's completely selfish and is willing to kill anyone who gets in her way. She tried to kill me and Score and Helaine before - and screwed up so badly it killed her instead."

"It was *your* interference that killed me," Destiny snarled. "It's your fault that I'm reduced to *this* - manipulating my former self."

"Uh, time out," Shanara called. "If you're dead, how come you're here? Are you a ghost of some sort?"

"A ghost?" Destiny considered the matter for a second and then laughed. "Yes, I suppose you might call me that. But a very special ghost."

"Well, I for one think you should be exorcised, then," Pixel said. "And if you think you can take on the three of us alone, you're crazier than I thought."

"But I'm not alone, lover boy," Destiny purred. She held up the diamond. "That's why I needed you to find this for me. I could travel back in time alone. And I could use Shanara's spell to send the five of you into the past - hooking into what she was trying to do and making it go awry. But to bring someone else into the past, I needed to make a pure time portal, and for that I need this." She stared into the gem in her fist.

"Pixel, Jenna!" Shanara whispered. "I know where - or, rather, *when*, Score and Helaine are! I had two visions in mind when I cast my spell - one to show you what happened to the Three - the one we're stuck in. The other was to show Score what happened to me. If we're here, then he and Helaine have to be three hundred years further back in time and on Ordin."

Jenna blinked. "How does that help us?"

Pixel gave a low laugh. "That diamond - if Destiny can use it to create a time portal, then so can we! We have to defeat her and take it away from her. Then we can use it to return all of us back to our own time. It's simple!"

"Are you sure you want to defeat her?" Jenna asked bitterly.

"What do you mean?" Pixel asked, clearly confused.

"Well, look at her! She's so gorgeous! And I'm… I'm…" She gestured at her own nondescript skirt and top.

"You're the one I love," Pixel told her, firmly. "Destiny might *look* beautiful, but she's got an evil soul. She's a killer, selfish and vicious. Don't let the packaging deceive you - there is no way I would ever throw you over for her. You have a beautiful heart, you're caring and you love me. I'm not stupid enough to give all of that up."

Jenna felt a little better, but she still hurt. "I notice you didn't say I was beautiful - which is understandable. Compared to her, I must look like a pig."

"Jenna, stop being jealous and *focus*," Shanara snapped. "We have to fight Destiny and win. Stop feeling sorry for yourself and deal with these feelings of inadequacy later, okay?"

Destiny looked up from the diamond. "You three…" She shook her head. "You won't be able to defeat me, and you won't get this gemstone. My assistant is on his way, and when he arrives we'll have you completely outclassed."

"Then we had better finish you off before he arrives," Pixel said. He made a gesture with his hand as he clutched his beryl in his left fist. The air about Destiny started to writhe and solidify, working to contain her in a solid block.

Destiny laughed and simply vanished from where she had been standing. She was on the far side of the room now, out of reach of the spell.

"Illusion spell," Shanara snapped. "I can feel it. Quite strong. She's not really there, either." She concentrated, and then threw up both hands.

Reality seemed to begin to peel back. The image of Destiny tore apart, shredded into nothingness. Instead she appeared from nowhere beside the door. Shanara gave a sigh, and staggered slightly, clearly drained from warding off the spell.

"Peekaboo," Destiny called, and laughed. "Oh, I knew you'd see through that spell soon enough. But the time it bought me was what I needed…" She gestured at the center of the room, where there were no books piled up.

The air shimmered and then something solidified into being.

"Here's Jagomath," Destiny laughed.

"That's the Great Wizard Jagomath to you," the new arrival snapped. He threw back his head and looked up at them all. "So - you're the villains I have to kill, eh?"

Jenna stared at him, then at Pixel, and then back at the Wizard. He was about four feet tall, and looked… "How old are you?" Jenna asked him. "Six?"

"Eleven," he said, haughtily. "I'm just small for my age."

Jenna looked at him, and then at Pixel and Shanara. "*You're* the big villain behind all of this?"

"Villain?" Jagomath looked annoyed. "Look, I know you're the bad guys, but there's no need to call *me* names."

"Bad guys?" Shanara glanced sharply at him. "Who told you we were the… bad guys?"

"Destiny." Jagomath turned to look at her, and then he stared, obviously surprised. "What did they do to you? You're *old*!"

"What?" Destiny was clearly annoyed. "What are you talking about? I'm as beautiful and young as I ever was."

Jenna caught on the same moment that Pixel did. "No," she said, stifling a laugh. This was not the time to find their situation amusing - but it really made her feel better that *somebody* around here didn't find Destiny the most beautiful creature imaginable. "He's right, you know - you *are* old. Much too old for him. Why, you must be almost thirty!"

"Twenty-seven," Destiny growled. "I'm at the height of my beauty - and power."

"And *he's* eleven," Pixel added. "When you were about fifteen, you were an exotic older girl to him. But now… now you're ancient."

"Well, at least they get it," Jagomath said, sulkily. "This game isn't turning out to be as much fun as I imagined it would be."

"Game?" Jenna asked. "This isn't a game - it's our lives."

"Don't be silly," Jagomath said. Then he snapped his fingers. "Of course - you're part of the game I created, so you have to *act* real. I don't know why I even bother talking to you like this."

"Humor us," Pixel suggested. "We're just trying to understand the… rules of this game of yours. However did you create something this wonderful and complex?"

"Jagomath, be careful," Destiny warned the youngster. "They're trying to trick you."

"How can we trick him if he created us?" Pixel asked innocently. "If he created us, then he's obviously smarter than us, isn't he?"

"Or maybe you lied to him, and he *didn't* create us," Jenna finished. "Which is it?"

Destiny clearly hadn't thought about that, but Jagomath didn't seem to care. "I did it with the stone," he said, proudly. He fished about in the long cape he was wearing over his jeans and t-shirt, and then pulled out a burnt-looking rock. "This stone. Once I had it, I discovered I could do all sorts of things - like create this world, and all the characters. It's *way* cooler than online gaming."

Pixel looked over the stone, and then he stiffened. "I recognize that…" he breathed. "It's a fragment of Zarathan."

Jenna remembered he had talked about this. "That planet where nightmares became real?" she asked. "The one that was actually the shell of an alien creature?"

"That's the one." Pixel looked thoughtful. "The creature fed off dreams and then made them come to life. But we woke it up, and when it broke out of its shell, Destiny died… Of course!" He gave Destiny a dark look. "Even though the main source of power was the creature itself, the entire world must have become imbued with mental energy. When it broke apart, the fragments retained some of that vast power. When you died, you must have been able to transfer your consciousness into one fragment that then landed on the Earth - where this kid found it."

"Who are you calling a kid?" the magician asked. "That's Great Wizard Jagomath to you."

"Isn't it past your bedtime?" Shanara asked him.

"You sound just like my mother," Jagomath complained. "Do you know I have a nine o'clock bedtime? I mean, who in their right mind sends their kids to bed that early?"

"How is it that he's so powerful, then?" Jenna asked. "Earth is one of the outer worlds of the Diadem, where magic is the weakest. Yet he seems to have been able to create time portals, and to mess with Shanara's spells. I didn't think that should be possible on the Outer Circuit."

"It shouldn't be," Pixel agreed. "But that fragment of Zarathan seems to have amplified his powers to an astonishing degree."

"Okay, that's enough," Destiny snapped. She glared at the boy. "Come on, I told you, these people are *evil* and have to be destroyed. You haven't forgotten it was they who broke up your clever game on Brine, have you?"

"So *you're* the magician who was stealing the gems from that world!" Pixel said.

"*Mining* them," Jagonmath growled. "Since I invented the whole thing, I can't have been stealing my own stuff, can I?" He glared at them all, sulkily. "Talk, talk, talk - you're as bad as adults, the lot of you. I don't want *talk*, I want to play!"

"Jagomath, she's been lying to you," Jenna said. "This is all *real* - you didn't invent it - you simply tapped into it. It wasn't a game on Brine - people were suffering and dying there. She's lied to you all along."

"What else would a villain say?" Destiny asked, sneering. "Come on, Jagomath - it's time to finish all of this. It's time to punish them for their crimes, and for us to take our rightful places as rulers of the Diadem."

"Is that what you want?" Pixel asked. "To rule the Diadem? That's a lot of work, you know. I thought you were just trying to have some fun."

"Yeah, that's right," Jagomath agreed. He looked at Destiny, clearly annoyed. "You're one of them - an *adult*," he complained. "This isn't as much fun as I thought it was going to be."

"That's because it isn't really a game," Shanara said, urgently.

"Well, it's *gonna* be one," Jagomath growled. Before they could react, he waved his arms -

- and the world dissolved and reformed.

They were on another world, on a vast, open plane. In the far distance were rings of mountains, but there was nothing else visible save for acre after acre of grass. There was the hum of magic in the air, and Jenna realized that they were no longer in the Outer Circuit of the Diadem. This was obviously one of the inner worlds, where magic was much stronger. She and Shanara and Pixel had more power here.

And so did Jagomath. He was almost blazing with the energies coursing through his young body. "This is more like it," he said, happily. "I can *feel* the magic." Then he blinked. "But there's something still missing…" He snapped his fingers, and Score and Helaine suddenly popped into being.

"No!" Score screamed, falling to his knees. "No! Send me back!" Helaine gripped his shoulder hard, he sword raised to attack.

"What happened?" she asked, confused. "Where are we? How did we get here?"

"I don't care!" Score yelled. "We have to get back." He looked around and saw Jenna and the others, but didn't seem to understand. "My mother! I have to save my mother! We almost had her rescued…. And now we're here! I don't know who did this, but we have to go back!"

Shanara, looking pale, stepped forward. "Score," she asked urgently. "What do you mean?"

Score barely focused on her. "Cathane," he breathed. "Cathane. They took her - and we almost had her back! But she's gone." He seemed to see her at last. "Traxis took Cathane," he said. "But you know that, don't you, since you're her. And you know what is going to happen to her."

"Yes," Shanara said, softly. "He's going to subject her to horrendous torture." She touched her face, where there had once been terrible scars - before Jenna had cured them - the remains of what Traxis had done to her.

"And I almost stopped him!" Score cried. "We have to go back and save her!"

"You can't save her," Pixel said, reaching out to touch his friend's arm. "It *happened*. Shanara is here, now, because it happened. If you try and change all of that, you could mess up all of reality."

"Screw reality," Score answered. "I don't want my mom hurt. I have to go back and save her."

"What is it with all of you?" Jagomath cried, annoyed. "All you do is *talk*! I brought you all here to play, so let's play. It's me and Destiny against all five of you villains."

Score seemed to see the youngster for the first time. "What's with this snotty-nosed kid?"

"That snotty-nosed kid is the one behind all of this," Jenna told him. "The one with the power to send you through time."

"Him?" Score snorted, and then looked grim. "If that's the truth, then he's going to get the spanking of his life." He stepped toward the kid.

Jagomath laughed. "That's more like it! Let the games begin!"

And the whole world seemed to explode…

Continued in: The Book of Games

Diadem #12

The Book of Games

John Peel

Prologue

Oracle walked straight through the castle wall and into the room beyond. There were sometimes advantages to being intangible. Doors and locks were no problem, for example.

But there were disadvantages, also. He couldn't pick anything up, or touch anyone. He couldn't even feel a breeze, or change his clothes. And if he wanted to check out what was inside a chest, he had to stick his head through it.

Still, he'd managed to learn to live with his ability/disability, and he only wished he were fully human… oh, every ten minutes or so. It was an improvement. It used to be every five.

He glanced around the room, but saw that there was nobody here. That was odd, because he'd zeroed in on Shanara, and this was her usual haunt. He tried his sense of tracking again - another of the advantages of his not being quite real was that he could somehow focus in on someone he wanted to see, and then moved through space to join them. But his sense was insisting that Shanara was here - when she clearly wasn't.

Puzzled, he tried to focus on Score instead.

And his sense told him that Score was here, too. And, in rapid order, so were Helaine, Pixel and Jenna.

But the room was completely void of life.

Ah! Not *quite* void. He could see in the corner, perched on a rather crowded table of books, was Blink. The red panda was - inevitably - sleeping. He was Shanara's familiar, a magical creature whose innate abilities worked with Shanara's to increase her own powers. He was also the laziest creature Oracle had ever run across. When he wasn't sleeping, he was eating. And when he wasn't sleeping or eating, he was thinking about doing one or the other. Obviously, with Shanara not here, Blink was taking full advantage of the time to catch up on his rest. He'd probably sleep forever, if she didn't return soon.

But where could she be, if his senses insisted she was here and his eyes said quite plainly that she wasn't?

There was only one way in which Oracle could interact with the real Universe: he could speak and be heard. It was clearly time to employ that ability. He walked across the room and stood beside the snoring panda. Leaning down, he yelled loudly: "BLINK!"

The panda literally jumped into the air. He came awake instantly, completely confused and spluttering. Landing awkwardly, he knocked several books flying and fell onto his back. He blinked in confusion and then managed to focus his eyes on Oracle.

"Oh; it's you. What do you want? Never mind, just let me get my rest." He started to right himself sleepily.

"Where is everyone?" Oracle demanded. "My senses tell me that they're here, but obviously they're not."

"Well, you've clearly lost your senses, then," Blink said, grouchily. "And I'm losing sleep. Leave me alone." He started to settle back down again.

"Blink," Oracle growled, "how much sleep do you think you'll get if I start singing *Ninety-Nine Bottles Of Beer On The Wall*... very loudly?"

"You wouldn't," Blink protested. Then, studying Oracle's face, he changed his mind. "You would, you sadist."

"I would." Oracle smiled grimly. "So, just answer my questions and I'll leave you in peace. Where is everybody?"

"I don't know where *everybody* is," Blink replied. "But I do know where *some* people are - the ones you're after, I presume. Shanara and the four noisy kids?"

"Yes, they're the ones. Where are they? I *feel* that they're here, but they obviously aren't."

"No. You can tell that because it's peaceful, and I was getting some well-earned rest after the spell they made me help out with."

"What spell would that be?" Oracle asked, rapidly losing his patience.

"The one to create an illusion of the past. The one Shanara wanted made so that she could show the four of them what had happened to her once upon a time..."

"Oh." Oracle thought he was starting to understand. "So they're *here*, but inside some sort of illusion so I can't see them? That doesn't sound possible."

"It isn't possible, you idiot," Blink growled. "I said they *wanted* an illusion created - I didn't say it had happened."

"Blink, I swear, if you don't tell me where they are, I'll make it my life's work to make sure you never get another second of rest."

"You *are* a sadist!" the panda protested. "Just give me a chance to explain. Well, when we cast the spell, there was *another* spell that hit them at the exact same second. It was really powerful, and it took control of the illusion and made it real."

"You're not making much sense," Oracle complained.

"It's hard to explain exactly," Blink said. "It hijacked the spell Shanara cast, and instead of creating an illusion of what she wanted them to see, it transported them to the reality. Back through time," he added, helpfully.

"Back through time?" Oracle was starting to understand. "Then that's why my senses are having trouble. They can only locate someone here and now - and they're not here and now."

"No, they're there and then," Blink agreed. "Now will you leave me in peace?"

"What?" Oracle glared at him. "Where and when *are* they?"

"What difference does it make?" Blink asked. "There's no way you can go back there, so you're stuck like me waiting for them to return. Why not take my advice and catch up on your sleep? You're getting very testy - a spot of rest would do you good."

"Sleep? How can you sleep? They're obviously in trouble!"

"They're *always* in trouble," Blink pointed out. "And they always manage to get out of it. They'll probably get out of this, too."

"*Probably*?"

"Well," the panda said, reluctantly, "they are up against somebody very powerful this time. It takes a *lot* of power to hijack a spell. And a lot of know-how to send people through time - even I don't know how to do that."

"Aren't you worried about them?"

"What's the point of worrying?" Blink asked. "Like I just said, I don't know how to time travel, so I couldn't go back and help them even if I wanted to. And you can't time travel, either, so you're as stuck as I am. Worrying about it won't help them, and it will ruin my sleep. So, no, I'm not worried."

"I thought you *liked* Shanara," Oracle said.

"I *do*," Blink answered. "She's the best friend I've ever had in my life, and I'm extremely fond of her. And if you ever tell her that, I'll find some way to make you tangible again and bite your head off. Literally." Blink and Shanara always pretended to dislike one another - it was a running game they always played.

"You're a vegetarian."

"I didn't say I'd *eat* it."

"I meant that it means you have blunt teeth," Oracle pointed out.

"Then it would take me a long time to bite your head off. It would be even more painful. Which is sort of the point." He sighed. "Anyway, worrying is pointless, so I don't do it. All that we can do is to wait and hope that they manage to come through, somehow. They have a pretty good track record so far, but they're up against somebody really tricky this time… So, I just don't know." He growled. "There ! Now I *am* worrying about them. I hope you're happy. I'll not be able to get back to sleep again." He stood up and looked around. "Well, I might as well eat instead." He jumped down from the table and headed off toward the kitchen.

Oracle let him go - there was no point in talking to the panda any more. Blink was right - there was nothing that they could do, and worrying about his friends was pointless.

Pointless - and impossible not to do…

Chapter One

Strain as he might, Score found himself unable to move a single muscle below his jaw. He was trapped like a fly in amber, standing just inside the doorway of his murdered father's room. Meanwhile, Traxis, Sarman and the turncoat Damon were off kidnapping his mother... Cathane - as Shanara was known on this world and in this time.

He was so overwhelmed by emotions that he hardly knew what he was feeling. King Caligan lay dead beside his bed, stabbed to death, apparently by the sword that Helaine was holding in her frozen hand. As soon as the alarm was given, people were going to rush in here and assume that he and Helaine were the killers and had been caught in a magical trap immediately after the regicide. Nobody was likely to believe the story of strangers against that of Traxis - Caligan's "grieving" brother... and heir to the throne...

Cathane was pregnant, here and now - and that child would be *him*, Score, one day. He had always believed that his father was Bad Tony Caruso, a minor would-be crime boss from New York. On his last trip to Ordin, though, he had been taken for the heir of King Caligan, which he had never been able to understand at the time. Now it was starting to make some kind of sense. He really *was* the child of Caligan and Cathane, and not Bad Tony's kid after all. Not that any of this made any real difference to him right now, because the father he had never known was lying dead in a spreading pool of his own blood.

"Score," Helaine said, urgently. "Are you all right? You've been quiet for almost two minutes, and that is so not like you."

"I've... got a lot to think about," he admitted. "It's hard to take it all in."

"Well, *we'll* be taken in if we don't do something fast," she pointed out. "And I doubt there will be much in the way of a fair trial planned after that."

"Yeah, that had occurred to me," he agreed. "So..." He had to put a lid on his emotions right now - he'd try and sort them out later. Helaine was right - there were more important things to consider right now. "First things first - getting out of this trap."

"I've been trying to think of a way out," Helaine told him. "But I can't figure out any way of using my powers that will help."

"Well, the two of us thinking together should be able to beat anything that creep Sarman could conjure up," Score said. "Okay, the spell didn't affect us till we walked in the door, did it? And it's not a spell that he cast."

"He said it would be found to be one set to protect the king," Helaine said. "So it's probably centered on this room."

"Right," Score said, a sense of excitement flooding over him. "So all we have to do is to get out of this room."

"Neither of us can move," Helaine pointed out. "And we don't have the power to teleport ourselves."

"You're thinking too logically - and that's something I never thought I'd accuse you of," Score said. "There are other ways to leave a room without walking out or teleporting. Get ready."

"Score!" Helaine yelled in alarm. "Are you sure you've thought this out? You have a habit of doing -"

Score concentrated his power through his citrine gemstone, which enhanced his power of transmutation. He turned the wooden floor they were standing on to oxygen gas.

They dropped clean through the space, and into the room below. Helaine screamed, and then they hit the floor together. Score rolled with the impact, and Helaine ended up on top of him, her furious face inches above his own.

"- stupid things!" she finished yelling.

"What are you complaining about?" he asked her. "It worked." He flexed the muscles of his arms happily, and then grabbed her and kissed her nose. "Much as I like you on top of me, this isn't the time to get romantic, is it?"

"I'm not getting romantic, you idiot," she grumbled. "I just wanted to fall on the softest thing around here - your head!"

"Complain, complain, complain," he grumbled, as she stood up. "My plan worked, and we got out of there in one piece."

"We could have broken bones or anything," Helaine pointed out, as he clambered to his feet.

"But we didn't," he said.

"You didn't think it through, as usual," she told him. "It's just pure dumb luck we aren't hurt."

"Hey, pure dumb luck and I are old friends," Score said. "Don't knock it."

Helaine had dropped her sword as she fell - thankfully, or it might have ended up in one of them - and she retrieved it now. It was still soiled with the king's blood. They were standing in another bedroom, so she wiped the blood off on the bed sheet, and then slid the sword back into its scabbard.

"Now what do we do?" Helaine asked him. "And this time *talk* about it before you act."

"Now we go rescue Cathane," Score said grimly. "Sarman and Traxis are going to take her out of this castle, and if we don't stop them now, we'll have no idea where they've gone."

"Do you think they'll use a portal?" Helaine asked.

"More magic?" Score didn't know. "Maybe. We don't know how good Traxis or Sarman might be at creating them. This is before Traxis becomes one of the Three Who Rule, don't forget, and it's not easy creating a portal on Ordin. The magic isn't strong enough here - we always had to have someone deeper in the Diadem create one to get us off this place. It's probably true for them, too."

"So then they'd probably have to get her out by conventional means," Helaine said. "And that means on horseback or in her carriage."

"Good thinking," Score said. "So our best bet is to head for the stables, then. That's where they'll be." He started for the door, but Helaine grabbed his arm.

"I can't walk about like this," she pointed out. "Girls aren't allowed to wear boys clothing or to carry weapons here, remember? And everyone thinks I'm a boy."

"I don't - I know better." He grinned at her. "Though if you want to change clothing, I'd be happy to help."

Helaine rolled her eyes. "Actually, I just wanted you to get me a hat I can hide my hair under. Mine's in the room upstairs, remember?"

"Right. Well, easy enough." Using his jasper, he was able to invoke his power of sight, and saw exactly where her hat was above them. Then he switched to the citrine and removed the floor below it. The hat fluttered down through the newly-created hole. "There you are. Now get dressed and let's go and save my Mom, okay?"

Helaine grabbed the hat and in a moment her thick, long hair had vanished under it, and she was back disguised as Raynard again. "Right, let's go."

"One last thing," Score said. He restored the two holes in the floor above them. "That should keep them puzzling about the killers for a while." He felt another sharp pang of sorrow about his true father, but suppressed it. This wasn't the time to get overly emotional about things; there was Cathane to rescue.

As they hurried out to the stables, he realized something very strange: even though Cathane and Shanara were actually the same person, he had no problems with thinking of Cathane as his mother… and yet he still somehow couldn't accept Shanara in the same fashion. It didn't make any sense, really, and there was probably some deep, psychological reason for it that Pixel would see through in a second.

Maybe it was simply that he still resented Shanara for not telling him the truth the moment she'd realized it. It hurt. It felt like she'd abandoned him again. And he still didn't know why she had abandoned him on Earth in the first place – in the none-too-tender clutches of Bad Tony.

"We'll get her back," Helaine said, softly, touching his arm.

"That's right, we will," he vowed. "I'm not going to lose her to those sadistic rats." They were out in the courtyard, where there was a lot of activity. Soldiers were hurrying toward the main entrance of the castle, and Lord Votrin was screaming orders. "Uh, looks like somebody's been clued into the murder."

The squad leader who had taken command of Helaine and Damon earlier blocked their way. "Where do you think you're going?" he demanded. "We're ordered into the castle to search for the king's killers. Come on."

"Sorry," Score replied. "We're needed in the stables. There are more than enough of you already to stomp about and cause confusion."

"You're not allowed in the stables," the captain growled. "Only the Prince and the Queen's guards are allowed there – they're protecting her in case she's the next target."

"They're *kidnapping* her, you moron!" Score yelled. "The Prince is the one who killed Caligan!"

The soldier's eyes narrowed suspiciously. "And just how would you know that?"

"Because I was with the Queen," Helaine snapped. "If you remember, I was assigned to help her. Damon is working with Traxis, and he betrayed us all."

The captain hesitated, clearly not able to work out the truth of the matter. "There's no time for talk," Score growled. "Get out of our way – you can think it through later."

"We'd better talk to Lord Votrin," the soldier decided. "He'll know what to do."

"*I* know what to do!" Score yelled, furious at the delay. His mother was in danger, and this idiot wanted to *talk*! He grabbed his chrysolite and concentrated. This gave him power over water, so he focused all of the water in the air around them onto the captain. Instantly, he was drenched, water pouring out of nowhere onto him. He was caught by surprise, and knocked from his feet, gasping and spluttering.

"That's going to cause trouble," Helaine warned Score as they dashed past the floundering soldier.

"Good," Score growled. "I'm really in the mood for trouble."

They were going against the flow, so they had to duck and dodge as they moved across the crowded courtyard. Then Score could see the entrance to the stables, and several people leading horses out. One of them he recognized instantly – Damon. "You traitor!" Score yelled, aiming to go for him. Helaine grabbed his arm.

"He's mine," she said, quietly. "Go find your mother." Score hesitated, and then nodded. As he rushed off, he half-saw Helaine facing off against Damon, who had drawn his own sword. He wished he could stay and help her, but she was more than capable of handling herself in a fight – and it was imperative that he find Cathane.

None of the servants working with the horses made any move to try and stop him. Most of them probably didn't know that they were helping to kidnap the Queen. Score ignored them in return and dashed into the stable. Since Cathane wouldn't go with them voluntarily, they'd have to imprison her in her coach, so –

There it was! The team of horses that would pull it had been harnessed to it, and it was clearly just moments away from rolling out of the castle. As he ran toward it, Sarman stepped around from the rear and saw him. There was a second's pause as Sarman's face registered incredulous surprise, and then Score had reached the coach. He had an instant to glance inside, and saw Cathane on the seat, clearly unconscious, breathing heavily. Then he turned to Sarman.

"How did you escape my trap?" the magician asked.

"The bottom fell out of your scheme," Score replied. "And now you and Damon and Traxis are really going to get it!" He threw a fireball at the man.

Sarman gestured, sending the flaming ball off to one side. "Did you think I was so easy to catch out?" he sneered.

"No," Score answered. "That was just to distract you so you wouldn't realize I was doing *this*." He was clutching his amethyst, which gave him the ability to change the size of things. He had concentrated on the hay-loft above Sarman, shrinking the boards and increasing the size of the bales of hay. The whole floor collapsed, sending a thunder of bales down on the startled magician. To add to the confusion, the discarded fireball ignited some of the hay.

Score moved toward the carriage. There were undoubtedly others around to guard the Queen, but he'd fix anyone who came in his way. He couldn't figure out exactly his emotions, but they were giving him an edge of anger that was helping him to fight.

Then, suddenly, he felt strange. He stopped in his tracks, his body tingling. He could feel some force dragging at him. Sarman must have recovered faster than he'd expected!

No… This wasn't Sarman's doing… It was some other force, stronger and more alien than Sarman. Score could feel it dragging at every atom in his body, forcing him to halt, and pulling at him.

There wasn't a portal as such, but he knew instinctively that he was being hauled into another world, very much against his will.

The stable vanished, and he was suddenly elsewhere. He was barely aware that Pixel, Jenna and Shanara were staring at him in astonishment, and that Helaine was somehow beside him.

"No!" Score screamed, falling to his knees. "No! Send me back!" Helaine gripped his shoulder hard, her sword raised ready to attack.

"What happened?" she asked, confused. "Where are we? How did we get here?"

"I don't care!" Score yelled. "We have to get back." He looked around and saw Jenna and the others, but he couldn't understand any of it. "My mother! I have to save my mother! We almost had her rescued…. And now we're here! I don't know who did this, but we have to go back!"

Shanara, looking pale, stepped forward. "Score," she asked urgently. "What do you mean?"

Score barely focused on her. "Cathane," he breathed. "Cathane. They took her - and we almost had her back! But she's gone." He seemed to see her at last. "Traxis took Cathane," he said. "But you know that, don't you, since you're her. And you know what is going to happen to her."

"Yes," Shanara said, softly. "He's going to subject her to horrendous torture." She touched her face, where there had once been terrible scars - before Jenna had cured them - the remains of what Traxis had done to her.

"And I almost stopped him!" Score cried. "We have to go back and save her!"

"You can't save her," Pixel said, reaching out to touch his friend's arm. "It *happened*. Shanara is here, now, because it happened. If you try and change all of that, you could mess up all of reality."

"Screw reality," Score answered. "I don't want my mom hurt. I have to go back and save her."

"What is it with all of you?" asked a new voice. Score looked around and saw two more people present. One was an annoyed-looking young kid, maybe twelve years old.

Beside him stood… Destiny? But she was dead, wasn't she?

The kid cried, annoyed: "All you do is *talk*! I brought you all here to play, so let's play. It's me and Destiny against all five of you villains."

Score couldn't take it all in. "What's with this snotty-nosed kid?"

"That snotty-nosed kid is the one behind all of this," Jenna told him. "The one with the power to send you through time."

"Him?" Score snorted, and then looked grim. "If that's the truth, then he's going to get the spanking of his life." He stepped toward the kid.

Jagomath laughed. "That's more like it! Let the games begin!"

And the whole world seemed to explode…

Chapter Two

"No!" Helaine yelled, furiously. "No, no, no, no, no!"

"But, my dear," the fat, white-bearded man pleaded, wringing his bejewelled hands together in frustration, "consider."

"I will *not* consider!" Helaine told him. "And I will not wear… this!" She gestured down at the outfit she was clothed in.

"But it's all the rage," the man protested. "Guaranteed, top of the market this year in every Gap in Bagdhad."

Helaine didn't understand most of what he had said, but she did understand that she wasn't going to dress like *this*! She took another look at herself in the full-length mirror a straining female servant was steadying. She was dressed in pink – pink! – if you could call this being *dressed*. She had on billowy pants of some very light, almost see-through material, and small slippers on her feet. Above the waist she had only a very narrow halter-top that covered only about two thirds of her breasts, leaving a lot of cleavage and very little to the imagination. And then in her hair she wore a stupid tiara of sparkling diamonds!

"This," she spluttered, "this is not the dress of a warrior!"

"Of course not," short, fat and bearded replied. "It's the dress of a princess. Which you are."

"I am *not* a princess!" Helaine screamed.

"Of course you are," the man replied. "All girls want to be princesses. And as my daughter, you are certainly one."

"I am *not* your daughter," Helaine growled.

"There are certainly times when I wish that were true," the man sighed. "Like now. But you're my daughter, and it's my duty to marry you off to just the right sort of suitor. And two are arriving today to woo you, so you have to look your best for them. And, if I say so myself, you certainly look a sight."

"You're a filthy old man!" Helaine informed him. "How could you let any girl dress like this – especially if you think she's your daughter?"

"You get this from your mother's side of the family," the man sighed. "I remember your Great-Uncle Rashid – he was quite mad. Thought he was a genie, and fell to his death trying to fly. Then there's Great Aunt Anitra, who –"

"Perhaps I'd better take it from here, your majesty," a vaguely familiar woman's voice said. "You know how willful Princess Jasmine can be."

"Oh, thank you," the man said, clearly relieved. "I'll leave you girls alone." He gave Helaine a big wink. "Time to talk about boys. I understand." He trotted out of the room as fast as his fat body could move.

Helaine had a second or two to think. She had no idea what was happening. One second she had been standing beside Score, her sword in hand. The next she was here, dressed in these appalling clothes and with that fat lunatic babbling on. "Here" was a room with white marble floors, tables laden with fruit, walls draped with filmy pastel hangings and large windows looking out over a city the likes of which she had never seen before. Many of the buildings had bulbous domes and tall spires, and from the heat she appeared to be in the tropics. To be honest, if she was dressed in her usual clothing, she would probably have been sweating like crazy right now.

She would also have been a lot more comfortable. She felt almost *naked* dressed like this! As well as really stupid. The only good thing was that Score wasn't here right now. He'd be drooling and making his sick, lewd jokes. She wished he was here, even if he did get to laugh at her expense.

She turned to see who was here, and then stiffened and wished she had her sword.

Dressed almost identically to her, only in blue, stood Destiny, a slight sneer on her pretty face.

"What have you done to me?" Helaine growled.

"Me?" Destiny spread her arms wide, showing off her slim figure. "Nothing. It was Jagomath who did this to us both."

"Jagomath?"

"The snotty-nosed kid as Score called him. He cooked this all up out of his imagination. And an eleven-year-old boy's imagination is bound to incorporate a few pretty girls." Destiny examined her critically. "Actually, you don't look half-bad once you're out of those boys' clothes you usually wear. Some guys might even mistake you for pretty. Until they met me, of course."

"I can see you haven't changed much," Helaine said. "Still the slut. Getting killed doesn't seem to have affected very badly."

Destiny scowled. "Oh, it affected me all right – and I aim to see that you all pay for it. Jagomath is working for me." She smirked again. "Like I said, an eleven-year-old boy likes pretty – and he's very taken by me."

"Taken in by you, you mean," Helaine said, recalling what she could of Jagomath's conversation before she had been blasted here. "He seems to think my friends and I are the bad guys."

Destiny laughed. "Well, I did sort of give him that impression. After all, you *did* murder me, the love of his life."

"As I recall it," Helaine replied, "you died because of your own stupidity whilst attempting to murder us. You seem to have misplaced ideas about who the villain is."

"You see things your way, and I see them mine." Destiny smiled. "More to the point, Jagomath also sees them my way, and he's the boy with all of the power."

"He created all of this?" Helaine asked.

"That's right. If there's one thing he likes more than scantily-clad girls, it's playing games. You and your friends ruined his game of pirates on Ocean, so he's determined to make you all pay for it by entering into other games of his choosing. Lucky you, you're in his Arabian Nights fantasy."

"That *game* of his was killing people," Helaine said, angrily. "He must be very wicked." She gestured at her clothing. "As well as even more lecherous than Score."

Destiny laughed. "Let me give you a little advice, girly, while you're still alive. Your body is your most potent weapon against the male sex. You're a warrior, so you should understand using any weapons you can to achieve your goal. I'm almost irresistible, and I use that power to twist the minds of men to do my bidding. Jagomath believes everything I tell him because he's so entranced by what he sees. If you used your… assets, instead of covering them up, you might be able to get guys to give you anything too."

"I *am* a warrior, yes," Helaine said. "And the first thing I learned is to know my enemy. Score and most men are not my enemies, and I do not need to defeat them or coerce them. You are a manipulative witch, unable to have a normal relationship with anyone. You're in love with yourself, and at war with everyone else."

"You stupid, naïve girl," Destiny said. "The Diadem will not miss you once you're gone. Such pathetic ideas as you possess will get you nowhere."

"I am done talking with you," Helaine informed her. "Prepare to do battle."

"Not quite yet," Destiny replied. "This isn't your game or mine, but Jagomath's, and you have to follow it through – at least for the time being."

"What are you talking about?"

"His game is simple, dummy," Destiny told her. "You're the daughter of the Caliph of Bagdhad, and you're to be married off to one of two suitors, who are arriving to seek your hand. I can't imagine why Jagomath cast you as the fairy tale princess, but he did. So you have to play along with him and meet the suitors. Then the game unfolds from there."

"Give me one good reason why I should even consider that course of action," Helaine demanded.

"Because you have no choice," Destiny said. "Jagomath is more powerful that you, or even you and Score together. Probably even stronger that all four of you. If he wants something to happen, then it *will* happen. Especially now we're no longer in the Outer Rim of the Diadem but on the Inner Circuit – just one step away from Jewel and the heart of magic. He is sizzling here."

"That's nonsense," Helaine said. "I shall find some suitable clothing and change out of these scandalous rags..." Her voice faltered as she discovered that she couldn't remove anything she was wearing. Her arms and hands simply wouldn't obey her will. "What has he done to me?"

"Nothing much – as long as you play the game. You can do anything and say anything you wish – as long as you follow the rules. Jagomath's only constraint is that you must act your character's part. So – skimpy costume is a must. You'll also discover that you can't hold a sword because princesses don't do that sort of thing. As long as you stay in character as a Disney princess, though, you've got free will."

"What is a *Disney Princess*?" Helaine asked, worried.

"A role model for little girls, apparently," Destiny said drily. "And an object of desire for little boys. Play the part and you'll be fine. Now come on – it's time to meet your would-be wedders. Let's go, cutie."

Helaine was furious – even more so when she discovered she didn't have any option but to follow Destiny. Apparently her foe was correct – Jagomath had the power to enforce his will that she play the game, whether she wish to or not.

"And what is your role in this… game?" she forced herself to ask Destiny. She needed as much information as she could get if she was to win this game.

"I'm the Grand Vizier," Destiny replied. "The Caliph trusts me implicitly; I'm second in command of the city."

Helaine was starting to catch on. "And, knowing you, you're going to betray him somehow. You'd never willingly be second to anyone."

Destiny laughed. "You know me so well," she agreed. "It seems that in all of these Arabian Nights tales, the Vizier is wicked, and plotting to overthrow the Caliph. And to do horrible things to his daughter. I do believe I'm going to enjoy my part in the game."

"But I know your aims," Helaine pointed out. "What's to stop me telling my so-called father?"

"Absolutely nothing," Destiny answered. "But, as I said, he *trusts* me, so I can guarantee he wouldn't believe any warnings. Until I actually kill the doddering old fool, he won't believe any evil of me." She grinned. "Like I said, I know how to use my stunning looks to win me every advantage. And since you're too dumb to do the same, I have you hopelessly outclassed."

They had arrived in a large hall. At the far end was an overly-ornate throne, raised on a dais, on which her supposed father sat, looking very self-important. Slaves were fanning him whilst others ran around the room on various tasks. There were low couches and plump cushions scattered about the room. It was all very decadent, and Helaine scowled in disapproval. All of the females wore costumes like hers, though not as rich, and in some cases covering even less skin than hers did. The male slaves wore only trousers and slippers, and their bare chests gleamed.

"Cute, huh?" Destiny asked her, seeing her looking at the slaves.

"Immoral," Helaine growled.

"Somehow that's pretty much what I expected you to think. You really have to loosen up a bit. Not that you'll be alive for much longer to benefit from a change in attitude."

There were several soldiers about the room, all with large swords that had curved blades that seemed impractical to Helaine. She preferred a good, honest broadsword. But her fingers itched to grip one of the scimitars. Only she discovered she couldn't even take a step close to a soldier with that aim in her mind. Jagomath was enforcing his stupid rule that princesses didn't use weapons.

"Are there you are, my dear," the Caliph said cheerily. "All excited to meet your suitors, no doubt. Well, let's not keep your eager little heart waiting any longer."

"I can hardly wait," Helaine growled, lying.

"Splendid! Splendid!" The Caliph clapped his hands loudly. "Right, bring in Sinbad!" He winked at Helaine. "He's a sailor, I know, but he's a rich one, as well as brave and handsome, so I couldn't just forbid him from wooing you. You'll have to forgive his manners, though – he's a trifle brash."

"This just gets better and better," Helaine complained.

The main doors to the room opened, and the attendants ushered in a person who was clearly Sinbad. He was dressed in blue and silver – pants, tunic, and turban – and had sensible boots on his feet. Helaine found herself envying the man those boots. She *hated* her slippers!

There was something vaguely familiar about the man, and as he drew closer Helaine realized what it was.

Score stood absolutely still, staring at her. His eyes widened, and his mouth opened.

"Not one word," she warned him, blushing heavily. "Not one word."

"Definitely not," he agreed, grinning foolishly. "This is going to require a lot more than one word."

"It isn't my desire to appear like… this," Helaine complained, indicating her clothing.

"I'm sure it isn't," Score agreed. "But you are *hot*. Woweee…" He looked her over critically, and Helaine blushed again. She wished she could cover up some of her exposed skin, but knew it was impossible.

"Do not make fun of me," she growled.

"Fun?" Score shook his head. "Trust me, making fun never crossed my mind. I was thinking more along the lines of whisking you out of here and whispering sweet nothings in those gorgeous ears."

"What did I tell you, Jasmine?" the Caliph broke in. "His sailor's language is a bit odd, but I do believe he's rather taken with you."

"I'd rather just take her, your rotundity," Score told him. "She's a knockout."

"Strange words," the Caliph said. "But I believe we understand the meaning."

"You're enjoying this, aren't you?" Helaine growled, clenching her fists.

"Every last little detail," Score assured her. "I didn't know you had freckles on your shoulders."

"You don't like freckles?" Helaines asked, suddenly worried.

"Trust me, on you they look great. So, how far down do they go?"

Typical! "You're not going to find out," she promised him. "Anyway, aren't you rather cheerful all of a sudden? The last time I saw you, you were howling mad and desperate to get back to save your mother. Has the sight of so much of my bare skin so affected you that you've forgotten about Cathane?"

"Who?" Score grinned. "Just kidding. And while you are definitely most distracting, it's not just you. I realized that this Jagomath jerk has the power to send me back to any time I choose, so all we have to do is beat him in his silly game." He glanced around the throne room. "I wonder if Disney can sue him for copyright infringement? Anyway, all we have to do is whomp him, then spank some sense into him, and then get him to send us back to save Cathane. Simple. Oh, speaking of simple, how are you doing, Destiny?"

Destiny glared at him. "So, the two of you have finally admitted you have feelings for each other? How sweet." She moved closer to Score and stuck out her chest. "But why go after her when you could have a *real* woman?"

"You?" Score laughed in her face, which made Helaine proud of him. "You're not a real anything, except bitch. And, since you're actually dead right now, I guess you're not even that. Besides, I can trust Helaine with my life – I wouldn't trust you with a stamp collection. And, finally, she's a lot more beautiful than you are."

"You fool," Destiny hissed, clearly stung by the force of his rejection.

"I thought it was rather sweet, actually," Helaine confessed.

"I'll remind you of that when we're alone," Score promised her. She believed him.

"Ah, I do believe I hear your other suitor arriving," the Caliph broke in suddenly. There was a fanfare of trumpets, and the doors to the throne room were flung wide. Several dozen girls in skimpier costumes than even hers entered the room to Helaine's amazement, strewing rose petals all around. They were followed by a dozen soldiers in smart uniforms, and then by six huge, muscular men carrying a large chair.

In the chair, smirking happily, sat Jagomath. He was dressed similarly to Score in pants, tunic, boots and turban, but his were gleaming white and trimmed with jewels. Strangely, at his belt hung a small lamp.

"Welcome," the Caliph called out, beaming like an idiot. "Welcome, Aladdin."

"Aladdin?" Score sounded vaguely worried.

"Aladdin," Jagomath agreed, as the slaves set his carrying chair on the floor and he hopped out. "And all ready to go into action…" He held up the battered lamp, and rubbed it. Helaine had no idea what he was doing.

Then smoke started to pour from the spout of the lamp. To her surprise it coagulated into a vaguely human shape, and then solidified.

Standing in the room with them stood a ten-foot tall man with a dark beard. He was naked from the chest up. He bowed impressively to Jagomath.

"I am the genie of the lamp," he said in a booming, echoing voice. "You have but to command and I will obey."

Helaine still didn't have a clue what was happening, but obviously Score did. His smirk had changed to an expression of deep concern. "This may not be as easy as I thought…" he muttered.

"No," Jagomath agreed. "As you are going to discover, I can do *anything*. And you cannot match my powers."

Helaine glanced from the genie to Score. "Is he telling the truth?"

"Uh," Score said, worried. "He may be. Genie's are very powerful."

"And let's start with a quick demonstration," Jagomath said. "Genie – he's a sailor. He must feel lost without the sea. Why don't you help him out?"

"Your wish is my command." The genie's hand shot out, and he snatched up Score. Then he wound up and pitched.

With a howl, Score went flying out of the palace window. Helaine had no time to react, and no weapon to use.

They had to be a hundred feet from the ground, and there was nothing between it and Score...

Chapter Three

As Pixel's vision cleared, he found himself instantly confused. He was standing still, but now he was dressed in some kind of high-tech armor, and he was holding what seemed to be some kind of ray cannon in his arms. He was standing in the midst of a city that had clearly been savagely attacked and partially destroyed. Tall skyscrapers were now as jagged as broken teeth, and many were still burning or smoking. Wreckage filled the streets, along with burning or smashed vehicles. A grey pall hung over everything, and dust blew around his ankles.

Beside him stood two similarly clad figures. It took him a couple of seconds to realize that they were Jenna and Shanara – partly because they also wore the armor and carried ray cannons, but mostly because they now had blue skin, dark hair and pointed ears. In fact, they looked as if they had come from his home world of Calomir.

Behind them, looming over them, was a spaceship of some kind. It was huge, vaguely circular, and with spars and antennae jutting in all directions. He, Jenna and Shanara stood at the foot of a ramp that they had apparently descended.

On the ground in front of them, battered and bruised, lay Destiny. Her skin was still white under the grime, so she hadn't been changed in the same way that they had.

None of this made any sense to Pixel. He glanced at Jenna, who appeared very worried. She was staring at her blue hands. "You look good in blue," he assured her.

"How could this have happened?" she asked.

"It's an illusion," Shanara assured her. "Merely an overlay on our real skin. But it's a very good illusion – and I know illusions."

"But… why?" Jenna asked. She glanced at Pixel. "Don't get me wrong, this color looks good on you – but I'm not used to it."

"I understand," Pixel assured her. "When I have to be disguised to go to Earth and other worlds it feels just as odd to me to be white. But your skin color is a minor issue – what's happening here?" He gestured at the burning city with the barrel of his gun.

"Another illusion," Shanara told him. "But this one is astonishingly powerful. Things not only *look* real, but we can touch them and they *feel* real. If we walked into a wall, it would really hurt us."

"This must have been caused by that Jagomath somehow," Pixel realized. He glared down at Destiny. "What has he done?" he asked her. "What's the purpose of this?"

"It's a game," she replied, then winced and touched her jaw. "The little rat! This *hurts*! I actually feel like I've been tortured. I'll kill the little jerk!"

"I guess that means he's disillusioned with you," Pixel remarked. "He liked you as a teenager, but when you appeared as an adult he seemed to go off you. But… a game? What's the purpose?"

"What's the purpose of any game?" Destiny asked, annoyed. "To *play*, of course. Jagomath is really into games, and he really loves to win."

"I see." Pixel considered for a moment. "So this appears to be some sort of world at war."

"Yes." Destiny glared at them. "You're the evil alien invaders, and you've attacked the city, leaving it in flames. He and I are members of the resistance. You've captured me to interrogate me about his plans. The game picks up from there." She rubbed at her arms and winced. "But he needn't have made it quite so realistic – these bruises really hurt."

"I did say his illusions were powerful," Shanara commented. "Anything we experience here is going to seem very real to us."

"Including death?" Jenna asked.

"Including death," Shanara agreed. "I believe that if we die in this game, we'll die in reality also."

"That may be the point of this whole charade," Pixel realized. "We're cast as the villains, and Jagomath appears to think that we really *are* villains. Apparently he believes Destiny's lies about us."

"So he wants to beat us – and then kill us?" Jenna asked.

"I suspect that's the plan, yes," Pixel agreed.

"The all we have to do is to convince him that he's got it backward," Jenna said. "That Destiny is the villain, not us."

There was a sudden scream of firepower, and an explosion erupted barely twenty feet from them. Pixel shielded Jenna with his body, and winced as shrapnel and mortar bounced off his body armor.

"It's a good thing these suits are efficient," he muttered. "And it doesn't look like he's in a mood to chat. Get to cover." Jenna and Shanara dived behind what was left of a wall. Pixel grabbed Destiny and shoved her ahead of him. "That includes you," he said.

"This attack must be his attempt to rescue you."

"That seems likely," Shanara agreed. "But what do we do now?" Further explosions burst all around them.

"We play the game," Pixel said. "We have no other option is we wish to live." He located a communicator built into his armor. "Pixel to base-ship," he called.

"Base ship," a harsh, metallic voice replied. "Awaiting instructions."

"It's a computer," Pixel realized. "It can't act without instructions. That's why it wouldn't fire back – it needs to be told to do so." He tapped the communications control again. "Fire two hundred feet from me in the direction I'm pointing." He gestured just to the right of where the firing was coming from.

Mighty blaster cannons roared above his head, making him wince. Beams tore through that section of the landscape, tearing it to pieces. Rubble exploded as the broken buildings were shattered further.

"You missed," Destiny said smugly.

"I *meant* to miss," Pixel said. "I don't actually want to hurt Jagomath – just make him stop his attack."

"He's not going to be so constrained," Jenna reminded him. "He's out to kill us."

"Is he?" Pixel asked her. "He's very powerful – maybe more than we are even working together. If he wanted to kill us, he could just attack. Instead he's playing games."

"He *likes* to play games," Destiny said.

"That's my point," Pixel said. He ordered up another barrage to the right of the place he was sure Jagomath was. After the roar of the guns, he added: "He's a *kid*. Kids don't generally want to kill people unless they're psychopaths. And Jagomath didn't strike me that way. I think he'd much rather play with us than murder us. So as long as we keep the game interesting, then he'll keep on playing."

"And how long do you intend to keep that up?" asked Shanara. "He doesn't seem to have a curfew, so he might want to keep going."

"Just long enough for you to sneak around behind him," Pixel said. "Jenna and I will keep Destiny here. The point of the game is for him to recover her, so he'll have to come here for her. I think I can keep him busy, while Jenna prevents Destiny from escaping. In the meantime, you sneak around back of him and grab him. I suspect the game will automatically end if he's captured."

"That makes sense," Shanara agreed. "Fine, let's try it." She gave him a smile. "It's been quite some time since I played games with a child…" She vanished into the rubble.

"And I'll be more than happy watching Destiny," Jenna said grimly. "I just hope she tries to escape, because I *really* want to hurt her." Destiny actually started to look worried, which amused Pixel. The woman didn't know how gentle Jenna really was, and that she probably wouldn't be able to bring herself to harm anyone.

"Then this becomes a strategy game between Jagomath and myself," Pixel said. "And I don't care how good he is at playing, I'm certain I'm better." After all, he'd spent a large portion of his life doing nothing much more than playing computer games in virtual reality. It was like reliving his own childhood again.

By experimenting, he discovered that he had a bunch of shock troops under his command on the ship. He deployed them carefully throughout the ruins. They were dim-witted, unable to think for themselves, but they obeyed orders perfectly. Jagomath's men, meanwhile, were working their own way through the wrecked streets toward the ship. Pixel's shock troops fired back at anything that moved, making the rescuers' progress extremely slow and costly for them.

But this was far too simple and straight-forward. Pixel thought about it even as he played. The resistance fighters couldn't possibly have more forces than the invaders, so simply trying to break through the enemy lines couldn't be all there was to Jagomath's strategy. He wasn't a novice player. So there had to be something else to consider. An aerial attack? No, the spaceship could shoot down any aircraft – plus there were small one-man (or one-alien!) saucers in the main ship that Pixel could launch any time.

Which left only one more possibility. Pixel had the ship scan below ground. As he'd suspected, there were tunnels for water delivery, electrical supplies – and sewers… Logically, the most likely rescue attempt would be through them. While the majority of his forces kept up a fake attack, Jagomath could lead an elite team through the sewers to come up and surprise Pixel and effect a rescue that would end the game. Pixel discovered that he couldn't get the ship to scan the sewers properly to detect any approaching troops. But he could position troops down there to cover the approaches. If Jagomath *was* planning a sewer attack, he'd be stopped.

There wasn't anything else Pixel could think of doing. He had Jagomath's main force pretty much pinned down, the "surprise attack" planned for, and his own sneak attack in the form of Shanara underway. Now it was simply a matter of waiting for something to happen.

Ten minutes later, the ground rocked with the impact of gunfire from below ground. Pixel grinned. "His rescue party might need rescuing themselves," he said. "I've got them bogged down in the sewers."

Destiny scowled. "If I weren't constrained by his stupid rules to be the damsel in distress I'd use my powers to beat the crap out of you," she growled. "It was stupid of him not to utilize me more fully."

"I don't think it was foolishness that prompted that decision," Jenna said. "I think it's simply that he doesn't like you the way you are now." She scowled. "Pixel, why *is* she an adult?"

"Because that's what she really is," Pixel replied.

"But she was a teenager when she died," Jenna pointed out. "Shouldn't she *still* be a teenager if she's been reborn from that rock fragment?"

Pixel slapped his head. "I can't believe I didn't think about that," he said. "Thank goodness you're around to stop me ever getting too arrogant. You're right – she *should* have come back as a teenager. So there must be a reason why she's an adult…" He laughed. "Of course! If she was simply being recreated from the planetary fragment, she'd only be an illusion, or a ghost. Unable to touch or interact with the world."

Jenna punched Destiny on the arm, and the woman yelped. "Well, she's no ghost – she's as real as anything around here."

"And there's only one way that could have happened," Pixel realized. "We're in the past – *her* past – at a time when she was still alive. She's simply possessed her current body, which happens to be an *adult* body, while she was working for the Three Who Rule."

"You think you're so smart, don't you?" Destiny sneered. "So, yes, that's what I've done."

"And you're now too old to interest Jagomath any more," Jenna said. "Your plan is backfiring on you, isn't it?"

"It's working well enough," Destiny insisted. "He's going to beat you all and then kill you. After that –"

"After that you don't need him," Pixel said. "But he trusts you, and won't be expecting treachery. And treachery is what you *always* do…"

Jenna laughed. "Of course!" she said, in sudden realization. "She doesn't want Jagomath at all – she wants that planetary fragment!"

Pixel was proud of her. "Smart girl," he agreed, "That's what this is *really* all about, isn't it? In this time, Destiny betrayed the Three to Sarman, and they found out. They then punished her by sending her spirit into the body of a baby about to be born on Earth. They used her to test their own escape plan, and, to cap it all off, they made the baby a cripple so she couldn't enjoy her exile."

"And the fragment contains a lot of power from Zarathan," Jenna said. "Power she can access because she's linked to it."

"Right," Pixel said. "That's what this is all about, isn't it?" he asked Destiny. "You aim to kill Jagomath and steal back the fragment and then use it to change the past – either so you won't be caught and exiled, or else to make the future-you on Earth more powerful. You're manipulating everything to save yourself!"

"So what?" Destiny snarled. "Wouldn't you?"

"Rewrite the whole of time just to save myself some anguish?" Pixel shook his head. "Only you could be that selfish, Destiny. You were always selfish, and that's what caused your exile initially, and then your death. Now you're just an echo of yourself, trying hard to cobble together a life again. You're clinging desperately to life even while you're really dead. This cannot possibly end well for you, no matter how you scheme and betray."

"You're bound to say that," Destiny said. "But I *shall* succeed – nothing you can do will prevent it."

"Wow," Pixel breathed. "You know, I used to think that maniacs like you were simply something some over-active writers dreamed up. But you really *are* unhinged, you know."

"Plus," Jenna added, "Jagomath is stronger than you – he's forcing you to play his game, and he's preventing you from using your powers. So you're helpless anyway."

"Only in *this* game," Destiny snapped. "And this one won't last…"

There was another round of explosions from below the ground. Pixel listened to a report from the strike team captain.

"That's the end of the rebels down there," he announced. "Jagomath's game strategy has failed him – he can't rescue you now. And I think that realization will distract his attention long enough for Shanara to strike…"

Suddenly, everything ground to a halt. Reality was on hold. That meant that Shanara *had* struck, and must have captured Jagomath. The game was over – and they had won.

Then everything shimmered around them. "What's happening?" Jenna gasped. "I can feel the magic altering… But we *won.*"

"One game only," Jagomath's voice cried across the world. He sounded very annoyed. "That was Pixel's game, and he beat me. But now it's *your* game, Jenna, and you can't possibly win this one…"

Chapter Four

Jenna stared down at herself in amazement. She was seated and dressed in a style she'd never before seen. She wore a heavy dress of a rich, deep-green material. Floral patterns were picked out on the bodice and the very puffed-out sleeves in what appeared to be gold. The skirt was edged with fur, as were the wrists of the dress. Beneath the dress she could tell she wore petticoats – more than one! There were thick, rich stockings on her legs and green slipper-like shoes on her feet. There was a choker of pearls about her neck and several gold rings on her fingers inlaid with diamonds and rubies. She knew that this had to be another of Jagomath's illusions, but the clothing felt very real – and a little too warm. Such clothing would cost a minor fortune to actually purchase. She had been raised the poor daughter of a hedge-witch and was completely unused to such finery. Even though it couldn't possibly be real, it made her very uncomfortable to wear it.

She became more aware of her surroundings. She was seated at a table in what appeared to be some sort of an inn. Remnants of an ornate breakfast were spread before her – half a large pie, a platter of vegetables and a couple of loaves – all started, but none finished. Beside her sat Shanara, as elaborately dressed as herself, but in blues and silver instead of green and gold. Shanara also had a tiara in her hair, studied with diamonds.

Pixel stood beside the table, dressed in livery of gold and black, clearly supposed to be their servant. He looked as confused as she felt. Shanara seemed more at ease – but, then, she had been a queen once, so this was probably nothing out of the ordinary for her.

"What's going on?" Pixel asked her. She became aware of other people around them, most of them definitely less well-dressed, and some of them actually looking like grubby peasants. Pixel had to speak up to be heard over the sounds of conversations. "Where are we? Jagomath said that this was your game, Jenna, so I'm assuming you recognize it."

"I do in a way," she said. "We're obviously in an inn in some wealthy town, presumably on my home world of Ordin."

"These dress-styles are very similar to ones I wore," Shanara confirmed. "I believe Jenna is correct. It would seem to be a little after the time when I... left Ordin."

"But I was never dressed like this in my life," Jenna protested. "I feel like a doll in all this finery." She stood up. "It's quite heavy and absolutely impractical."

"That's the point of it," Shanara explained. "It's designed to show that you're so wealthy you not only don't have to work, but that you couldn't possibly, even if you wanted to."

"I'm starting to think that might be also true if I have to visit the bathroom," Jenna grumbled. "It would take forever to get under these layers of clothing!"

Shanara grinned. "If we're here long enough to need that, I'll show you how it's done," she promised. "But since we haven't actually eaten or drunk any of this meal, I hope it's a problem that doesn't arise."

"Well, the two of you seem to have done very well out of this," Pixel complained. "How come I'm just a servant?"

"It's Jagomath's game," Jenna said. "Maybe he's trying to punish you for beating him in the last one?"

"Maybe," Pixel said. "But it is a good point – we *did* beat him."

"Yes," Shanara mused. "Despite the fact that he's got so much magic, he can still lose."

"That's because Pixel can think rings around him," Jenna said, proud of her boyfriend. "And I'm sure he'll do the same in this game."

"Thanks," Pixel said, frowning slightly. "But I was at home in that last game – I've played hundreds like it when I used to live on Calomir. But I don't have a clue what's supposed to happen here."

"Nor do I," Jenna admitted. "I'm completely out of my depth – I'm not used to being rich – even in a game."

A stout man wearing an apron came across to them, a humble look on his face. "My ladies," he said, bowing deeply. "Your coach is ready."

"We appear to be intended to take a trip," Pixel murmured.

"Yes," Shanara agreed, thoughtfully. "We've broken our fast, and now are supposed to be on our way. You'd better go ahead of us and clear a path to the door. It wouldn't do for any of the peasants to even touch the hems of our dresses."

Jenna felt her face growing red. "I don't like being the lady," she growled. "Not even in play. I'm nothing but a peasant myself."

"Perhaps not," Shanara said. "But you'd better get used to playing one if we're to win this game. Jagomath said it was *your* game, so it's important you pay attention to behaving properly, at least until we know what the game *is*."

Jenna growled again. "I've always hated the nobility," she said. "They oppressed us and abused us – and then ignored us when we were inconveniently dying or suffering. I'll *never* get used to playing one."

"You have no option," Pixel said, gently. "For now, just try and fit the part. We *must* win this game."

Jenna nodded. "I'll try," she promised. "But I can tell you now that I won't like it."

"Oh, this sort of life has its rewards," Shanara told her. "You'd be surprised how quickly you might get to enjoy it."

"*You* were born into this," Jenna said. "I was born into poverty. And I think I'd prefer poverty."

Shanara's lips twitched. "We'll see," was all she said.

Jenna was momentarily annoyed with the older woman. Did Shanara really think she could be seduced into *enjoying* being obnoxious and selfish? If she *really* owned a gown like this, she would sell it and use the money to help her village. To simply *keep* wealth like this when there were suffering people around was incredibly immoral. How could anyone enjoy it?

And yet – so many did. The nobles of Ordin thought very little about the lives of the peasants, who they considered to be beneath their notice. And in some ways it was better for the peasants to be unnoticed. When the rich *did* notice them, it was usually for bad reasons – to steal their crops, to carry off their children to be raised as servants, or the older girls for mistresses. Jenna knew what being rich meant – thinking only of yourself and your own desires and ignoring everyone else. Especially those you were certain were far beneath you.

She hated the nobles with a passion. It had taken her the longest time to be able to get along with Helaine, who was the daughter of a noble. And Helaine wasn't a bad person – she *did* think about others, and she had a good heart. But she, too, had been filled with her prejudices and initially had loathed Jenna. Now, though, they were able to relate and even to like one another. Both had been forced to admit their prejudices had been wrong. Helaine proved that not all nobles were evil. Oh, and Shanara also – the sorceress had accepted Jenna without a problem even though Shanara had once been a Queen, the worst of all possible nobles.

But… even so! Jenna felt almost physically sick even playing the part. But she lifted her skirt slightly, following Shanara's lead, and walked behind Pixel to the door. Pixel – clearly getting into his role – opened the door for them with a low bow. Jenna walked outside into the morning light.

There was a carriage awaiting them, staffed by a driver and a footman who was holding the door open for them. The vehicle itself was as ornate as their clothing – made from aromatic wood, lavishly painted with crests on the doors. It fairly shouted out that its owner was wealthy. Four impatient white horses were ready to run like the wind. Jenna was getting an awfully bad feeling about this.

The innkeeper had accompanied them to the door, fawning and scraping as they left. "A good journey, my ladies," he called. "May the Good God keep the Silverhawks at bay."

Jenna felt a real shock at his words. Pixel realized that there was something wrong and caught at her elbow to steady her. "What is it?" he asked her. "Why are you so pale?"

"Because now I know what it is we're facing," she replied, grimly. "We *can't* get into that coach!" She tried to turn and hurry back into the inn for safety, but her feet refused to obey her will. They carried her steadily toward the waiting trap. "We've got to escape!" she cried desperately.

"I can't turn back," Shanara said in a low voice. "I'm being forced to go into the carriage."

"Me too," Pixel confirmed. "This is Jagomath's game, isn't it?"

"This is no game!" Jenna said desperately attempting to force her feet into some other path, without success. She found herself getting into the carriage, helped by the footman who was paying no attention to anything she said. "This is planned murder!" She sat down on the padded bench. Shanara sat oppose her, and Pixel closed the door. There was a running board around the base of the coach, and he stood on this, holding onto the door for stability, as the coachman cried: "Ha!" and there was the crack of a whip.

With a rattle and several bumps, the coach trundled into motion. It swiftly picked up speed as it headed down the unpaved road. Each bump was painful for her behind, but she barely noticed the discomfort. She was too frightened.

"What is it?" Shanara asked. "It was the mention of that name, wasn't it? The Silverhawks."

"Yes." Jenna shuddered, feeling chilled to her bones. "It was after your time, of course." She saw that Pixel was leaning in at the window and paying rapt attention as she spoke. "We peasants always hated and resented the Lords and the other nobles, but there was nothing we could do about it. We were forbidden by law to own weapons and in any event had no training to use them even if we had them. The soldiers of the local castles made certain that we were kept in line and paid the dreadful taxes imposed upon us. They also brutalized and terrorized us so that any sort of fight was unthinkable. As so it was – except to the Silverhawks.

"They were a family who lived in a mountain pass that was difficult to reach. Thanks to this, they were left pretty much alone for the most part and unmolested. But the local lord, Catrain, didn't like the thought that he was losing taxes he felt that they should be paying. So he organized his troops to raid the Silverhawk village. They attacked it while the men were hunting, and there was only a small resistance. The soldiers killed all of the men who were present and all the male children. Then they raped and killed the women they could find, and carried off the girls as slaves.

"Naturally, when they returned the Silverhawks were furious. They buried their dead, and gathered in all of the survivors. Then they vowed vengeance on Catrain. Lord Catrain never left his castle again – and any of his men or family that ventured outside were brutally slaughtered by the Silverhawks. These men finally worked out a way to undermine Castle Catrain's walls and they managed to get into the castle. They slaughtered the entire Catrain family, down to the last child.

"When news of this massacre got out, the other Lords nearby were stunned – and angry. They were desperately afraid that the example the Silverhawks was setting might influence their peasants to risc in rcvolt, so they banded together to destroy the clan. In response the Silverhawks now started raiding anyone who was a noble. They killed and vanished for several years."

"But they were stopped eventually?" Pixel prompted.

"Oh, yes," Jenna admitted. "At least, that depends on who tells the story. The bards employed by the nobles all say that the Silverhawks were wiped out, their stronghold burnt to the ground and the land salted so it would never be useable again. In the villages, though, the peasants tell a story that says the Silverhawks were never caught, and that they retreated deeper into the woods and mountains, and would return someday to wipe out the rest of the nobles." She shuddered as she spoke.

"A charming story," Pixel observed. "Obviously the two versions are for two different audiences. But which one is true?"

"It doesn't matter," Shanara said. "Because I see what Jenna is getting at – we're now dressed as nobles and in a very rich carriage, heading obviously into Silverhawk territory. Jagomath's little game is clear enough – we're to be attacked and become victims of the Silverhawks." She shivered also.

"Exactly," Jenna said, grimly. "This is a game he's determined that we will not survive. And the odds are very clearly in his favor."

"But it doesn't make sense," Pixel protested. "Jagomath is from *Earth*, not Ordin. How does he even know about the Silverhawks?"

"He said it was *my* game," Jenna reminded him.

Pixel abruptly grinned. "Of course! That's it exactly! It's *your* game – not his." He laughed. "And that last game was mine, not his. He's taking the format for these games of his from our minds. Well, that makes sense- he's only a kid, and doesn't have much imagination, obviously. He has to raid our thoughts as the basis of his games."

"And how does that help us?" Shanara asked. "His imagination may be limited, but his power clearly isn't. We may be providing the concepts he's using, but he's bringing them to life – to kill us."

"His lack of imagination is what helps us," Pixel said. "He's limited in what he can do. I managed to out-think him in the last game, and I suspect it's possible that Jenna can do the same in this one. All you have to do is figure out a loophole, some way to stay in the game but win it."

"Pixel," Jenna said, shaking. "You don't understand – there isn't any way to win this time! The Silverhawks killed everyone that they attacked! As soon as they appear, we're doomed. This time there isn't any sneaky way for us to win – all we can do is die…"

At that moment, the coach driver gave a yell of fear. "Armed men!" he cried in terror. "It's the Silverhawks! They're attacking!"

Chapter Five

Score had one brief moment of extreme terror as he was flung by the genie out of the palace window. Then it settled down to sheer terror and he was able to think again. That is, for the few remaining seconds he had before gravity took over and pulled him rather messily back to earth again…

He had four jewels to amplify his magic. Amethyst affected the size of things, and seemed useless. Emerald worked on transforming things – maybe making the ground nice and rubbery? No – he'd just bounce up and then come down again, probably elsewhere and probably very hard. Jasper gave him Sight, which wasn't helpful. That left his Chrysolite and the power of Water.

Why couldn't it be air? He had plenty of that!

Whoa… And the air held a lot of water vapor. He'd learned a few things in school. Now if there was just some way to use that water to save himself… He didn't have much time left… The ground was starting to look an awful lot closer. He had a second to observe that the "city" looked like a cartoon backdrop – Jagomath's powers didn't extend to making everything real, it seemed. Or maybe it wasn't a lack of power but a lack of imagination? Either way, it suggested weakness, something to exploit once he'd saved himself.

He focused quickly, using the chryosite and emerald together. He isolated the water vapor in the air and changed it to ice, forming it as he did so into a slide, like in a children's playground. He felt the weight of it below him, buoying him up, as he feverishly formed it, and then began to shape it to curve back toward the palace he's so recently left. It took all of his concentration and power, but it was working. He was sliding along now and no longer falling.

Now his immediate panic was dying down, this was starting to be almost fun. Jagomath liked cartoons, did he? Well, he wasn't the only one who'd watched TV around here… And Score had some favorites of his own to bring into play. He slid down the ice he was creating as he went along, and was aimed squarely back into the window from which he'd been thrown out.

He even managed to land back on his feet as he slid back into the palace room. Helaine looked startled and then very happy, which pleased him immensely – she must have been scared he was dead. Jagomath looked almost as startled and certainly *not* pleased. Destiny simply scowled.

Score grinned at the young magician. "Of course you know this means war," he said in his best Bugs Bunny impression. "What's up, doc?" And he replayed his trick by making the floor under Jagomath's feet sheer ice. Then, for good measure, he did the same to where Destiny stood. Both of them cried out in shock and lost their footing. Score couldn't help laughing and he ran across to join Helaine. "Try and out-cartoon me, will he?"

"I don't know what you're talking about," Helaine admitted. "But I am really glad you're safe."

"Me too, toots," Score said, laughing. He turned back to where Jagomath was trying unsuccessfully to get back to his feet. He was slipping and falling. So was Destiny, in quite interesting ways… In that skimpy costume, something was liable to burst out soon. The genie was standing still, doing nothing. Interesting… Of course – it wasn't really alive. It was animated by Jagomath's magic, and as long as he couldn't command it, it wouldn't act.

Right, next trick, then. "Helaine," he said, quietly. "Levitate Jagomath into the air and spin him around as fast as you can." She looked puzzled, but did as Score ordered.

Jagomath lifted off the ground about four feet, and then started to revolve fairly rapidly. He started to wail. "I'm getting giddy!" he complained. "I'm gonna heave!"

Score laughed again. "He can't order the genie around in that state," he said, happily. "It doesn't matter how much power he has if he can't use any of it."

Helaine looked mildly surprised. "That's quite clever," she admitted. "But how long do I have to keep this up?"

Score hadn't thought that far ahead. "Until he throws up?" he suggested. "Or gives in? Do you give in?" He called to Jagomath.

"I'm gonna get you for this!" Jagomath wailed. He was starting to look very white-faced and sickly.

"Yeah, right," Score said. "Here – have a cigar." He used his power of transformation to make one out of the oxygen in the air and then slammed it into Jagomath's mouth. A moment later, it exploded in true cartoon fashion. "Ain't I a stinker?" He was really starting to enjoy this.

"You stupid brats," Destiny growled. While they were dealing with Jagomath, she had managed to get off the patch of ice and back to her feet. She used her own powers to hurl a fireball straight at Score.

Score barely blinked. He turned the oxygen in the air in its path into carbon dioxide – and the fireball spluttered and died, without oxygen to keep it burning. Hey, middle school chemistry had its uses after all! Then, before she could react again, he turned the floor under her feet into maple syrup. She yelped as her feet sank six inches into the sticky stuff. Score then turned the syrup into hard chocolate, trapping her very effectively. As an afterthought, he conjured up more syrup from the air and poured it over her. "You always were quite a dish," he commented. Thankfully, that one went right over Helaine's head – he didn't want her getting jealous.

"Surrender, Dorothy!" he yelled. "Oops, wrong movie… Okay, Jagomath – do you give in yet? Or do you need longer to think about it?"

"No!" the boy wizard gasped. "Enough – you win this one, I admit. Let me down!"

"There's a good little maniac," Score said approvingly. He nodded to Helaine, who let the youngster flop to the floor. The boy was looking definitely unwell, but he hadn't actually thrown up yet. "Now, behave yourself, and we can talk this all over."

Jagomath scowled. "You think I'm defeated because you won one game?" he snarled. "Maybe you beat me in this one, but there's still *hers* to go!" He gestured, and the world about them vanished…

…To reform moments later, before Score had a chance to react.

He blinked in surprise as he discovered that he and Helaine were now standing in thick woods. Tall, angular trees surrounded them, towering over their heads and casting dark, oppressive shadows across them. Score was now dressed in a tunic, leggings and a long cloak – which helped to shelter him a little from the cutting wind whistling through the eerie trees. Helaine was in similar attire, though the tunic looked far better on her. The leggings showed off her limbs rather nicely. If they weren't about to be fighting for their lives again, Score might have enjoyed the sight. As it was…

"Any idea what's going on here?" he asked her. "I have to confess, I liked you better in Bagdad and that harem gear."

"I'm sure you did," she growled. "I feel more comfortable like this, though. You won't be staring at my cleavage quite so much."

"Wanna bet?" he asked, with a cheeky grin.

"I do not yet know what this place is, or what the game will be," Helaine said, ignoring his crack. "It does appear to be Ordin, but beyond that I can't say much. I am certain Jagomath will reveal himself shortly."

"Yeah, that seems to be his game plan," Score said. "You know, though – I've been thinking…"

Helaine glared at him. "Those words usually preface a ridiculous plan that gets us into trouble."

"Hey, not always!" he protested. "Sometimes they preface a sensible plan that just goes a bit screwy and gets us into trouble. Anyway, what I was thinking was that Jagomath is getting things too much his own way."

"He lost the last game," Helaine said. "And I doubt he's doing too well against Pixel and Jenna. If he was, then either he or Destiny would be bound to mention it. So how can you say he's having things too much his own way?"

"What I mean, o skeptical one, is that he's the one who decides the setting and the rules," Score replied. "We then have to counter him. What we need is a weapon we can use against him."

"Like what?" she asked.

"Like his real name." Score folded his arms and smiled smugly. "It would be great if we had the Book of Names here, but we don't."

"He's not likely to be in that anyway," Helaine pointed out. "He's only recently discovered his powers, don't forget."

"Well, anyway, there's another way to try and find his name, and I think we should give it a go. Surely you'd agree that there's no harm in trying?"

Helaine frowned. "None that I can see," she agreed. "But there may be a hidden problem we've yet to discover."

"Wow, listen to miss negativity!" Score laughed. "All we need to do is to set Oracle on his trail. Dark, tall and miserable is good at ferreting out stuff."

"But he's not here," Helaine said. "Or did you forget that part?"

"No, smarty pants, I didn't," he replied. "He's right where he needs to be – in the future. Where Jagomath comes from. Where he can track him down on Earth."

"And how do we contact Oracle?" Helaine asked with a sigh. "Do you have one of those cell phone devices they're so fond of in New York? One that can let you talk through time?"

"Helaine, Helaine," he said in mock sorrow, shaking his head. "Only thinking of technology. We have *magic,* remember? Better than a cell phone."

"Oracle's in the future," Helaine repeated. "How do you propose to get around that?"

"Listen, kid, you stick to being the brawn in this partnership and let me be the brains." He grinned at her. "Okay, you can be the beauty to my beast as well, if you like."

Helaine sighed again. "Your idea?" she prompted.

"We do what we do best, sweetie – join forces. My jasper gives me the power of Sight, and I don't think it's limited to seeing just what's here and now. And your agate gives you Communication. Joining the two together should enable us not only to find Oracle but then to talk to him. Agreed?"

Heleaine looked surprised. "You know, I think it might just work… Score, there are times when you appear to be positively brilliant."

"I know," he said modestly.

"And that's usually when you screw up the worst," she added. "But in this case I have to confess I do not see a negative side to this plan. Let's try it." She gripped her agate firmly in one hand, and then took his hand with the other. He appropriated his jasper and cling tightly.

"Focus," he ordered. "Concentrate on Oracle." He followed his own order, striving to reach out with all of the power of his mind…

"Score! Helaine!"

"It's Oracle!" Helaine exclaimed. "Your plan worked!"

"Of course." Score tried to hide the fact that he hadn't been certain it would. She didn't need to know that.

Oracle's vague form took shape uncertainly in front of them. "What's happened?" he asked. "Where are you? *When* are you?"

"It's the same answer to all the questions," Score said. "Don't know. Okay, listen, we need you to track somebody down for us." He explained as best he could what they knew about Jagomath and his plans. "He's eleven years old, and from the sound of his accent, he's from the Midwest somewhere."

"That's not a lot to go on," Oracle complained.

"That's because we don't do easy," Score growled. "Can you get to work on finding out who he is?"

"Of course. I have a few ideas of my own, you know." Abruptly Oracle smiled. "It's good to hear that you're safe, anyway. Blink and I were very worried."

"We're *not* safe," Score pointed out. "Jagomath aims to kill us. And, trust me, we're far more worried than the pair of you."

"If you find out what we need," Helaine added, "will you be able to contact us again?"

"Yes," Oracle said confidently. "Now you've linked with me, I can use Blink's powers to keep the link alive. Then I just have to follow it to get back to you. I don't know how long this will take, so be careful till I return." He gave a small wave of the hand and vanished again.

"Yay for me," Score said, rather pleased with himself.

Helaine rolled her eyes. "So, we contacted Oracle. I'll give you that. But we don't know if it will do us any good."

"Wow, have you ever considered developing a sunny side to your nature?" Score asked her. "You don't have to be down all the time, you know."

"I'm attempting to provide a balance to your puerile optimism," she countered.

"Well, I'll take my optimism over your negativity any day, In fact…" He stopped talking as the sound of a horn broke the silence all about them. "What's that?"

"A hunting horn," Helaine said. "A lot of nobles use them when they're out in the woods. It helps them to keep their dogs centered and…" Her voice trailed away. Score looked at her and saw she'd gone pale.

"What's wrong?" he asked her.

"Score," she said urgently. "I think I know where we are now – and we're in very grave danger."

"When are we *not* in grave danger?"

"I'm serious!' she yelped. "One of the stories I heard as a child was of Lord Arvin's Hunt… He was a vicious and sadistic man who had a pack of half-starved hounds. He'd use them to go hunting." She stared into his eyes and Score was amazed to see that she looked absolutely terrified. "Score, he hunted *people* – and his dogs would tear them to pieces…"

Chapter Six

Helaine couldn't suppress a shudder that shook her entire body. When she had been young, one of her older brothers had loved to terrify her by telling her the story of Lord Arvin's Hunt. Peder had been sadistic like that, and it had taken her a long time to get over the nightmares she would have following his recounting. Now it looked as if the nightmares were about to all come true.

"It must have been fun being you growing up," Score muttered. "All those creatures you conjured up on Zarathan, and now this... Didn't they have any *nice* stories on your world?"

"Like yours are any better," she snapped. "I've been reading some of those Brothers Grimm stories – and *grim* is the word for them."

"You read books?" Score asked, pretending to be amazed. "Wow. We'll have you surfing the internet next."

"I can still beat you up with one hand tied behind my back," she reminded him.

"Big deal. So can Oracle – and he's intangible."

Helaine knew he was trying to distract her from her fears by being silly, and she was grateful for the attempt... even though it failed. "Score, *please* be serious for once," she begged him. "If Jagomath has brought Arvin to life from my memories, then we could very well be killed."

"Well, if we're about to die, is there any chance of you showing me your legs first? Then I'll have something nice to think about as I'm being torn to death."

"Score, *please* take this seriously!"

"I *am* serious. Believe me, I really want to see your legs when they're not encased in chain mail."

"Fine. If we survive this, I'll wear a skirt for a week." It was amazing how he could manage to be so childish and annoying at times.

Score grinned. "Now that's what I call incentive. Ain't nothing going to kill me till I get to enjoy that," he promised her.

"Honestly, there are times when I don't know why I like you," she informed him.

"I've never figured out why you like me, either" he said. "But it's not something I'm going to complain about. Okay, now I've got motivation to live, let's think about this one. This Lord

Arvin hunts people down using a pack of dogs, right?"

"Right," she agreed. "Big, hungry, man-eating dogs." She shuddered again at the mental image of large teeth ripping into her flesh…

"Then we'll be fine," he told her. All we have to do is to climb a nice big tree and wait them out. Dogs can't climb trees but we can."

"It's not going to be that simple," she replied. "So can Arvin."

"Big deal," Score scoffed. "Let's find an oak tree and pelt him with acorns."

"He'll be armed," she pointed out.

"And we can do magic," Score said. "Remember when I told you to not be so negative? You're doing it again. Stop picking holes in my plans."

"Stop coming up with hole-ridden plans!" she snapped.

"Fine," he said, folding his arms stubbornly. "It's *your* turn to come up with a plan."

"I don't have one," she confessed.

"Then we go with mine by default," he said. "Come on."

There was another peal of the hunting horn, this time definitely closer. Helaine felt as if she could almost see the dogs in their pack, running hard, jaws ready to crunch her bones… She felt Score shaking her.

"Snap out of it," he ordered. "Helaine, you're worrying me – I've never seen you as scared as this before."

"I've never been as scared as this before," she admitted. "Score, I've had nightmares about this for years."

"Then move it, so you'll live to have nightmares about it for years to come," he snapped. He grabbed her arm and dragged her along.

Helaine forced herself to calm down, to stop picturing evil teeth ripping at her flesh… Score was right, she had to stop reacting in fear and force herself to focus. She was a warrior, not a child whimpering in her bed at night. She could face her fears and defeat them, no matter how ingrained they were. But she couldn't stop shaking. Terror like this was too much to ignore. It had become a part of her life.

"This looks likely," Score said, stopping by a tall, majestic tree of some kind she didn't recognize. "Come on, I'll give you a boost up, then you can help me." He held his hands clasped together, and she lifted her foot into it. She scrambled up into the first branch, and lay across it. She reached her hand down, and helped Score up beside her. He gently touched her shoulder. "You can let go of that branch," he said. "We have to get higher."

Helaine managed to nod, but it took her a few seconds to force her fingers to release the branch. Then she managed somehow to follow Score up about twenty feet. Every time she heard the horn sound, though, she started shaking again.

"You know, you're right," Score said. "This plan isn't so hot. Not an acorn in sight." She realized he was trying to cheer her up, but it wasn't working. She couldn't even manage to get annoyed with him. Instead, she moved to sit behind him and held him tightly. "Whoo!" he gasped. "Hey, I'm starting to like this new side to your character. We get to cuddle. Of course, I'd like it better without the pack of hounds after us. And you back in that harem gear. Something nice and sheer and silky…"

"I might have known you'd start thinking things like that," she growled. "You have a very low-bred mind."

"Good, you're sounding more like your old self again." Score grinned and then kissed her forehead. "Maybe I should just do something to really annoy you, and then you'd forget this funk you're in. Of course, if I did what I'm thinking about, you'd probably push me out of the tree…"

Helaine felt her face blush. "Don't you dare!"

"Ha! Talk about low-bred minds!" he gloated. "If you didn't have one yourself, you wouldn't be thinking such naughty thoughts."

"You're impossible."

"And you've stopped shaking," he pointed out, accurately enough. "Just in time, because I think we're about to get dogged."

Helaine listened, and realized he was right. She could hear *things* moving through the forest. It wouldn't have been so bad if the dogs were barking or growling, but now they were silent as they moved on the trail. They didn't want to alert their prey, obviously.

And then they came out into the open. There were probably twenty of them, though she couldn't make an accurate count as they milled about so much. They were huge, much larger than any dog she had ever seen. They each had to be the size of a small horse. Their eyes were cold and dangerous, their mouths large and filled with razor-sharp teeth, drool dripping copiously. When they had spotted their prey in the tree, their silence ended. Snarling, growling, howling, they flung themselves against the bole of the tree, clawing and frantic.

Score stuck his tongue out at them and made a rude noise. It served only to annoy them more. He reached out and started plucking leaves.

"What are you doing?" she asked him.

"Transformation," he said. "My special gift, remember?" He held up a leaf, and it turned into a cookie. "Doggie treats... Your Lord Arvin keeps his dogs nasty by starving them. Let's see if we can calm them down a bit with treats." He started dropping the transformed leaves down to the vicious beasts.

At first the hounds didn't seem to notice. Then one broke off and nosed a fallen treat. With one quick gulp the dog downed it and then started looking for more. After a moment, a second dog saw what the first was doing, and started to grab for treats himself.

Astonishingly, his silly plan seemed to be working!

There was the sound of the horn again, this time almost on top of them. The dogs immediately forgot the treats and started leaping and snarling again. They were too well trained to be distracted quite so simply. Helaine touched Score's arm. "It was a good attempt," she told him.

Two horses broke into view through the foliage below. On one, grinning nastily, sat Destiny. Jagomath was perched on the other, his face lit up with amusement.

"You won't win this one!" he yelled up at them. "This time, I'm going to beat you."

"As if!" Score called back, scornfully. "You can't get us up here, and your puppies can't climb trees."

"I'm in no hurry," Jagomath sneered.

"Well, wait till Fall – maybe we'll come down with the leaves," Score jeered.

"Oh, I think I can hurry it up a bit," Jagomath replied. He gestured, and there was a cracking sound within the branch. Score grabbed Helaine's arm and pulled her closer to the tree. The branch they'd been on went crashing down to the ground. The dogs attacked it, and then ignored it when they realized their prey was no longer on it.

"No fair," Score muttered. "Okay, sweetie, I think it's time for you to come up with a plan."

"I'm too scared to think," Helaine confessed. All she could picture were those horrible creatures tearing at her flesh… She was shaking again, uncontrollably.

"Hey, brilliant!" Score said. "That's my girl – use your fear."

"What are you talking about?" she demanded. He was making even less sense than normal.

"Your agate," he said, softly, so Jagomath wouldn't hear him. "It gives you the power to communicate with anything. So use it to project your own fear – at the dogs. Make *them* as scared as you are!"

Amazingly, it sounded workable. She clutched her agate, and then focused. She felt all of the terror and panic in her soul, and *threw* it with all of her power at the snarling, murderous beasts below. She willed every ounce of power she had to funnel her own fear into the dogs.

For a second, nothing happened, and she was afraid that she was going to fail. But she was a warrior, and would not give in to fear, no matter how powerful it was. Sweat dripped down her face as she fought to project.

Then the dogs stopped snarling. They started to back away from the tree, their ears and tails flattening. They began to whimper, and to scurry for cover.

It was working! She had to be careful to feel no triumph or hope – nothing but fear to feed to the dogs.

"What's happening?" Jagomath asked, confused. "Come on, you stupid animals! Go after them!"

But the dogs backed away, whining, and then they broke, running away as fast as they could as if all of the devils in hell were on their tails.

"No!" Destiny growled. "You can't win – not again! You can't – Jagomath is much stronger than you are!"

"It's not just strength," Score called down. "It's also skill and, well, mostly being low and tricky. And we've got him licked on that. Come on, Jaggy – admit it, you're outclassed!"

"No!" he yelled. "I won't let you beat me again – I won't! This is *my* game, and I'm going to beat you!"

"Wow, what a sore loser," Score jeered. "Loser! Loser!"

"Stop it!" Jagomath howled. "I'm better than you! I'm stronger! You've got to lose – you've got to!" He was almost crying in frustration. Well, for all of his power, he *was* only an eleven year old boy playing games.

"I hope I didn't come at a bad time."

Helaine saw Oracle standing in the air beside her. She was starting to feel hope again, and trusted it wasn't getting through to the dogs. She let go of her agate, and realized her palms were moist with sweat. "I'm glad to see you," she told him.

"And I have news," their friend replied, smiling. "I managed to backtrack that young boy to his home."

"Who is this?" Jagomath demanded. "What's going on? He's not part of the game!"

"You demented little creep," Score snapped. "It may be only a game to you, but it's life and death to us. And all's fair in love and war." He turned to Oracle. "So, what's the scoop?"

"Well, it seems he's really a school child from Chicago," Oracle answered. "And his real name is –"

"No!" Destiny screamed. "No!"

" – Timothy Reichart," Oracle finished.

Helaine felt a surge of satisfaction and peace. With the possession of Jagomath's true name, they now had power over him. And since he didn't know *their* true names, he would be unable to fight back the same way.

He clearly didn't understand this, though. He scowled. "Shut up!" he told Destiny. "You're annoying me."

"You idiot!" she snarled. "Don't you understand? They know your name! It gives them power."

"So what?" Jagomath looked more irritated than worried. "You told me they're only characters I created anyway. That they're not actually real."

Helaine had almost forgotten that he seemed to think this. "If that was true," she called down, "then you'd know *our* true names, wouldn't you? But you don't – and neither does Destiny. Which should prove to you that she's been lying all along. We're not characters in a game you're playing – we're real people who you're trying to *murder*."

"Well done, Helaine," Oracle said. "That's well thought out."

Jagomath was red-faced and furious. "You're ruining it!" he yelled. "You're ruining the game! It's all *your* fault!" he howled at Oracle. Since you came, it's all going wrong." He made a gesture and shot a ball of blazing fire at the dark man.

Naturally, it passed harmlessly through Oracle. It came dangerously close to the tree before fizzling out. Oracle merely crossed his arms and smiled down at the enraged child. "Your magic can't touch me," he said. "I'm not entirely real myself – I'm a sort of projection. Nothing can affect me."

"You think so?" Jagomath growled. "Well, I'm used to creating projections myself, and I have a *lot* of power over them!" He scowled and gestured darkly.

Helaine felt the magic grow, accumulating and solidifying about the tree. She wasn't sure what Jagomath was up to, but it felt really, really strong and potent. "Score," she gasped.

He looked as worried as she felt. "What's happening?" he muttered.

Power surged, and Jagomath threw out his hand. "Now!" he howled.

Oracle gave a startled look, and then he was inundated by the surge of magic. He screamed, and then fell to the ground – hard.

"That hurt," he sobbed. "That…" His voice died out. He held up his hand, which was cut and bleeding. "It *hurts*," he whispered. "I'm *real* again…"

Chapter Seven

Pixel felt a shudder of fear as the coach came stumbling to a halt. The Silverhawks were attacking… The terror in Jenna's eyes was vivid and he realized that she was on the verge of complete panic. He wasn't used to that in her, because Jenna was one of the bravest people he had ever known. But Jagomath was preying on stories she'd been told as a child, stories she believed in implicitly. Stories that had terrified her then and still held their dreadful power over her even now.

As the coach came to a halt, Pixel realized that their coachman had fled, abandoning them. He couldn't blame the "man", because he was nothing more than a constructed puppet, but the action was annoying. He simply didn't have a clue how to drive a coach – it simply wasn't in his upbringing. He could ride a horse now, having learned this skill since entering the circuit of the Diadem, but he knew that handling a team of horses pulling a coach was a skill that took a long time to acquire. Jenna had been brought up the daughter of a poor folk-healer, and had never ridden a horse either until recently. That left Shanara.

"I don't suppose you can drive a coach?" he asked her.

"That's not one of my skills, no," she replied. She wasn't as scared as Jenna since she'd never heard of the Silverhawks before, but she was clearly concerned. "I think we're meant to be abandoned to our fate. It's part of this stupid game of Jagomath's." She put her arm around Jenna, who was now shaking from fear. "He's managed to get Jenna terrified. I doubt she'll be able to help much."

"Then you don't know Jenna," Pixel said firmly. "She's capable of almost anything."

"Perhaps not of defeating this," Shanara said softly. "This strikes to a very deep level of primitive emotions. It's fear from her childhood that has never completely gone away. She might not be able to beat it."

"She will," Pixel insisted. "I just have to get through to her." He shook the trembling girls' arms. "Jenna! Focus!"

Her eyes were wild and unfocused, her mouth slightly open, but without uttering any sounds. Pixel was really worried for her, but he couldn't let it show. He had to act confident, so that perhaps his faith in her would break through Jenna's barrier of fear and reach her thinking mind. He shook her again.

"Jenna! We need your help! You have to overcome your fears – if we are to stand a chance. Come on, I love you! I know you can beat this! Jenna!"

Slowly, he could see the intelligence returning to her eyes, and she finally gave a huge shudder. "Oh, Pixel, I'm so scared!"

"I know," he said. "But you can't let it defeat you before the game gets moving. You're the only one among us who knows the stories, so you're the only one who can defeat Jagomath. He's relying on you being too terrified to be able to think straight – but if you *can* think properly, then we can defeat him again."

"What's the point?" she asked. "He'll just start up another of his horrible games. He's so powerful, and he's in charge of everything that happens to us here."

"Up to a point, you may be right," Pixel agreed. "But if there's one thing I've learned from being in the Diadem, it's that power isn't everything. Score, Helaine and I have faced a lot of pretty powerful foes, and we've beaten them all because we work as a team. Individually, maybe we're not as strong as Jagomath – but the three of us together should be able to take him out. We've done it once already, after all."

"But that was in your game," Jenna said. "And you're so much smarter than anyone else. I'm just not as bright as you, and wouldn't be able to see how to win."

"Well, you certainly won't with *that* attitude," Shanara snapped. "Pixel couldn't love somebody who's stupid, so if you don't have any faith in yourself, have faith in *him*. If we don't beat Jagomath, we *die*."

"Oh, right," Pixel said. "Don't put any pressure on her, will you?"

"If she can't take pressure, then the Diadem is no place for her," Shanara said coldly. "It's always been a dangerous place, but wonderful if you've got the courage to face up to it." She glared at Jenna. "Do you have that courage? Or are you just going to roll over and die? And then let Pixel die too?"

Jenna swallowed hard. "I'll try."

"Try?" Shanara shook her head. "That's not good enough. Jenna, you have to *fight*. To your last breath and final drop of blood if necessary. But you have to *believe* you can win, otherwise you'll let us down and we'll all die because of your weakness."

Pixel scowled at the sorceress. "I know that's your idea of encouraging her," he complained, "but I think it's unnecessarily harsh."

"No," Jenna said. "She's right – if I don't give this everything I've got, I'm letting you both down. And I can't do that." She steeled herself visibly. "I'm ready to beat the little brat."

"That's my girl," Pixel said, proudly. "Now, since we're apparently stuck here, driverless, we'd better try and come up with some sort of a plan to beat Jagomath. First of all, I don't think we'll be very safe inside the coach – it will hamper our abilities to fight."

Jenna nodded. "Maybe we can unhitch the horses and ride away?" she suggested.

"I doubt Jagomath will allow that," Shanara said with a sigh. "We're supposed to be spoiled rich bitches – I doubt that type has ever ridden anywhere for fear of hurting their backsides."

"Lots of rich women ride," Jenna pointed out. "It's an acceptable pastime for them. We could at least try."

Shanara managed a smile. "Touché," she agreed. "Now I'm the one being defeatist."

They scrambled from the coach and glanced around. The four horses that had been pulling their coach were now standing, snorting and glancing about nervously. Evidently they could sense the trouble about to arrive. There was no sign of their driver. Pixel looked at the fixtures that held the horses in place. There seemed to be an awful lot of straps that would need to be unfastened in order to free the animals.

And there clearly wasn't the time for that. He could hear the sound of horses pounding down the road toward them, though there was nothing visible as the road curved ahead of them. There came another winding of the horn, this time a lot closer.

"No time," Shanara snapped. "We need to come up with another plan."

She was right. They'd be caught for certain if they started messing with the horses. Pixel glanced around. "Is there somewhere we can hide?"

"I shouldn't think that Jagomath has forgotten something that simple," Jenna said. "But he really doesn't know our powers, does he? Or does he? He's created these games from our minds, so maybe he's read them thoroughly."

Pixel laughed. "I don't think he's had the time for that – it's more likely he's just skimmed them quickly to find a source of games. Besides, if he'd *really* read our minds, he'd know that we're not the villains that Destiny claims, and he'd know what kind of a nasty creature she really is."

"That's true," Shanara agreed. "And he's already underestimated you once, Pixel."

"And now he's going to underestimate Jenna, too, isn't he?" Pixel smiled at Jenna, and saw how much it encouraged her. "Right, this is *your* game, so think of something he's probably overlooked."

Jenna nodded and thought for a moment. Then she glanced down the road as the sound of horses drew nearer. Pixel saw the shadow of fear flicker through her eyes, but she managed to bury it again.

"I think I have an idea," she said, slowly. "The Silverhawks killed the rich and powerful – but you're a servant…"

Pixel laughed. "And that makes me neither. So he's going to target the two of you, and ignore me, at least a little."

"I'll try and give you a chance to do something," Jenna promised. "I can't run, but that doesn't make me powerless." She gave him an unexpected quick kiss. "Thank you for your faith in me."

Then there was no more time; horses dashed around the bend in the road and reined to a halt.

"So," drawled Jagomath, "more victims." He was dressed in what had to be finery stolen from his "many victims", including a long coat with ornate silver buttons that were shaped like skulls. He wore a large belt with pistols and a long saber. On his head was a large tricorn hat. He looked like an overdressed pirate, which no doubt amused him.

There were four other riders with him, all dressed in stolen jackets and such. Closest to him, naturally, was Destiny. She wore a tight-fitting blouse, emphasizing her figure, a loose tunic and large black boots. All she was missing was an eye-patch to complete her piratical appearance. "Kill them all," she said, flatly.

"Where's the fun in that?" Jagomath objected. "We have to play with them a bit first."

"Haven't you learned the danger in that?" Destiny snapped. "Kill them and have done with it before they outsmart you again."

"No!" Jagomath growled. "This is *my* game!"

"Actually," Jenna said, stepping forward slightly, "I believe it's *my* game. You stole it from my mind."

"Doesn't matter," Jagomath replied. "It's my game now, and this time I'm going to win because the Silverhawks *always* won. You know that."

Smart, Pixel realized – he was using her own beliefs to attack her with. He might only be a kid, but he was a smart one. And powerful…

But Jenna was refusing to allow her fear to control her. Pixel was so proud of her. He could see the beads of sweat on her forehead, but she was keeping her face impassive. It had to be taking a lot of courage to stay as calm as she was. "Why don't you ask Destiny why she's so eager for you to kill us?" she suggested. "Maybe it's because she doesn't want you to hear what we have to say?"

"You're the Silverhawk," Destiny snapped. "Kill them now! It's what you're supposed to do!"

Pixel could see the confusion in Jagomath's face. Jenna seemed to be getting through to him – Of course! She had to be using her citrine and the enhanced power of persuasion it gave her! Smart girl! He wanted to hug her, but it was important he stay in the background, so that Jagomath would ignore him…

"If you're so eager for us to die," Jenna said softly, "then why don't you try to kill us yourself? You've got that great big sword – it's almost as big as your mouth…" Then she deliberately turned away from Destiny to look at Jagomath. "We're not the villains she claims," she said. "Think about it – which one here is trying to get people killed? Not us…"

Destiny was obviously worried that Jagomath might start listening to Jenna. She snarled, whipped out her sword and spurred her horse on toward the helpless Jenna. Pixel was terrified for one long, agonizing instant, as Destiny brought her sword down –

Onto nothing. Jenna wasn't there. Jenna, apparently, wasn't anywhere.

Brilliant! Jenna had switched to obsidian and the power of invisibility. For that moment, both Jagomath and Destiny had their attention firmly on where Jenna *wasn't*, freeing Pixel to act.

He was already clutching his beryl, which enhanced his control over Air. He concentrated and slammed two blasts of wind at their foes. Something unseen but powerful sent both Jagomath and

Destiny howling from their mounts and tumbled them to the ground.

Jenna reappeared just a foot from Destiny. Her fist crashed out, catching the woman by surprise and sending her reeling again. Jenna snatched the sword from Destiny's faltering grip and held it to her throat, grinning. Pixel, meanwhile, moved to stand over Jagomath, who had been badly winded when he'd hit the ground.

"You may be a powerful wizard," Pixel informed him, "but power isn't everything. You have to have brains enough to use that power. Luckily for you, we're neither the villains you take us for, nor simply figments of your imagination. When are you going to get it through that thick skull of yours that Destiny's being lying to you?" He held out his hand. "Come on, back on your feet."

The boy accepted his help and then stood there, dusting himself off and looking confused. "I don't understand it," he admitted. "Destiny told me that you were the bad guys I'd conjured up in my dreams so I'd have good villains to fight in my games."

Pixel sighed. "Look, you're not the only one who's fallen for her lies. For a while I believed her stories, too. But she's a self-centered little witch whose dreams of power outweigh her tiny abilities to achieve it. She's been using you to get her revenge on us for beating her the first time we fought."

"And you killed me," Destiny snapped. "Not bad for people who aren't supposed to be evil."

"It was *your* trap that backfired on you," Pixel pointed out. "You died because you were trying to kill us."

"Stop it, all of you!" Jagomath yelled. "I don't know who to believe! I just want to have some fun, that's all. I just want to play games!"

Shanara stepped forward. "That's not such a problem," she said. "If you come with us, you can play with unicorns. *Real* unicorns, not something you've dreamed up. Jagomath, you have no idea what is possible once you enter the circuit of the worlds of the Diadem. You have genuine power and true abilities as a magician. We can show you how to use them properly."

"Don't listen to her," Destiny said. "She's an *adult* – she's just trying to control you."

"And what are you?" Jenna asked, sweetly. "You must be at least thirty-five."

"I'm twenty-three!" Destiny yelled, annoyed. Her vanity had clearly been punctured.

"An *adult*," Jenna said, pouncing. "And not to be trusted."

"I can't take all of this squabbling," Jagomath complained. "It's not fun any more. You're ruining it, all of you!" With a growl, he gestured.

They were no longer in the forest in their finery. Instead they were in a stone room, large and dimly lit. They were back in the clothing they had been wearing before all of this began.

And with them were Score, Helaine – and Oracle, lying on the floor, a strange expression on his face.

"That's it," Jagomath announced. "This game officially sucks. I'm not playing with any of you any more. You guys can sure ruin a person's fun." He crossed his arms, scowling.

"What just happened?" Score asked, bewildered. "Did we win?"

"Maybe by default," Pixel said. "Jagomath's had enough."

"Timothy Reichart," Score informed him. "Oracle discovered his true name. Speaking of which…" He moved to where Oracle lay and reached out, helping him to his feet…

"What?" Pixel was stunned. "You can *touch* Oracle?"

"More than that," Oracle said, wonderingly. "I can touch the world again…" He turned to Jagomath. "I don't know how you did it – but *thank you*! You've made me real again!"

The boy was having a hard time maintaining his scowl. Finally he stopped trying and grinned. "I did, didn't I?" he said. "I'm some magician, huh?"

"I'll say you are," Score agreed. "You know, when you're not trying to be a homicidal maniac, you're almost likeable."

"Enough!" Destiny yelled. Her fist flew out and she caught Jenna hard across the jaw. Jenna yelped in pain, falling back. Destiny used the few seconds she had to leap forward, grabbing hold of the startled Jagomath. Her arm circled his throat and she whipped the saber from his belt and held it against his neck. "All this good humor is getting very annoying," she complained. "I think it's time for the rightful balance of power to be restored."

"Give it up, Destiny," Pixel said. "You can't possibly beat all of us. We're all stronger in magic than you are."

"You sniveling simpleton," she spat. "You have no idea what strength is – or what I'm *really* up to." Before any of them could react, she slashed out with the sword. Jagomath gave a howl of pain before he realized that he hadn't actually been hurt – Destiny had simply severed the bonds of a small bag he had tied to his waist. She snatched the bag as it fell, and then kicked the boy away from her and threw aside the sword. "*This* is what I've been after all along!"

She opened the bag and drew out a small piece of dirty, rocky-looking substance. Pixel suddenly realized that they had all made a dreadful mistake.

Destiny hadn't done all of this simply out of revenge.

She'd been after the piece of Xarathan that had kept her spirit alive… and now she had it.

"You morons," she told her all, moving slowly back from them. "*This* is the power! Not that simple idiot. This is a piece of the dreaming stone of Xarathan. This makes thoughts into reality – and reality into whatever I choose it to be." She grinned, feral and evil. "The games are over, boys and girls. It's time to face reality.

"*My* reality…."

Chapter Eight

Jenna sighed, wearily. Was this never going to end? She glanced at Pixel, who looked really worried. "You know the nicest people," she murmured. "This isn't one of them."

Score gave a sharp laugh. "Destiny – delusions of grandeur now? You couldn't beat three of us before. And I can count six magicians facing you this time. Even with rocky there in your greedy little paw, you don't stand a chance." He grinned. "But maybe you're not too strong on math? It's not my best subject, either."

Destiny gave him a mock-sweet smile. "Trying to talk me back to death, are you? Well, that won't work – and neither will anything else you have in mind. And I'm not stupid, no. But *you* are."

Jenna could feel a surge in the magic in the air. She saw the others starting to move toward Destiny, but it was too late. The woman raised the first with the rock in it and muttered a few indiscernible words. Power pulsed, and Jenna felt it grip her and shake her entire body. There was a single agonizing moment in which she thought she was on the brink of death and then her vision and pain cleared.

She had fallen to her hands and knees on stony dirt. Her body felt as if she'd been battered with large, prickly sticks, and she felt like throwing up. As her head and vision began to clear, she collapsed to the ground and looked around.

She was in some sort of woods, and night was falling. She'd clearly either been transported somewhere or this was another illusion. But the last times the world had shifted there hadn't been pain or nausea, so she suspected that this time the move was real. There was a groan close to her and what she had initially dismissed as a rock moved. Helaine sat up, moaning. Jenna felt a touch of hope; if Helaine was here, then perhaps Pixel was also. No matter how bad things were, she could face anything as long as he was with her.

"What has that psycho bitch done now?" Helaine asked, wincing with pain. "I feel terrible."

"I think it must have been a transfer spell," Jenna said. Her own pain was ebbing a little, and she was able to stagger to her feet without immediately falling over. "Can you see any of the others?"

Helaine also rose, though very shakily. "No," she finally replied. "I think it's just the two of us here. Wherever here is."

"We're probably still on Ordin," Jenna answered. "There's something about the atmosphere that seems very familiar to me. It *feels* like home."

"Yes," Helaine agreed. She scowled. "But why are the two of us here alone?"

Jenna was trying to puzzle that out. "Destiny appears to be smarter than Jagomath," she said. "Jagomath split us into teams that were stronger than he was, and smarter."

"Ah." Helaine nodded. "Destiny's split us up, too, so she doesn't have to face us all at once. And she's split us into teams she thinks are less likely to work effectively together."

"Right," Jenna agreed. "She's been on Ordin as a servant of the Three Who Rule, so she could tell you were a noble and I'm only a peasant."

"So she thinks we couldn't possibly get along," Helaine finished. "There's no way she could understand that we're friends. Friendship simply isn't something she's familiar with. She only *uses* people."

Jenna felt a sudden twinge of jealousy. "What's this about her being Pixel's girlfriend?" she asked, trying to sound casual.

"That's just nonsense," Helaine reassured her. "Yes, Pixel found her attractive – but you know how he is. Boys are easily attracted to a pretty face. But she quickly revealed that her only feelings are selfish ones. She only made those comments in an attempt to hurt you. That's her way. You can trust Pixel, you know that."

"Of course I know that!" she replied, maybe a little too sharply. Then, sheepishly, she added: "It's just that she's so *beautiful*, and I'm kind of plain."

Helaine gave a sharp laugh. "I think Pixel would dispute that! Besides, in her case, the beauty really *is* only skin deep. Inside she's a seething cauldron of pure nastiness."

Jenna felt relieved. She hadn't *really* thought Pixel could prefer Destiny to her. But... She wrenched her thoughts back on track. "So, what is she after? What's all this subterfuge for?"

"Well, Pix is the one who usually figures things out," Helaine answered. "And he's not with us. But... Well, in the real history of things, Destiny was working with Sarman against the Three Who Rule. They discovered her treachery, but by the time they did they realized that they couldn't defeat Sarman. They decided to flee from him for a while in hiding – as Pixel, Score and myself. But being reborn as children and growing again was something that had never been done before, so they decided to test the process out, using Destiny. They sent her to the Earth as a baby, and crippled her as punishment. But because it was experimental, they'd left her with some of her memories, and she worked out a way to get back to the Inner Worlds to try and reclaim the power she didn't have on the Earth. She took Pixel to Zarathan, the world of nightmares. The planet itself was actually an egg enclosing some sort of a creature. Its dreams were able to interact with those of anyone on the planet, causing whatever they were afraid of to come into existence. She died when we woke the infant... creature up and the world cracked open."

Jenna had heard the story before from Pixel, but now she was beginning to see how this was fitting together. Maybe hanging around with Pixel was improving her ability to think! "But her... spirit survived in that fragment of the planet shell," she said slowly. "Somehow it came to Earth, where Timothy discovered and used it. Destiny used him to get the shell back to the Diadem and into the hands of her still-living self, *before* the Three sent her into exile to Earth."

"Right," agreed Helaine. "And now her future self has informed her past self what is to happen, and she must be intending to use the shell somehow to change her impending fate."

"And if she changes her own fate, then that will change the past completely." Jenna was very worried. "How will that affect Pixel – and Score and yourself?"

"Knowing Destiny? Very badly. The only way she could stop herself being sent to Earth as a baby is if she kills the Three Who Rule. And that would kill the three of us as well, since we are in some way Eremin, Trantor and Traxis. Or could be."

Jenna was getting scared. Pixel was in danger! "Then why are we here?"

Helaine looked grim. "My guess is that Destiny's simply blasted us all in different directions. Score was right, she couldn't possibly hope to defeat us all together. But she doesn't have to! If she can get to the Three, then by destroying *them,* she destroys *us.*

And if *we* die…"

"Then you can't ever have rescued me when I was facing death," Jenna said. "So *I'll* die, too."

"I could be wrong," Helaine added, but didn't sound too hopeful. "I'm not the thinker that Pixel is. Or even Score. But I think I've managed to work out what Destiny is aiming to do. Unlike Jagomath, she doesn't feel any need to fight and beat us *now*. I think she's simply shot us here and gone on with her plans, feeling she can ignore us. All she needs is time, and she'getting that."

"I'm sure you're right," Jenna replied. "And that means she's just made a big mistake. We're not simply fighting for our own lives, but those of the boys as well. And I won't let Pixel down."

"Nor I Score." Helaine scowled. "A pain he might be, but he's *my* pain."

"Well, that's great," Jenna said, slowly. "We're in agreement that we have to do something – but what?"

"Well, the first thing we need to do is to discover where we are," Helaine answered. "Then we have to find out where Destiny is – and then get there. Then we have to figure out some way to stop her."

Jenna laughed, sourly. "That's not much to ask, is it?"

"No," Helaine said, fiercely. "It's *not* too much to ask. We can do it. We *have* to do it – for Score and Pixel as well as for ourselves. Besides, I'm sure the two of them are working at doing the exact same thing that we are. They may even beat us to it. But we don't want to leave everything to them, do we?"

"No." Jenna took a deep breath and fought to squash her feelings of fear and inadequacy. "Right, let's see… You have your agate, right?"

"Of course." Helaine took it from the pouch at her waist and grinned. "And I can use it to communicate with the boys!" She gripped it tightly, and then appeared to go into a trance for several moments. There was nothing Jenna could do, so she simply stood by and worried. There was so much that could go wrong…

Then Helaine gave a gasp and came out of it. She blinked several times and shook her head. "It's worse than we thought," she reported. "Pixel and Score aren't together, and they don't know where each other is. Score's with Jagomath, and you can just imagine how well those two are getting along. Squabbling, mostly, with Score threatening to spank Jagomath. And Pixel is with Shanara and Oracle. Pixel is going to use his ruby to Find Destiny, and I'm going to talk to him again in a few minutes. Once we have information, we can try and work out some sort of plan."

"We could certainly use one," Jenna commented. She was glad to hear that the others – especially Pixel – were all right so far. They obviously had a few minutes to wait, so she brought up something. "I've been thinking about this whole plan of Destiny's," she said. "I know I'm not as quick as Pixel at catching on, but... Well, doesn't it seem horribly coincidental to you that the one piece of Xarathan that contained her soul should just happen to land on the Earth of all places? And that it should be discovered by a child who happened to be an unknown magician?"

Helaine looked surprised. "I hadn't considered it," she admitted. "But now that you mention it – yes. What are the odds of all that happening?" She laughed. "I'll bet Pixel's got a theory about it, though. And I'm *certain* Score will have something to say, even if he doesn't know anything."

Jenna looked at Helaine. "You two are very fond of one another, aren't you? Why do you fight so much, then?"

"I don't know," Helaine admitted. "It's just... Well, I'm really fond of Score, but there are times he makes me so mad I could just beat him up. And... Well, I've always been brought up to believe that the man should be the strong one in the relationship, and Score is so..."

Jenna laughed. "I think that's your father talking, not you. I'll admit Score isn't the most physical of people but he *does* always seem to get things done when it counts. And he's a lot braver and smarter than he pretends to be. I suspect he's so used to hiding his abilities from people and simply can't be open any longer. I don't think he'll ever be the man you *want*, but I do think he's the man that you *need*."

"That's what bothers me the most," Helaine answered. "I'm so used to being reliant only on myself. It's very hard to share any part of me with somebody else. Especially somebody who seems to make fun of a lot of what I believe in."

"He makes fun of *everything*," Jenna pointed out. "Including what *he* believes in. It's just Score's way – a self-defense mechanism, as Pixel would say. I think he finds it hard to share himself with another person, too, so he makes jokes about it."

"Not very funny jokes," Helaine growled.

"Maybe not," Jenna agreed. "But it's just his way of dealing with life. You just have to deal with him."

"I think…" Helaine began, and then grew stiff. "It's Pixel," she said, softly. "Wait a moment." She seemed to go into a trance again for a few minutes. Jenna watched her, realizing how used to Helaine she had become – and how much she actually liked the other girl. It would have been unthinkable for her at one time that she could even *speak* to an aristocrat, much less actually *like* her. But both her own and Helaine's prejudices had been stripped away over the months they had come to know and rely upon one another. From barely concealed enmity, friendship had grown.

Helaine blinked and sagged slightly. "Right," she said. "Pixel has a plan – as always. And we're in the forefront of it." She shook her head. "Where to begin? Well, I asked Pixel your question, and he says he doesn't think that what is in that rock is Destiny's soul. He used a computer analogy I didn't quite follow, but he said that it's not really her. When Destiny died, Xarathan was fragmenting, but it could see, feel and feed from our thoughts. Somehow it absorbed parts of her thoughts and mind as she died, sort of like splinters from a broken tree-branch. What is in the rock isn't Destiny exactly, just a sort of copy of her most basic thoughts and desires. Most of the rocks that broke off from Xarathan probably contain the same sort of stuff in them, and there could be millions of them, scattered all over space. This rock just happens to have landed on Earth, and near a budding magician."

Jenna paled. "You mean there could be *other* Destiny's still alive all over the Diadem? And that she could come back again and again?"

"I hope not," Helaine said. "But *this* one only came back because everything fell into the right order for her – so other rocks might be scattered around and there's nobody near them that she can contact. And Pixel said that the imprint will fade over time, so soon enough none of the others would be strong enough to contact anybody else. It's probably only this one we have to worry about."

"But *one* is enough," Jenna pointed out. "So, what do we have to do?"

"It seems we're the closest to her current position. I think she felt we were the least challenging to her, so she used more power on sending the boys away." Helaine gave a grim smile. "That's not her first mistake. Anyway, she's about ten miles from us, heading toward the lair that the Three Who Rule use on Ordin. Pixel says that they aren't here, though. Destiny probably has to get to them through a portal to reach Jewel and kill them, and he thinks that the portal is easier to create if she's in their lair."

"So we're supposed to somehow cross those ten miles and stop her before she can get to Jewel?" Jenna guessed. "Or does Pix have some idea how we can do it?"

Helaine smiled. "He says he's sure we'll come up with something."

"Typical," Jenna said. "Leave the hard part of the plan to us. Well, I suppose we'd better get started – maybe inspiration will strike us on the way." Together they set off in the direction Pixel had transmitted to Helaine.

The woods, it turned out, weren't very deep. After only about a half mile of walking, they emerged onto a pathway that was obviously well-traveled. There were ruts in the muddy roadway that showed carts passed this way fairly frequently and there were even hoof-marks showing that sometimes horses were used. Since peasants couldn't afford the upkeep of more than farm horses, any riders around here had to be nobles. There was, however, nobody at all in sight at the moment. Since the pathway went the way that Pixel had indicated, they began to follow it.

Soon the trees thinned out and the two girls could see grasslands around them, and then, farther away, what was clearly a group of buildings and irrigated farm lands. There were shapes moving about among the fields, clearly the local peasants.

"Maybe we can find some transportation there?" Helaine said doubtfully.

"There's unlikely to be anything but old plough-horses there," Jenna commented. "We'd probably be faster walking. We need the sort of steeds that nobles ride."

Helaine broke into a grin. "Like those?" she asked, pointing. Jenna followed her lead and saw that there were three riders on large mounts heading toward the village from another roadway to their right.

"Just like those," Jenna agreed. "Maybe we can borrow their horses?"

"Two young girls?" Helaine shrugged. "They're not likely to agree very readily."

"Of course they are," Jenna responded. "Honestly, Helaine, you have to have a better opinion of the kindness of people. Besides," she added, "I have my citrine." The gemstone enhanced her natural ability to persuade people to do as she wished them. It couldn't *force* them, but it did make people more amenable to her will.

The riders caught sight of them at that moment. There was a little conversation amongst them, and then the horses were turned to intercept them. Jenna's stomach clenched. "It's not a good thing when nobles notice you," she muttered to Helaine.

"I *am* a noble," Helaine stated.

"Dressed as a warrior," Jenna said. "You lost your hat a while back, and they can see you're female, I'm sure. I doubt this conversation is going to go too well."

"Now who needs a better opinion of the kindness of people?" But Helaine looked quite grim as they drew closer to the three young men on horseback. They were indeed nobles – Helaine's own class – and dressed in fine riding clothing, with flowing capes. Each had a sword at their side, though none were making any move toward their weapons – yet.

"Well," drawled the first one, obviously their leader, "what do we have here? A peasant and a girl who dresses like a boy!"

"Maybe that's because she doesn't have too much to offer when she's dressed like a girl?" the second suggested.

"Maybe we should have her take those clothes off," the third added, a nasty grin on his face. "She should learn not to dress to ape her betters."

That was too much for Helaine, of course. Before Jenna could do anything, Helaine had drawn her sword. "Apes you may be," she growled. "But betters you most certainly arcn't. I am a Votrin of the House of Votrin, and I take my clothes off for no man."

"A Votrin?" The leader laughed. "Girl, you must be crazy. Even a Votrin wouldn't allow one of their daughters to dress like a boy – and everyone knows that Votrin arc scum."

"Draw your sword and back up your words with skill," Helaine ordered. "Or I'll open up your throat to make it easier for you to take back your words."

So much for simply persuading the boys to hand over their horses – they were all too angry now to even think that such an idea was their own.

"Take off those boy's things," the third boy ordered her, "or we shall be forced to show you how nasty a sword in the hands of a real fighter can be."

"You think so?" Helaine gave a mischievous grin. "Then come and show this poor Votrin scum how brave and strong you are."

The boy didn't even hesitate. He jumped from the saddle and withdrew his own weapon. "When we're done," he promised her, "you'll feel the flat of this blade across your naked backside." He grinned. "I'm looking forward to that."

"You have to fight me first," Helaine informed him. "Talking won't win any battles." She waved her sword under his nose. "Or is talking your only fighting skill?"

The boy gave a growl and lunged at her with his sword. Helaine parried the clumsy thrust with ease. Puzzled, the boy struck again, and was just a simply pushed back. He was finally starting to understand that this fight wasn't going to be quite as simple as he'd imagined. Now he roared, and jumped at Helaine, swinging his sword with grim intent to harm her. Helaine stepped lithely aside and dodged the blow. She rammed the hilt of her sword into his stomach, winding him badly. The youth gasped hard, staring at her in fury. His two companions had started laughing at his plight, but their laughter was dribbling away as they started to understand that Helaine could really fight.

"Help Marc," the leader ordered the other boy. "Get that little tramp. I'll see to the other girl."

The second boy vaulted from his steed, drew his sword and closed in on Helaine. The leader moved his horse in front of Jenna. "Are you a fighter, too?" He growled at her.

"Not I," Jenna answered him cheerfully. "I'm a witch." As he leaned forward to try and grab her, and gripped her obsidian and vanished from his sight. He gave a startled gasp, and then a howl as she grabbed his outstretched hand and yanked him hard. He came tumbling from the horse to the ground, and as he scrambled on his hands and knees, Jenna kicked him hard in the backside. He went sprawling in the mud. She laughed, and caught the horse's reins. The mount whinnied in fear, feeling itself grabbed and unable to see what was effecting this. Jenna turned visible again and vaulted into the saddle. "My thanks for the ride," she told the mud-splattered youth.

She glanced over at Helaine, who was truly in her element now. Facing two armed opponents didn't seem to bother her in the least. She was laughing, her sword dancing from one clashing blade to the other. The boys had weight and strength on their side, but Helaine was far nimbler and infinitely more skillful. She parried each crashing blow, and twisted her own sword to nick and draw blood. The boys cursed and strove to beat her, but each was fighting independently and they frequently got in each other's way. Helaine danced around them, her sword flickering and striking.

"Helaine," Jenna pointed out, "we are in a hurry, you know."

"I'm sorry," Helaine replied. "But this is so much fun." She sighed. "Well, all good things..." She saw an opening when one of the boys lunged and missed. She brought the flat of her blade across his behind, sending him sprawling, and then whirled as the other youth attempted to stab her in the back. With a grin, she forced him back, and then nicked him in the thigh. As he cried out and stumbled, she slammed the hilt of her sword hard into his stomach. With a whoosh of expelled breath, he collapsed. "It's been fun, lads," she told them. "But we have pressing business elsewhere. If you follow us, you may be able to get your horses back when we're finished with them." She dashed to the closest horse and leaped into the saddle. With her sword, she whacked the remaining steed across the withers. It gave a huff of surprise and ran off. "You'd better catch him first," she added, "so you won't all have to walk."

Jenna joined her laughter as they rode off. "I just hope they don't catch up with us," she said, finally. "They might not be as easy to beat next time – they did rather underestimate us, you know."

"They're not warriors," Helaine said, contemptuously. "Attacking two poor, defenseless girls... and losing." She grinned again.

"Well, they weren't much of a challenge," Jenna agreed. "But it won't be as simply to beat Destiny."

"Perhaps not," Helaine said. "But at least we can reach her now..."

Chapter Nine

Score groaned and rolled onto his back. "There are days," he muttered, "when I really hate magic…" He forced his aching body into a sitting position and looked about. He was sitting on the ground amid a bunch of rocks. The travel spell he'd been zapped by had clearly shot him onto the slopes of a mountain somewhere. He had no idea how far he'd been sent – or, for that matter, where any of the others might have ended up.

He heard a groan and somebody moving nearby. "Helaine?" he called, anxiously. "Pix? Jenna?" He scrambled wearily to his feet and moved toward the sound.

"None of the above," said an all-too-familiar voice. Jagomath, looking as shattered as Score felt, came into sight. "What happened to us?"

"A pretty powerful travel spell," Score replied. "Are there any of the others with us?" After a few moments searching it became clear that they were alone. "Great. I'm stuck out here with a Munchkin. I always knew Destiny hated me the most."

"Knock it off, motor mouth," Jagomath complained. "You think I want to be wherever we are alone with you?"

"Stop complaining," Score replied. "This is all your fault for being so gullible as to be taken in by that pretty face and not seeing her evil heart."

"As if you're any better," the youngster snapped. "Don't think I haven't noticed you making goo-goo eyes at that bimbo with the sword."

"That's *Miss* Bimbo to you," Score growled. "And only I get to insult her. *You* treat her with the respect she deserves."

"Or else what?" Jagomath demanded.

"I'm thinking you're not too big nor too powerful to spank. Maybe your Mommy should have done it more often – you might not have turned out to be such a dim-witted brat."

"You want to try?" Jagomath sneered. "You don't scare me, you moron."

"You should –" Score broke off as a powerful mental blast reached him. Helaine! He grinned. "Attagirl!"

"What's wrong with you?" the boy asked.

"Helaine's contacting me. Shut up and let me concentrate."

"You're hearing voices now?" Jagomath smirked at him. "Where I come from, they lock you up for things like that."

"They also lock you up for murder, which is what I'll do to you if you don't shut up." He concentrated on listening to Helaine, thankful that she was alright, at least for the moment. He listened to her familiar voice in his mind as she explained how matters stood. Then she broke contact and he blinked several times. "Great."

"So, what's wrong?" Jagomath asked him.

"You mean aside from me being stuck playing babysitter to you? Plenty. Destiny split us all up. Helaine's with Jenna in a forest somewhere. Pixel's with Oracle and Shanara in a desert. And none of us are anywhere near Destiny, apparently."

"Why would you want to be near her?" Jagomath glared. "I thought you'd be happy to be as far away from her as possible."

"You haven't been paying attention, have you?" Score sighed. "Okay, let's try it one more time to explain to Your Density... Destiny is really dead. Extinct. Not living."

"So what is she? A vampire?" Jagomath sounded almost eager. He'd obviously watched *Twilight* a few times too many.

"No. Trust me, a vampire would be a step up from what she is. She's basically an animated memory. That rock you were using to help do your mystic mumbo-jumbo was kind of like a recording device. It had part of her mind in it – enough for it to think it was really her. And to formulate a plan." An idea suddenly occurred to him. "Hey, short and stupid – what's your magical talent?"

"Being smarter than you? And better looking?" Jagomath suggested.

"Being delusional, it would appear. No, I mean, without any gemstones or magic rocks, what can you do? All magicians seem to have a special gift. Mine is the ability to change things from one thing to another. Helaine has an incredible gift for detecting trouble. Jenna can heal people. Pix is just super-smart. You must have something you can do, besides being obnoxious."

"Oh." Jagomath thought for a moment. "I never really thought about it, but I can muck about with time, I guess. My mom always tells me I'm wasting time playing games on my computer and so on, but actually I spend *way* longer than she thinks doing it. I can kind of bend time so that it lasts longer than it should. Or speed things up – I once grew a plant from a seed to a flower in ten minutes." He sounded proud of himself.

"Well, that's really great if you forget your girlfriend's birthday," Score commented. "But I can see why Destiny used you – with that power over time, enhanced by the rock fragment, she could get you to come back in time. She's planning on warning her living self here in the past of what's going to happen to her. She works for a bunch of really evil creeps called the Three Who Rule, but she betrayed them and got caught. As a result, they banished her to the Earth in a crippled body. It was when she tried to cure herself and kill us that she died on Zarathan. She's planning to make sure none of that happens."

Jagomath shrugged. "Well, you can't blame her for trying to save her own life."

"That's not the problem," Score answered. "The problem is that she wants to change the past. And if she succeeds, then the Three Who Rule might not get defeated. And, definitely, Helaine, Pixel and I will never be born. If she keeps herself alive, we die. And if we die, everything we've ever accomplished doesn't get done. The Diadem will fall back into chaos. Maybe the Three will control it, maybe it'll be Sarman – who's just as evil as they are. In any event, it will be bound under an iron grip of tyranny. We can't allow that to happen, so we have to stop this memory Destiny from meeting her past self."

Jagomath considered all of this. "Well, a future without you in it sounds like a great idea," he finally said. "But I don't like the thought of this Three Who Rule or Sarman taking over everything. So I guess I'm on your side. But I've lost a lot of my power now that the rock's gone."

"Yeah." Score reached into his pocket and pulled out his four gemstones. "We all use gemstones to enhance our natural abilities," he explained. "That would probably work for you, too – but we don't have the time to go gem hunting right now."

"Can't I just borrow a couple of yours?" Jagomath asked.

"They wouldn't work for you. The gems have to call to you. If you were in a treasure chamber, you'd find your stones without a problem. For now, you'll just have to stick with whatever you *can* do without them. Maybe we'll stumble across the right ones for you later. For now, we just do what we can with what we've got." A sudden mental blast reached him. "Hang on, I'm on call waiting," he said. It felt nice to be able to make jokes somebody else could understand – even if it was just a midget magician with delusions of grandeur. After a moment, he blinked and refocused on the young boy. "That was Helaine again – she's had a chat with Pixel. He's the brains of the outfit."

"Well, I'm glad you don't think *you* are," Jagomath said with a smirk.

Score decided to ignore the comment. "They've located Destiny – she's heading for what appears to be some sort of a base the Three Who Rule have on this planet. It's quite some distance from here. The others are all heading that way, so we'd better get moving, too. The problem is, she's made certain she's got quite a head start on us – I don't think any of us stands a chance of beating her to it."

"You're forgetting about me," Jagomath said, with another of his infuriating smirks.

"Trust me," Score assured him, "I really wish I *could* forget about you."

"I meant my ability to mess about with time," Jagomath said, sighing. "If you can whip up some way to get us moving, I can speed us up."

Score frowned. "You really think that ability of yours is going to be of any help?"

"You asked for it, jerk-face," the kid replied. Suddenly he seemed to almost disappear, blurring almost into invisibility. Score gasped as he was struck at least a dozen times in quick succession, but without seeing any of the blows. As he reeled back from the attack, Jagomath came into focus again. "You want to not see me do that again?" he asked, with his usual infuriating smirk.

"How did you do that?" Score asked, wincing. The blows hadn't been particularly hard, but there had been plenty of them.

"I slowed down your personal time," the youngster replied. "All I had to do was to walk around you and hit you when and where I liked. You couldn't even move."

"No, I couldn't," Score agreed. "Maybe you *do* have a power we can use." He glowered at the kid. "And just so you realize that *I* can do some magic that's useful, too, I'll provide the transport."

"Wow, can you magic up a car?" Jagomath asked. "I'd like a BMW."

"You're not even old enough to drive," Score growled.

"Not on Earth, true," Jagomath replied. "But there's no traffic cops here, are there?"

He did have a point... "Actually, I *might* be able to make a car," Score said. "Using my power to Transmute things from one element to another. But I'd need to make all the parts individually and then check that they worked together... I had something a little easier in mind. I used my Sight to find a river close by. That would get us really close to where Destiny is headed."

"Uh, I'm not the world's best swimmer," Jagomath admitted, looking a little pale.

"Relax, I wasn't thinking of swimming – I had something a little less strenuous in mind."

"Amazing," Jagomath said.

"That I have good ideas?" Score grinned.

"That you have *any* ideas," the youngster replied. "I didn't think there was room in your head for thoughts considering the size of your ego."

"You're not too old nor too powerful to spank, you know," Score warned him.

"Yeah? You and what army? I can freeze your time frame so you couldn't even get near me."

Score was getting really annoyed with this kid's attitude. He seemed to think that his power to manipulate time made him super-powerful or something. It was time to cut him down to size. He made a swift gesture, and Jagomath found himself suddenly encased in a block of ice from his toes to his neck.

"Hey!" he exclaimed. "What are you doing?"

"Showing you you're not the only one who can do things," Score replied. "I can leave you here in that thing and go off to save the day on my own."

"All I have to do is to speed up time and this ice cube will melt away."

"But you're in it," Score replied. "That means you'll have to speed your own time up as well. That thing will take almost two days to melt. You can speed it up so it'll seem like ten seconds for me – but it'll still be two days for you. Two long, freezing cold days..."

"You rat," Jagomath growled, as reality finally sank in. "I could die."

"Yes, you could," Score agreed. "Look, kid, you're a pain in the butt, but you're not really bad. I'm just trying to show you that your tricks may be powerful, but so is what other people can do. If you think you're better than everyone else, you're going to end up learning that you're not – right before you learn what it's like to be dead. Trust me, Destiny, or the Three, or Sarman wouldn't hesitate to kill you if you give them a chance. So stop being so big-headed and start listening to me and the others for a change. You might live to grow another inch or two that way." He used his power to change the ice into oxygen, so it vanished from around Jagomath. "So let's declare a truce for now and try and stop super-bitch before she changes history, okay?"

Jagomath was shivering, but he nodded. "And *then* I get to kick your butt."

Score grinned. "Then you get to *try*," he answered. "Okay, this way." He led the way to the river he'd located. It was a few hundred yards across and flowing quite swiftly – luckily in the direction they needed to go. "Okay, here goes…" He grasped his emerald and focused his power. He Changed the water into solid form, shaping it into the design of a sleek boat. He added a couple of comfy seats. "Right, hop in."

"You forgot to make an engine," Jagomath pointed out. "I don't intend to row this thing."

"Nor do I," Score answered. "And we don't need an engine – I have power over Water, so I can use the river itself to power us along. And if you can speed up time for us so we can move faster, we should be able to catch up with Destiny before she reaches her goal – her younger self."

"And then it's payback time," Jagomath said grimly, getting into the boat.

"And then, as you say, it's payback time," Score agreed.

Chapter Ten

Helaine signaled to Jenna to halt, and the two girls reined in their horses. They had made good time, as their mounts were in excellent shape. If you're going to steal horses, she thought, at least steal the best… But even the best needed a break from time to time. She dismounted and walked to where Jenna was getting down a little less easily.

"You must have a cast-iron backside," Jenna muttered, rubbing her own. "I'm not going to be able to sit down for a week after this."

"It's all a matter of practice," Helaine said. "I've been riding since I was three. You get used to it."

Jenna glared at her horse, which was grazing placidly. "I don't think I want to get used to it. They're big and they smell."

"You get used to that, too."

"Like I said…" Jenna shrugged. "Do you know how well we're doing?"

Helaine touched her agate and linked her mind with Pixel's. "Pixel says we're getting very close – just a few miles now. We'll probably be there in twenty minutes when we start up again."

"Shouldn't we push on then?" Jenna asked, "instead of wasting time here?"

"We're not wasting time," Helaine corrected her. "If the horses aren't rested for a while, they might give out on us. That wouldn't save us time. Besides, Pixel says that Destiny isn't at the castle yet. Apparently she's being very cautious."

"She probably doesn't want to risk getting caught by one of the Three Who Rule. Even with that rock of hers, I doubt she'd be powerful enough to take any of them on."

"I'm sure you're right," Helaine agreed. "Of course, we'd better be careful, too – they'd be quite happy to kill us, too. Or torture us. Or both."

"Nice people." Jenna sighed. "We *really* have to make certain that the past isn't changed. Aside from the fact we'd all die if it did, we simply can't allow the Three to keep the Diadem in their nasty grasp."

"You don't need to convince me of that," Helaine said. She was just as impatient as Jenna to be off again, but she couldn't risk the horses. At this point, they'd probably not be able to find any more. To take her mind off her worries, she contacted Pixel again and asked if he had any further news about Score. She wasn't exactly worried about him, but she was always afraid he'd get up to something stupid if she wasn't there to keep an eye on him.

"He and Jagomath are heading in your direction," Pixel informed her. "They've made a boat and are travelling quite fast. They'll probably meet up with you just before you reach the castle."

"How are you doing?" she asked him. She knew Jenna was worrying about him.

"We're on our way also," Pixel said. She could feel him laughing. "We managed to make a sort of boat on wheels between us, and I'm powering it by Air. We're fairly whipping along. But I doubt we'll reach you in time, though Oracle thinks he might be able to help out. He won't say how, though. He does seem to be enjoying being solid again."

"That's one good thing to come out of this so far, then," Helaine said. "At least *he's* better off." She relayed the news to Jenna, who seemed to be relieved. Helaine could understand this – Jenna and Pixel had grown very dependent on one another. They weren't like her and Score – independent people who were simply fond of one another. Pixel and Jenna were more like two halves of a whole, and they actually seemed to suffer when they were apart. She couldn't quite understand this herself. Sure, she *liked* Score, and she definitely had romantic feelings for him. But the thought of having him around all of the time was quite awful. She *liked* being herself, on her own, also. And she knew Score felt pretty much the same way. She had no doubt he liked her, but he also enjoyed being off on his own, doing whatever silly thing he'd dreamed up. When she spoke with him mentally, she could feel the fun he was having in the boat he'd created. He was thinking of her, certainly, and he missed her – but not in the way that Pixel and Jenna felt about one another.

Love, she supposed, was different for different people. Or maybe she and Score weren't in love, as such, but some other emotion that was similar. She didn't really know. She'd been so used to being on her own all these years, being unable to share her secrets and desires with any other person, that it was still very difficult for her to consider it. And she knew that this was pretty much how Score felt, also. He'd been on the streets, alone, for years, without parental guidance. She and he had faced very different lives, but they had ended up curiously similar in many ways.

And, of course, completely different in others. Every time she linked her mind with his, she could feel his desire to see various portions of her body unclothed. When she'd visited New York with him, she had seen that girls there didn't seem to be bothered about showing off their bare legs and arms – and even portions of their waist. It went against everything that Helaine had been raised to believe was respectable, but New York was, after all, an alien world. She couldn't expect people there to behave as thought they were civilized… Besides, who was to say that she was right and they were wrong?

But that was a matter for another time. "I think we've rested long enough," she decided. "We'd better get going again."

They were swiftly on their way again. Helaine, used to riding, could feel the difference the short rest to graze had had on her mount. It moved more fluidly beneath her, pounding along the narrow road they were following through the countryside. It wouldn't be very long before they reached their destination.

And then what? Planning wasn't Helaine's strong point. She generally left all the scheming to Pixel, or even (when she felt she could trust his reasoning) to Score. She herself preferred simply confronting a problem head-on and using her skills and strength to overcome it. That wasn't likely to work here, though – Destiny was a powerful magician in her own right, and now she was coupled with the power of the dreaming planet through the rock she held, she might well be almost invincible. True, there was the element of surprise on their side, but would that be enough to help out when she and Jenna came across Destiny? Somehow she doubted it. Destiny was without morals and very vicious – which would probably help her win any fight.

There was only one thing that Helaine could think of doing, and it really went against everything she had ever believed in. She had to ask Jenna for advice.

Not too long ago, the idea that a noble of Ordin would be seeking the opinion of a peasant would have been completely unthinkable. But Helaine had come to… well, *like* Jenna, after a fashion. Certainly to respect the other girl. She might even go as far as saying they were friends. In some ways, she felt closer to Jenna than she did to her own sisters – though that was more a measure of how far she was apart from her sisters than close to Jenna. But taking advice from the other girl… it still rankled her.

On the other hand, Jenna was a resource, and a smart warrior always made the best possible use of every resource at hand. It would be foolish to allow her pride to prevent her from taking advantage of any ideas Jenna might have.

She knew what Score would say at this point. She didn't need to contact him for his opinion. In his usual blunt fashion he'd tell her she was stupid even to have doubts about Jenna's advice, and to smarten up and do the right thing. And then he'd make some inappropriate comment about her legs or other portion of her anatomy. She missed him.

What was happening to her? Was she really falling in love? Was she forgetting all of her heritage? Was she – as Score always said – overthinking everything as usual? Was she simply trying to put off doing what she knew she had to do?

"Jenna," she called, steeling herself to the decision finally, "do you have any idea what we can do when we catch up with Destiny?"

Jenna gave a nervous laugh. "I was rather hoping you did," she admitted. "This is likely to be some battle, and you're far better in a fight than I am."

"This will be a magical fight, not combat," Helaine answered. "I doubt most of my skills will be useful. Destiny is not likely to allow me to get close enough to punch her on the nose."

Jenna laughed again. "No, otherwise I think I might enjoy trying that with her. She really annoyed me with her comments about my Pixel."

"You wanting to punch somebody?" Helaine laughed herself. "That hasn't happened since you met me."

"Well, I got over wanting to hit you," Jenna admitted. "But I don't think I'll manage that with Destiny."

"Me either," Helaine agreed. "She's nasty, through and through. But she does have the advantage in this fight – that rock makes her pretty invincible."

"Then we have to use the only thing we have that she doesn't," Jenna decided.

"And what would that be?" Helaine asked, puzzled.

"Each other. Destiny is a loner, but we can cooperate. If we use our powers in conjunction, maybe we can do something that she can't stop."

Jenna made a good point. "That's also what defeated the

Three," she said. "Together, they were pretty near invincible – but they were such obnoxious people that they simply couldn't get together very much."

"Well, I think the fact that you and I can get along proves that you'll never become Eremin," Jenna said. "If she couldn't get along even with people she needed, she'd never have tolerated me at all."

Another good point, and one that brought a slight relief to Helaine. The thought that she might one day become Eremin was her worst nightmare. She could see and feel the roots of that ice-cold witch within herself and she was terrified that one day they might win out over her better nature. It was an on-going struggle not to give in to certain flaws in her character. But she *had* learned to bend a little from her own rigid nature. She had formed genuine friendships, and maybe even loved Score… Certainly they were achievements that Eremin would never have attempted.

Well, they would have to defeat Destiny in order for any of that to matter. If the Three weren't forced to be reborn as herself, Score and Pixel, then none of her fears mattered – she would *be* Eremin, right up to the point when Destiny killed her.

Then, ahead, she could see the castle! Her heart raced as fast as her steed – the enemy would soon be in sight, and then the battle would take over her thoughts. And battle she could understand.

"There's Score!" Jenna called out, pointing to their right. Helaine glanced across, and saw that there was a river only about a quarter of a mile away, and racing down it was a strange, transparent boat-like affair. She could make out Score and Jagomath in it and laughed. Things were working out!

"I can see you," she called mentally to Score, glad he was so close.

"Hiya, kid," he answered. "Any sign of Destiny yet?" She could feel the warmth he felt toward her, and that pleased her.

"No, but she's got to be close…"

"And there's Pixel," Jenna added. The affection in her own voice could hardly be missed. Helaine looked to the left, and saw Pixel's odd craft racing across the fields toward them. It was still too far off to make out individuals, but she mentally called a greeting.

And then she saw Destiny. The sorceress seemed to be unaware of their approach, focusing all of her attention on the dark-walled castle ahead. It was a huge, imposing place, gloomy and oppressive, clearly meant to intimidate anyone who approached. It was typical of the thinking of the Three – scare people. Helaine had a moment to wonder what to do, but knew that the important thing right now was to stop Destiny getting into the castle. She was far too close to it now, and she couldn't take the chance that the sorceress might slip in before she could be stopped.

There was only one thing she could to at this distance to halt her. Helaine gathered all of her mental strength and sent a mental scream ripping through Destiny's mind.

Ahead, the witch screamed and fell, writhing on the ground. Helaine strained to keep the mental explosion she was causing going. It was taking all of her strength and concentration, but it was working. They were drawing closer every second.

Then her horse stumbled, and Helaine had to focus on her riding, breaking the mental hold she had been projecting. Destiny managed to scramble to her feet and Helaine could feel a mental blockade come down over the other woman's mind – one she wouldn't be able to penetrate without a lot of time and effort. Destiny was clutching the rock in the crook of her left arm, and she glared back at Helaine.

"I don't know how you managed to get here," she growled, "but this time I'll kill the both of you." She gestured, and the earth started to shake and rip apart.

Helaine's steed whinnied in terror, and reared up as the ground broke beneath its feet. With sudden horror, Helaine saw that there was a gaping pit forming below them, one that they would never manage to bridge...

They would fall to their deaths...

Chapter Eleven

"Brace yourselves!" Pixel yelled. He allowed his madcap vehicle to dissolve from under himself, Shanara and Oracle as he focused all of his efforts through his Beryl, which gave him control over Air. He firmed up the air beneath Jenna and Helaine as they fell, slowing their drop, and then solidified it, bringing them to a halt. Helaine, now she was able to think clearly, used her own powers over Earth to carve a set of stairs back to the surface of the ground.

Pixel fell back to the ground himself, staggering, but managed to remain upright, Shanara fell, but Oracle helped her to her feet again.

Destiny spun around, startled and furious. "You again!" she snarled. "Why can't you all just leave me alone?"

"Because you're a miserable human being and misery loves company?" Score suggested.

"And it's payback time, bitch," Jagomath added.

"Hey, watch that mouth on you, squirt," Score warned him. "I don't want your Mom complaining we're a bad influence on you." Score sent a blast of fire toward Destiny, who deflected it without much of a problem. Pixel knew that it hadn't been a serious attack, merely something to keep her occupied while everyone had a chance to regroup about her.

Destiny looked around wildly, obviously caught out by this fresh attack. Like many crazed people, she couldn't accept easily that her plans had gone wrong. She thought she was so much smarter than everyone else, mistaking viciousness for intelligence. The idea now was to keep her off-guard. Helaine had informed him that Oracle had apparently concocted a plan and it was important to buy him time to accomplish it.

The easiest way was to rattle Destiny again. "Face it," he told her, "you can't beat us – we're smarter and faster than you. You died facing just three of us once – and now there are seven of us. You don't stand a chance."

"But I have the power of Zarathan, and you don't," she snarled.

"Dream on, dummy," Score mocked her, loosing another fireball. She batted it aside again, but Pixel could see she had a twitch in her left eye – the strain was starting to tell on her. She really had thought she had won, and dealing with yet another failure was starting to get to her. He used his own power over Fire to take the blazing remnants of Score's attacks and whipped up a ring of fire around Destiny. She tried to douse it, but he poured his strength into sustaining it. It became a battle of strength between them.

Which meant she wasn't focusing on the others. Helaine was back on the surface again, a grim expression on her face. She used her own power to open a pit beneath Destiny. The sorceress caught herself in time, managing to stand on thin air. Score, meanwhile, in his usual silly approach to fighting, was making it rain on her now.

Destiny screamed in anger and frustration, lashing out with waves of psychic energy. Pixel was able to block a lot of it, but some got through, sending him staggering backward. There was strength in the attack, but it was unfocused and none too successful. The strain was really starting to tell on Destiny now. Clutching the rock-fragment, she poured everything she had into her assault on the three of them.

Which was what they had been planning on, because it left the others unaffected by the raging storm of power. Shanara and Oracle started to circle Destiny also, and then Jagomath started to mutter to himself, getting ready to cast some sort of spell. Destiny simply didn't know where to expect the next attack to materialize from, and her eyes were wild and wide with fear.

A *second* Oracle suddenly appeared from nowhere right behind her. He tapped her on the shoulder and, as she started to turn, ripped the Zarathan fragment from her grasp and vanished again.

"No!" Destiny screamed, clutching at empty air. Her power boost was gone, and without it she was helpless. The power from Pixel, Helaine and Score hammered her, sobbing, to the ground.

"I think we can stop now," Jenna said, gently but firmly. "She can't hurt us any more."

"Okay," Score said. "I'll admit I may be kind of slow on the uptake, but what just happened there? *Two* Oracles?"

"One and my illusion," Shanara said, laughing. The "Oracle" standing beside her faded away. "I created this one so Destiny wouldn't realize the real one was missing."

Oracle popped back again, without the rock. He was grinning cheerily. "It seems that although I'm now solid once again, I still have my powers of transportation. So I jumped in and grabbed the rock – which I dropped off a few miles away, just to be sure she couldn't grab it again."

"So now we do horrible things to her to pay her back for what she did to us?" Jagomath asked, eagerly.

"No," Shanara said. "That's not how we act, young man."

"Speak for yourself," he argued. "I owe her for what she did to me – lying, and making me believe this was all an illusion I'd created. I almost killed you all because of her."

"Almost?" Score laughed. "You weren't even close, squirt. We've defeated stronger foes than you in our sleep."

Jenna sighed. "Are you two going to be like this full time?" she asked. "Can't you just get along?"

"Of course we can," Score said, sanctimoniously. "Right after I spank him so hard he won't be able to sit down for a week."

"You and what army?" Jagomath howled. "I'm not afraid of you, you big idiot!"

"Stop it," Helaine ordered. "Now. Or I shall spank *both* of you."

Score grinned. "It might be fun to have you try," he said.

"Yeah," Jagomath agreed. "You're kind of cute when you're being bossy."

"Stop hitting on my girlfriend," Score warned him.

"Yours?" Jagomath laughed. "She's too smart to stick with you when she could have me. She'll wise up."

Pixel tuned the two of them out. It was obvious that both boys were actually enjoying their feud and that it wasn't likely to grow into a real fight.

"He does have a point, though," Jenna said. "What *are* we going to do with Destiny?"

"Nothing," Pixel said. "We don't have to do anything." Seeing Jenna's puzzled look, he explained: "Without the rock, Destiny's back to where she always used to be – here at the castle of the Three. They know she's betrayed them and they're going to send her to the Earth as a crippled baby. History is back on track and she no longer has the ability to change it. Everything is at it should be."

Destiny seemed to be suddenly aware of what he'd said. "No!" she screamed. "It means my death! You can't do that!"

"You will cause your own death," Pixel told her. "All of this has been because of your own selfishness and lust for power. You've brought your fate upon yourself."

"You can't leave me," Destiny begged. "You *can't!*"

"We don't have a choice," Pixel replied. "For history to play out as it must, you have to fulfill your role. Even if we wanted to, we couldn't save you."

"And we don't want to," Score added. "You're one sick puppy, consumed with your own wants and willing to destroy anyone and anything else to get what you want. The Diadem is better off without you."

"That's a bit harsh," Jenna objected.

"Hey, for once I'm with idiot," Jagomath said. "Everyone is better off without her."

"I think there's a certain amount of anger within you over her using you," Jenna said. "It colors your outlook."

"And you're too soft-hearted," he snapped back. "You're not even mad at me, like the others are, are you?"

"Don't worry," Score assured him, "I'm mad enough at you for two. Or maybe four. "

"I didn't know you could count to four," Jagomath jeered.

"Enough," Pixel insisted, seeing that the pair of them were likely to argue for quite some time. "I think it's time we left this place – and Destiny to her destiny." He turned to Oracle. "Can you transport people with you now that you're solid?" he asked.

Oracle looked surprised. "I don't know – I've never tried it."

"He doesn't have to bother," Jagomath said. "I can transport people through time and space, remember?"

"Without the rock fragment, your powers are greatly decreased," Pixel pointed out. "I don't know if you'd be able to take all of us at one time."

"He could borrow energy from the rest of us," Shanara suggested. "We'd help boost his power for one leap, at least."

"Take me with you," Destiny begged. "Don't leave me here! I don't want to die!"

"Then learn to behave yourself," Helaine snapped. She turned to Jenna. "Can you stop her whining like this? If she annoys me much more, I'll end up hurting her."

"No problem." Jenna turned to the defeated sorceress, using her citrine to increase her powers of persuasion. "You have to go meet the Three now," she said, gently. "There's nothing for you to worry about. Everything is happening as it should."

Destiny nodded, finally looking composed. "Of course," she agreed. "Bye now." She walked off toward the looming castle.

"I know she deserves everything that will happen to her," Jenna said sadly, "but I still can't help feeling sorry for her."

"It's your wonderful, sweet nature," Pixel told her, kissing her forehead gently. "It's one of the reasons why I love you so much." He turned to the rest of the group. "So – where do we go from here?"

"Are you kidding?" Score asked angrily. "Isn't it obvious? I was going to save my mother when she was being kidnapped before I was brought here. We need to go back and stop her being abducted, obviously."

"No!" said Shanara sharply. "You can't do that."

"But she's going to be horribly tortured!" Score objected. "I've got to save her from that!"

"Not *she*," Shanara snapped. "*Me*! Hasn't anything sunk in from all of this? You can't change *anything* that has happened – and that includes what happened to me."

"I can't just leave her…" Score said, on the verge of tears. "She's my mother…"

Pixel sighed. "Score, you're suffering from a major disconnect. What's wrong with you?" He gestured at Shanara. "*That's* your mother, right there, and you're acting like she's someone else entirely."

"Well, that's how *she's* acted for years!" Score cried. "She abandoned me when I was just a child and ran off to have fun in the Diadem without me. But Cathane is my mother – she wouldn't leave me."

Pixel could sense all of the anguish and betrayal Score was feeling – he had never gotten over his mother's supposed death, and he was having real problems accepting that Shanara and Cathane were one and the same person. Perhaps Jenna could help him out later, but right now logic had to win through. "Score, you're not thinking this through."

"Score not thinking?" Jagomath scoffed. "Wow, how unusal is *that*?"

"Knock it off," Pixel said sharply. Jagomath didn't needle him the way he did Score, but the young kid could be very wearing on the nerves. Pixel turned to Shanara. "There's a lot about this that you're not telling us, isn't there?"

"What do you mean?" Jenna asked, puzzled.

But Shanara knew what Pixel meant, and she sighed and nodded. "There's a lot about this I *can't* tell you," she said.

"I admit that I don't understand this either," Helaine said. "What are the two of you talking about?"

"Shanara knows everything we're going to do," Pixel said, simply. "This is our future, yes, but it's her past. She lived through all of this as Cathane, remember, so she knows what we're going to do."

"And if you know that," Shanara pointed out, "then you know why I couldn't say anything before this."

"Because *we* didn't know what would happen," Pixel said, understanding. "If we'd known, we might have done something different."

"Exactly," Shanara agreed. "Besides, I *didn't* know everything that would happen. I had no idea how you'd defeat Destiny, for example, because I was never here before. At this moment, I'm off being tortured by Traxis. That's all I know of this instant."

"But you do know how we'll rescue you," Pixel said.

"Yes," she agreed. "And, clearly, I can't tell you how to do it. And I can't go along with you for it, because I daren't meet myself, even in disguise. Anyway, I know I didn't go along, otherwise I'd have remembered meeting myself. And Oracle doesn't go along because I didn't meet him for the first time until much later."

"I am getting a headache from trying to follow this," Helaine complained. "Can we stop trying to understand it and simply get on with the rescue?"

"It seems to me," Oracle offered, "that I'd best try transporting Shanara and myself back to her castle, and we'll await you there for news on how you succeed."

"I'll fill you in on the details while we're waiting," Shanara murmured. She took his hand, and the pair of them vanished.

"Well, that proves he can take at least one person with him when he travels," Pixel said. "Now – the rest of us. We have to save Cathane/Shanara from Traxis, and it has to be *after* she's tortured, but before she gives birth." He gave Score a sharp look. "I know you want to spare her the pain, but that *happened*, and it must remain fixed in time, whatever you feel about it."

"I guess I'm out-voted," Score growled, clearly unhappy. "But I can see that you're right – much as I hate it."

"Good boy," Pixel said. He turned to Jagomath. "So, can you transport the five of us to Traxis's castle at the right moment in time?"

"Hey, I can do anything I want," Jagomath answered.

"Want to be a nicer person, then," Score suggested.

"No more arguing!" Pixel said sharply. "Nothing will get done if we let the two of you bicker all day. Right now we have to save Cathane, so let us focus on that."

Jagomath nodded. The five of them gathered together in a circle, holding hands. Pixel concentrated on his ruby and the Finding ability it enhanced in him. Using this, he could focus on the spot where they must be…

And Jagomath took them….

Chapter Twelve

Nowhere.

Well, nowhere *different*. They were at the same castle, in the same place, Jenna realized.

"Hey!" Score protested. "We didn't go anywhere, squirt."

"We may not have gone *anywhere*," the youngster replied, annoyed, "but we did go *anywhen*."

"He's right," Pixel said, before Score could start an argument. "Look at the trees – they're all a little older-looking. And it's summer now, not spring."

"I took us to the point in time we needed to be to rescue Cathane," Jagomath explained. "It happens she's being kept in the same castle. I expect an apology, jerk," he added to Score.

"Expect away," Score replied, and then looked over at the castle, his face twisted in concern. "Right, how do we get her out of there? I'm thinking frontal assault might not be the best idea?"

"You're right there," Pixel agreed. "When we met the Three, they had no idea who we were initially, so obviously they aren't supposed to see us here and now. We have to get in and rescue Cathane without interacting with them directly."

"Fine," Helaine said. "Then let's plan this fight properly. Are any of the Three in the castle right now?"

Pixel clasped his ruby and concentrated on Finding the Three. "Only Traxis," he said. "The other two are off-world right now and unlikely to be back while we're here." He thought for a moment. "We have to get him out of the way to be sure he doesn't see us."

"No," Jenna said, slowly. An idea had come to her, and she was certainly it was the right thing. "You have to make sure he doesn't see *you* – and Helaine and Score. It doesn't matter if he sees me or Jagomath. We can distract him while the three of you pull of the rescue."

"No!" Pixel, Helaine and Score said, almost together. "You have no idea how dangerous he can be," Pixel added.

"I met Nantor, remember?" Jenna reminded him. "Believe me, I have a healthy respect for the powers of the Three."

"Jaggy there doesn't," Score growled. "He doesn't even have a sickly respect. He's likely to do something dumb and get you both killed."

"No, I leave the doing something dumb to the experts – you," Jagomath snapped. But he did look worried. "Jenna, do you really think we can pull this off?"

"We *have* to," Jenna replied, though she was nowhere near as certain as she tried to sound. "Remember – we know that it's going to work. Shanara *did* get away, with their help. It's not a very difficult rescue, after all – if Traxis isn't there, there's just some guards to face. The three of you should be able to handle them without any problem. Helaine can let me know when you've escaped, and then Jagomath can bring the two of us to meet up with you." She stared earnestly at Pixel, knowing that if she could convince him, then it would work.

He gripped her hands tightly. "We may know that part," he agreed. "But we *don't* know if you and Jagomath will be able to escape – *that's* not part of history, as far as we know. The two of you might be captured – or killed." She could see the real worry in his face and loved him for it.

But she *knew* she was right. "I promise you that we will take care. But it *must* be done this way – surely you can see it?"

"Yeah," Jagomath agreed. "Foxy here and I can take care of anyone who's related to Score."

"Why doesn't that reassure me?" Score asked. "Oh, yeah – it's arrogant, ignorant and stupid. I knew there was a reason."

"But Jenna is correct," Helaine said. "We have to save Shanara, and we can't risk running into Traxis. That means she and Jagomath *have* to get rid of him somehow. Come on, Pixel – I know how difficult a decision it is for you, but you must know it's the only logical way."

"It may be logical," he admitted, "but it scares the hell out of me. I don't want to lose you, Jenna."

"You won't," she promised him, hoping she was telling him the truth. "We won't take any crazy risks – we'll just lure him away until the rescue is over."

There was a long pause, and she could see the conflicting emotions chasing across his scared face. Finally he sighed and nodded. "You're right – I hate it, but you're right. We'll wait here until you've distracted Traxis, and then we'll go in and rescue Shanara. As soon as we're clear, Helaine will contact you and then Jagomath – you jump the both of you out of there as fast as you can, understand?"

"Yeah, I think I can wrap my brain around that," the kid agreed.

Pixel rolled his eyes. "And try and restrain that sarcasm," he advised. "Traxis won't appreciate it, and he can extinguish your life like flicking off a light switch – and with as little effort. Bear in mind at all times that you're going into a potentially lethal situation and that he will stomp the life from you with the slightest provocation."

"I will watch over him, I promise," Jenna assured Pixel. "We will be fine." She gave him a quick kiss, and then turned to the younger boy. "Come on – we'd better get moving."

She glanced back only once, feeling her courage ebbing. She could face anything the Diadem had to throw at her with Pixel by her side – but with just this unstable young boy… She shook her head, trying to bury her fears.

"If I offered you a penny for your thoughts," Jagomath asked her, "would I regret it?"

"Most likely," she agreed. "I do not feel as confident as I tried to sound whilst reassuring Pixel. I didn't want him to worry about me."

"Not to worry, sweetie," Jagomath said. "I've got confidence enough for the both of us. Stick with me and you'll be fine."

Jenna sighed. "Your confidence is born of youth and naivety," she pointed out. "You have virtually no experience in fighting evil magicians – Destiny is a rank amateur compared with Traxis."

"And he has no experience fighting me," Jagomath answered, not at all bothered. "Besides, we don't actually have to fight him, do we? We just have to distract him."

"And do you have anything in mind to accomplish that?" she asked.

"Well, you could take off all of your clothes and walk in naked," he suggested. "I'm pretty sure that would distract him. I *know* it would distract me."

"You and Score seem to be fascinated with seeing female skin," she said. "I suppose it must be an Earth thing."

"So does that mean you don't like my plan?"

"That's not a plan – it's an adolescent fantasy. Forget it. But there is one point you made that I like."

"The taking off the clothes part?" he suggested, hopefully.

"No – the *create a distraction* part. We won't need to worry about fighting him if he doesn't even see us." She studied the castle carefully. "That's a large establishment, and there must be a large number of staff working there. So what will they need for a large staff?"

"Very good toilet facilities?" he suggested.

"No. Well, probably yes. But I was thinking more of the kitchens."

"Yeah, that was my second guess," Jagomath agreed. "So, why should I be happy to hear about kitchens? Except it's about lunch time?"

"There's just so much that might go wrong in a kitchen in a rather spectacular way."

His face lit up. "Yeah! Grease fire! Cooks chopping off their hands instead of fish heads! Lots of knives…"

Jenna glared at him. "I was thinking of less violent actions," she said. "We really don't want to hurt anyone, especially not simple servants who are working there through no choice of their own."

Jagomath sighed. "Wow, you're even more of a wet blanket than Score – and I didn't think that was possible."

"We don't want to hurt anyone," she repeated. "All we have to do is to create a distraction. Now, what abilities do you have except for creating your time warps?"

"I don't know," he admitted. "Score did say something about finding me gemstones that would enhance my abilities, but we haven't had much chance to do that. We haven't exactly stumbled across a lot of treasure troves recently."

"We've stumbled across one," Jenna said, smiling. She pointed at the castle. "Given the nature of the Three Who Rule, I'm willing to bet they've been collecting tribute in there."

"And we just walk in and ask them to let me rummage though their treasury?" Jagomath asked her.

"Yes," she replied. "We do exactly that." She held up here citrine. "This enhances my powers of persuasion. I can convince most people to do almost anything."

Jagomath grinned widely. "Hey, this is starting to sound really cool. I hope I get some really neat powers from this."

"There is no telling what may happen," Jenna informed him. "Though I suspect that one's personality has something to do with it. My powers are almost all gentle and constructive, which suits me well."

"Well, I guess one of Score's powers must be super-talking," the youngster muttered."

They had reached the castle by now, and one of the four guards at the gate stepped forward. "Halt!" he ordered, leveling a wicked-looking pike at them. "State your business."

Jenna touched her citrine. "We are allowed inside," she suggested, gently, enhancing this with Persuasion.

"Pass," the guard agreed, moving aside to allow them through. Jenna led the way into the main courtyard.

"Impressive," Jagomath admitted. "Can I hear you say 'These are not the droids you're looking for' next?"

"Why would I wish to say that?" Jenna asked. Then it dawned on her. "Ah! Another obscure cultural reference that I cannot be expected to understand. Score does that constantly. It appears we will have to suffer twice as much of it from now on."

Jagomath actually looked surprised. "You mean you'll let me hang around after all of this is done? After what I did to you all?"

"It was not entirely your fault." Jenna led him across the bustling courtyard toward the main part of the castle. "Besides, you do possess quite impressive magical abilities – I think you will need our assistance in learning to use them correctly."

"And you could keep an eye on me to make sure I don't misbehave again?" Jagomath suggested.

"That too," Jenna agreed, honestly. She stopped the next soldier she saw. "Can you tell me where the treasury is?" she asked him, again using the citrine.

"Down this corridor, then take a left. There's a stairway up to the second floor. The treasury is the door with the guard." He nodded politely and then went along his business.

"Again, impressive," the youngster said. "I'm starting to think that hanging with the four of you won't be entirely dull."

"I'm fairly certain I can guarantee that," Jenna replied. "We do seem to have a predilection for falling into trouble." She led the way she'd been directed and came to the treasury doorway. Once again they were challenged by an armed man. "We have business inside," she assured him. He nodded and unlocked the door for them.

"I'll just wait outside here for you, miss," he said, politely.

"Thank you." Jenna took Jagomath inside the room.

It was some twenty feet square, and piled with "tribute" –

treasures looted from the many worlds of the Diadem and piled here. There were dozens of chests, tables laden with chalices, plates and crowns, and cupboards filled with richly woven robes. Light came from huge candelabras, causing gold, silver and jewels to sparkle and gleam.

Jagomath stared around in amazement. "Wow, being the wicked witch of the West really pays off..."

"We're only here for you to find your jewels," she reminded him. "We're not tourists and we're not thieves."

"Hey, this is all stolen in the first place," he complained. "So where's the harm in taking a little extra?"

"We take only what you need," Jenna said firmly. "Aside from anything else, what possible need could you have for any of this stuff?" She held up a cup that was solid silver, with gemstones inlaid about the rim. "You can't even drink water from this."

"But you could sell it for a fortune back on Earth and never need to work a day in your life," Jagomath suggested.

"Idleness is not fulfilling," Jenna said. "And neither of us needs a fortune back on Earth. Besides, how would you be able to account for where you'd gotten it?"

"With your powers of persuasion, who'd care?" he asked. "Maybe that's one ability I'd get..."

"Well, reach out with your mind," she told him. "Feel for the gems that call to you. Once you have them, you'll be able to discover your gifts."

"Right." Jagomath concentrated, his hand quivering in the air. Jenna remembered when she had sought her own stones, and how they had felt so right when she found them. It was clear that Jagomath was being led.

He went to one trunk, and threw it open. It was glowing with diamonds, rubies and sapphires, but he dug down and pulled out a fist-sized garnet. "This," he said with certainty. Then he moved on, drawn by the powers he possessed. In moments he had added a tourmaline, an opalite and finally a malachite. "These are the ones," he said with absolute conviction. Then he grinned, slyly. "But can't we take just a few extra as souvenirs?"

"No we can't." Jenna grabbed his hand. "Now we have to go to the kitchen and see what we can do. On the way, try and use the gemstones and see what they may be for." Jagomath grumbled a bit, but followed along.

"How do you know where the kitchen is?" he asked her.

"Follow your nose," she suggested. "Plus, it's always close to the courtyard in case of fires, and for ease of bringing in supplies. It's not hard to find."

They reached the large room in a few minutes. It had a lot of staff, as she had expected, working away. There was a spit in the huge fireplace with what looked like an entire cow on it, roasting away and providing most of the aroma that had led her here. There was a second fireplace, not much smaller, with other roasts and pans on stands containing vegetables and sauces. There were bakers making breads and pies for the ovens that were beside the two fireplaces. There were cooks, scullery maids, serving girls, and others moving about the room. It was organized chaos.

It was time to turn it into disorganized chaos.

"You all set?" she asked Jagomath.

He gave her a wide grin. "I think I have the perfect gemstone for this," he told her, clutching his tourmaline. "It creates Chaos." That certainly seemed like an appropriate magical power for him! He concentrated, and then –

One of the pots started to bubble and froth, and then it spewed a thick soup up into the air like a volcano. Hot, scalding soup started rain down on anyone near it. People screamed and ducked for cover. One brave soul pulled the pot from its position by the fire, obviously thinking this would calm down the problem. It didn't work; the soup merely blew over a different area of the room.

Bread started to explore like rockets. Pies began to whirl around the room, throwing their contents everywhere. Eggs started to fly, then drop onto the heads of anyone close by. Milk jars exploded; flour cascaded everywhere. People, stumbling and screaming, spilled even more stuff in their efforts to escape the mutinous food. Within minutes, the kitchen was a horrible mess.

A large man came dashing through the doorway. "What is going on in here?" he yelled, furiously.

"Sire, I don't know," one of the cooks answered. His pallor wasn't entirely caused by the milk and flour he was drenched in. "Everything simply started to go... wild..."

The man – obviously Traxis - glared around at the chaos. "Of all the incompetent idiots," he growled to himself. Then he started casting spells to stop everything that was going wrong. Flour started to settle, the soup stopped erupting, and the milk calmed down.

It was time for Jenna to take a hand. She projected her power of invisibility, making various chairs and table vanish. People scurrying to help clean up in case Traxis blamed them for this mess, slammed into furniture they couldn't see. They went spinning or crashing to the floor, knocking invisible chairs ahead of them and making other people fall. Despite Traxis's best efforts, everything was still insane.

Traxis glanced around wildly. "Clear the room!" he ordered. "I can't work with you fools underfoot!"

This didn't help matters. Jagomath used his tourmaline to make some of the fleeing servants slip and slide into others; some of the rest tripped over invisible chairs of ran into tables they couldn't see.

Jenna grabbed Jagomath's arm. "Time to go," she whispered. "It's going to take a while before this gets straightened out. We'd better see how the others are doing." They slipped out of the kitchen and ran down the corridor with the fleeing staff. The first soldier she saw, she grabbed. Using Persuasion, she asked him: "Could you tell me where the prisoner is being kept?"

"Certainly," the man answered, cheerfully. "Which one?"

Oh. She hadn't thought about it, but it made sense Traxis would have more than one. A despot like him was bound to have many enemies. "Queen Cathane," she said.

"Oh, she's in dungeon number four," he said. "End of the corridor, second door on the right. Down the stairs and straight ahead. Just follow the screams – you can't miss it." Jenna thanked him and then persuaded him to forget talking to her.

As the man had said, they heard screams coming from ahead of them as they dashed down the stairs. Several startled soldiers looked up as they approached and started to draw their weapons. Jagomath used his tourmaline again. Weapons jammed in scabbards, pikes mysteriously broke in half, trousers started to fall down and people began itching like crazy.

"Chaos," he laughed. "Gotta love it!"

Screams were coming from behind the next door. Jagomath zapped it and the wood rotted as they watched. Inside was an emaciated trio of men, covered in festering sores. Rats were nibbling at their feet. Jenna was disgusted and furious. Using her power of healing, she made the men strong enough to escape.

"We're looking for Cathane," Jagomath reminded her.

"I can't leave these people to suffer," she replied. "We have to help all of the prisoners."

Jagomath shrugged. "Hey, freeing them all should create more trouble," he agreed. "Come on." He ran down the corridor, leaving shattered doors and tortured people in his wake as they staggered from their tiny, filthy cells. Jenna followed, spreading as much healing as she could as she passed.

Then, up ahead, she saw a wonderfully familiar face – Pixel! With a cry of joy, she ran to join him. He gave her a relieved hug.

"The others are up ahead," he told her. "Score's fighting mad, and he and Helaine have Cathane between them. The problem is getting out of this dungeon with her. We have to go back the way you came – it's the only exit."

"The only exit for everyone but me," Jagomath said, grinning. "Remember, my specialty is creating wormholes in time and space." He held up his garnet. "And this little baby amplifies my powers."

"Terrific," Pixel said, happily. "Okay, let's join the others and get out of this horrible place. He gave Jenna an admiring glance. "Whatever you guys did, it seems to have distracted Traxis very well."

"We'll tell you later," she promised. "Right now, let's go before he comes back."

Ahead of them, she saw Score and Helaine. They were gently supporting Cathane. Jenna gasped with shock as she saw the scars cut into Cathane's flesh. She could read terrible pain in the Queen's eyes, but Jenna lacked the strength to be able to heal her immediately. Instead, at Pixel's urging, they all formed a circle and then Jagomath used his garnet. Jenna felt the world tumble around her, and then they were out in the open, and she knew that they were far, far away from that evil castle. She allowed herself to collapse, exhausted.

Everything was now almost the way it was supposed to be…

Chapter Thirteen

Score tried to keep his anger under control as he and Helaine carefully helped Cathane to stand. The fight to free her had been swift and almost silent. With Traxis distracted, it had been a simple matter to break into the dungeons and for Pixel to Find the captured Queen. Score and Helaine had taken out the guards before they even realized there was an attack under way, and now Jagomath had taken them far, far away using a portal. Score looked down at the woman who was to become his mother in a few short months and winced in pain.

Traxis had tortured her, slowly and painfully, leaving scars all over her face and neck. It broke his heart to see the livid red gashes, but he knew that there was nothing much that could be done about them – Shanara had only been cured of them recently by Jenna, so he knew that they had to remain for now. Thankfully, Cathane's ability was that of creating illusion, so she could hide her injuries from the rest of the world once she had recovered her strength.

She looked up at Score and smiled, brokenly. "You came for me, Matthew," she said, her voice barely more than a whisper.

"I told you I'd look after you," he said, fighting back tears. "I'm sorry I couldn't get here any earlier."

"You're here now," Cathane said, gratefully. "Before that monster could harm my baby. You and your friends have saved its life – and mine."

"We're going to get you out of here," Score promised. "We're going to take you somewhere Traxis will never be able to find you. You're safe from him." He glanced over at Pixel. "You know what we have to do, right?"

"We have to make sure that what happened before happens now," Pixel agreed, softly, so that Cathane wouldn't hear him. "I can arrange that with Jagomath. You tend to your m... To Cathane."

Score nodded. They were in a forest clearing, so he and Helaine were able to sit Cathane down against the trunk of a tree. She winced at the pain it caused her back, and Jenna moved forward.

Score grabbed her arm. "You can't heal her," he said. "I wish you could, but you can't. You don't heal her until she's Shanara."

"I don't heal her *scars* until then," Jenna agreed. "But I can help her with the pain now."

A wave of relief swept over Score. "Thank you," he said. Jenna nodded, and moved to use her skills on the wounded Queen.

Helaine looked up at him. "Are you okay?" she asked, gently.

"I am now," he replied. "Now she's out of that chamber of horrors." He felt weak with relief. "Now we just have to ensure things happen as they must, and I'm sure Pixel and the squirt can arrange that."

Jenna had finished her work with Cathane. She looked tired but pleased with herself when she touched Score's arm. "She wants to talk with you."

Score knelt down beside his mother-to-be. "I'm here," he said simply.

Cathane clutched his arm. "You've been quite amazing," she said. "Matthew, you've risked your life to save mine, and I'm grateful. If my child is a boy, I promise I shall name it after you."

Score choked up. "I think you can be fairly sure it will be," he informed her. "And he'll grow up… well, with you for a mother."

"I'm sure he will," she agreed.

Pixel moved to join them. "Right," he announced. "Jagomath can manage what's needed – a portal to Earth. New York, to be exact."

"Earth?" Cathane frowned. "I've heard of the planet – isn't it a bit far from here?"

"Trust me," Pixel said, "Traxis will never find you there. You will be safe."

"But I don't know the planet, the customs…" Cathane protested. "I'll be all alone, and with a child on the way…"

"No," Pixel promised. "You won't be. Come along." He and Score helped Cathane to her feet again, and then Jenna and Helaine joined them. Jagomath, grinning as usual, completed the circle and touched his garnet again. A portal formed, bright and beckoning, and they all stepped through…

Hours later, Score and his friends returned to their own time and the castle they shared. Jagomath was still with them, but quieter than he normally tended to be. It had been a hectic few hours.

Jagomath had taken them to the house Score knew well from his childhood, the house he'd grown up in. A startled Bad Tony Caruso had been stunned when they had all popped into his den, but

Jenna had quelled his anger and fear. Using her power of Persuasion, she had convinced him that Cathane was a distant relative from the Old Country – he'd have been stunned to know just how old and far away! – and that she was his new wife. The child she was carrying was theirs, Jenna had made him believe.

Cathane was safe – at least for now – and Score would be born and raised as he had been. The future was safe once again. So, reluctantly, Score had said goodbye to his mother, and the five of them had left Earth.

"Are you okay, Score?" Helaine asked him.

"Fine," he told her. "You know, this explains a few mysteries about my past that had never made any sense before – how I could be the heir to the throne on Ordin, even though I was born on Earth, for example. And why my father had always thought my mother had possessed magical skills. Of course, I still don't know why she abandoned us when I was a child…"

"You could ask Shanara," Pixel suggested. "After all, she is Cathane, and she would know."

"Hey, this whole mess started with me asking her about the past," Score said. "I don't think I could take any more explanations from her right now."

"I can understand that," Jenna said, smiling. "It has been something of an adventure. But we did get a new friend out of it." She put her arm around Jagomath's shoulder.

"Hey, cutie, let's go smooch somewhere," he suggested. She dropped her arm immediately.

"You may regret the new friend," Score told her. "I know I do." He glared at the kid. "Look, squirt, shouldn't you go home? Your mummy will be worried about you."

"I can time travel," Jagomath sneered. "I can go back before she even knows I've gone." Then he looked almost vulnerable. "But I can come back, can't I?"

"Yes," Pixel said, before Score could say anything. "You've got a lot of power, but you're undisciplined. You'll need training."

"And your backside kicked," Score added. "And we're just the magicians to do it. That part I know I'll enjoy."

"You just try it, and you'll regret it!" Jagomath yelled. "I'll send you somewhere you won't even be able to breathe in, let alone escape from!"

Helaine stepped between them. "No fighting," she said

firmly. "Or I shall deal with both of you."

"You can spank me any time, sweetie," Jagomath told her.

"Hey, don't you try hitting on my girl!" Score yelled.

"Maybe she'll wise up and dump you," the kid snapped.

"Home," Pixel told him. "Now!"

Jagomath stopped scowling. "Do I have to?"

"Yes," Pixel insisted. "We need to rest, and we can't possibly do that with the two of you yelling at one another. Go home now, and come back tomorrow. We'll start your training then."

Jagomath sighed and then nodded. He blew Helaine a kiss and then vanished.

"Peace at last," Score said, happily. "All's well that ends well, and all that garbage." He was grinning happily.

"You're looking awfully pleased with yourself," Jenna observed.

"And why not?" he asked her. "Cathane's safe, and she's going to name her baby after me. I must be the only person in the Diadem who's named after himself!" He laughed. "And Helaine owes me."

"What?" Helaine looked startled. "What are you talking about?"

"Your promise," he reminded her. "That if I saved us from Destiny, you'd wear a skirt for a week. Get ready to show off those legs, lady – I am *really* looking forward to this part. And no trying to get out of it."

Helaine blushed, but stuck her chin up. "I honor my promises. Even if they *do* involve a skirt…"

Score sighed in contentment. "I am so happy right now," he said. "Nothing could bother me now."

The door opened and Shanara and Oracle walked in. Oracle smiled. "I am very glad to hear that," he said. "It's wonderful to be solid once again, and I can do normal things again. Oh, Score, I think I should tell you – I'm dating your mother…"

About the Author

John Peel was born in England and moved to the U.S. in 1981 to get married. He and his wife live on Long Island with their pack of miniature pinschers. He has written over a hundred books, including the "2099" series and "Dragonhome", along with tie-ins based on "Doctor Who", "Star Trek" and "The Outer Limits".
You can find him at:
www.john-peel.com
and on Facebook at www.facebook.com/JohnPeelAuthor

About the Artist

"You'll never make it as a professional artist!" spat his venomous art teacher.

Since then he has gone on to a career where there is scarcely an area for which his professional illustration work has not been used.

Pete jokes that he was, in a previous incarnation, a Doctor Who illustrator and he now maintains that he has since regenerated into something entirely different and infinitely more agreeable!

These days, the kind and generous patronage of his work by others means more than ever - thank you.

With grateful thanks to Auntie Deb and Mollie for helping to create the pose for the cover of this book.

Visit him at: **www.petewallbank.org.uk**

Also from Dragonhome Books

The Slayers of Dragonhome (ISBN 9780615567082)

The sequel to the popular *The Secret of Dragonhome*!

Melayne is still in trouble – lots of it. Her brother wants her dead. Sea-Raiders are trying to kill her. Her dragons are growing up and want mates. Her husband is missing. And then the dragon slayers arrive in force…

Forced to fight to protect everyone and everything she loves, Melayne must abandon her family and chase down answers. It seems that all roads are leading back to Dragonhome. But what awaits her there apart from a deadly family reunion? And what is the terrible danger from her distant past?

Manufactured by Amazon.ca
Acheson, AB